Mary Gillies, Myles Birket Foster

The Carewes

A tale of the civil wars, with twenty-four illustrations

Mary Gillies, Myles Birket Foster

The Carewes
A tale of the civil wars, with twenty-four illustrations

ISBN/EAN: 9783337412135

Printed in Europe, USA, Canada, Australia, Japan

Cover: Foto ©Andreas Hilbeck / pixelio.de

More available books at **www.hansebooks.com**

THE CAREWES:

A Tale of the Civil Wars.

By MARY GILLIES,

AUTHOR OF "THE VOYAGE OF THE CONSTANCE."

WITH TWENTY-FOUR ILLUSTRATIONS BY BIRKET FOSTER.

LONDON :

W. KENT & CO., 23, PATERNOSTER ROW.

MDCCCLXI.

PREFACE.

In describing the lives and adventures of the characters in the following tale, I have endeavoured, (guided by the best authorities) to give a true picture of the customs and manners of the time, and to be strictly accurate in every circumstance touching on historical events. Above all, it has been my wish to give some idea, capable of being understood by my young readers, of the pure motives, the brave struggles, and the noble deeds, of those great men to whom our country probably owes its present liberty under a constitutional queen.

M. G.

CONTENTS.

LIST OF ILLUSTRATIONS.

THE CAREWES.

CHAPTER I.

CREWHURST HALL.

IN the year 1637, the twelfth of King Charles the First, there stood, not far from the skirts of Windsor Forest, a fine old hall belonging to a branch of the ancient family of Carewe. A deer park of considerable extent, adorned with magnificent trees, among which were some oaks and beeches, and a few stately cedars close to the hall itself, which were remarkable for their size and beauty, ended in a wild woodland, or chase, of some miles in extent, which at one point almost joined the royal forest. This chase had been granted to the Carewe family by a charter of King Henry the Second, and from it the whole manor took its name of Crewhurst—*Hurst* signifying, in Saxon, a woody region. The parish church stood close to the park wall. In fact, the mortuary chapel or burial-place of the Carewe family, which was part of the church, formed a portion of the wall, and had a private door entering from the park.

Sir Arthur Carewe, the present proprietor, had sat in the last parliament, but that was eight years ago. The king had never in all this time summoned another, nor was there any sign, as yet, of his doing so. Sir Arthur had taken no part in public affairs during this period, but had devoted himself to study, to the improvement of his property, and the care of his people. He was not fond of field sports himself, but he had a pride in keeping up the establishment in the order in which he received it from his father, who was devoted to them, so that the sporting establishment at Crewhurst was a model to the neighbourhood. Equally celebrated were Sir Arthur Carewe's farms. The new taste for improvements in agriculture met with a keen supporter in him. Nowhere were finer crops of wheat, rye, and barley, nor better pastures, nor finer breeds of sheep and cattle to be found, than on his estates. He also took great interest in the welfare of his tenants and dependants ; many of the retainers of the family had been born and grown old in its service, and for the special accommodation of such as were not the domestic servants in the Hall itself, but acted as keepers, foresters, gardeners, or in similar capacities, he had cleared a corner of the chase where his experienced eye detected an especially favourable soil, and had built a pretty village ; the neat thatched cottages peeping out from under the old trees, which had been left here and there. He had also been active in promoting the making of roads and building of bridges, which were both much wanted in those days.

While Sir Arthur carried on his improvements on a large scale, Lady Carewe took up the good work at the

point where he left it. A taste for flowers, and the adorn-
ment of gardens, was arising at that time, together with the
increasing interest in agriculture; and this she cultivated
successfully. She beautified the gardens while he improved
the farms; she also cared for the comfort and happiness of
the people who inhabited the cottages he had built, and
shielded them from want and suffering: so that Sir Arthur
and Lady Carewe found plenty of employment, though there
were no parliaments, and though they had not visited London
for several years. .   •

But besides all these interests, they had a family of five
children, four of whom were educated at home, by Lady
Carewe herself, with the assistance of the chaplain of the
family, a young man of great learning, and as Lady Carewe
was a devoted mother, and a careful mistress of her large
establishment, looking into every department of it, it is not
necessary to say that she led no idle life.

It is a bright sunny morning towards the end of July,
and a young party may be seen resting under one of the
spreading oaks in the park, on their way to the end of the
avenue to meet their brother Valentine, who was expected
home from Oxford for the long vacation that day.

First there is the eldest daughter, whom we should now
call Miss Carewe, but who was then called Mistress Edith.
She was a graceful fair girl of fifteen, with golden hair flowing in long ringlets down her back, from under a hat and
feather, not very unlike what young ladies wear now. She
sat, as if tired with the heat, on a stool which a servant had
carried for her. On her finger she held a beautiful falcon,
which she was caressing, having just taken off his hood and

jesses to cool him, as she said: but tame as he was, she had
secured him by a little silver chain that was fastened to one
of his legs; at her feet lay a very small Italian greyhound,
that whined every now and then, and looked wistfully in her
face, as if jealous of the bird; close behind her, cropping the
fine grass, was a much larger favourite—a tame stag: so it
was easy to see at the first glance, that Mistress Edith was
very fond of pets.

Next in succession is Master Henry. He was about
thirteen; a square-made, sturdy fellow, and was at that
moment stretched full length on the grass, with one arm
thrown across the neck of a fine handsome mastiff called
Lion, almost as large as his name-father, and very much of
the same colour. The dog was asleep, or looked as if he
was, but his young master was wide awake, and apparently
in deep thought. Beside him lay a large knotted oak stick,
which it was his fancy to carry, and perhaps, as the other
companion of his walks was always the huge mastiff, any
one might have said he was right to have a weapon of defence; but never had the stick been used on Lion—Henry
and he were much too fond of each other. Henry had none
of the graceful beauty of his sister; and his hair, which was
dark brown, grew in short clustering curls, so that he had
received from his elder brother, who was remarkably handsome, and wore a profusion of long wavy hair, after the
fashion of the time, the nickname of "The Puritan" because
those strict sectaries disapproved of the fashion. Sometimes,
also, from the contrast between the two brothers, the country people had called them Valentine and Orson; and perhaps
it was in a sort of proud defiance of these insults, and with

a determination to show that he did not care the least about
them, that Henry chose to carry his oak stick, as Orson
carried his club, while Valentine, like a gay knight, would
have a hawk on his hand, or a cross-bow, or fishing-rod, or
gun, and a hunting-horn slung at his back; but then, as old
Nurse Crairy used to say, "Our honourable young master,
Sir Valentine as will be some day, bless his handsome face,
and long may it be before his honourable father, our dear
and worshipful master, gives up his place to him—a better
will never fill it; our young Master Valentine is four years
the oldest. He'll be seventeen come Martinmas, and Master Henry, bless him, he was only born in the year of grace
one thousand six hundred and twenty-four, just the very
year before the king's majesty King Charles came to the
throne; more by token, I remember, just as if it was yesterday, when Ralph Ditchly, the carrier, came down from London, when he was a baby of one year old, and brought the
news of the proclamation, and I had the baby in my arms,
and he gave a frown, as he always did, pretty fellow, if a
stranger looked at him; and Ralph says, why marry, says
Ralph, young master, you be not going to frown at the King,
he says, and so we laughed, and Master Henry he stared out
of his great eyes at us, just, for all the world, as he do now
when Master Valentine teases him a bit, not angry like,
but grave; and then I says to Ralph, says I, some day this
babe here on my arm will be a judge, and so I say now;
and judge or no judge, see if he don't turn out as good a man
and as worshipful a gentleman as ever bore the name of
Carewe."

Nurse Crairy was not singular in her love of young

Henry. His mother said little about it, but she knew there
was a good heart, and good head too, under his rough outside; he was a favourite with every servant about the place,
and there was a friend besides who loved and valued him,
and was dearly loved by him in return. This was Mr. Russell,
the chaplain mentioned before, who acted as his tutor.

Little Mistress Alice, the next of the family, was only
eight. She was now seated beside her brother Martin, who
was but four, in his new little coach, or, as the two under-
nurses, Cicely and Mary, who drew it, called it, *coroach.* It
was quite a new invention for children, and indeed it was
not very many years since coaches had been introduced into
England for their elders, and most people still preferred
riding on horseback, in the country, to incurring the risks
and delays of the bad roads, where ruts and holes were apt
to cause overturns, or accidents of one kind or other. Alice
was nursing a doll which she called a baby, though it was
dressed like a lady in a court suit; and as to Martin, he was
fast asleep, his flushed cheeks bearing witness to the heat
of the sun.

The party was aroused out of its repose by the sound of
a man's voice, but as Lion was not at the trouble to raise
his head, and only half opened one eye, it was very sure that
no stranger had approached. It was in fact Woodruffe,
the keeper.

"I have been thinking, so please you, Mistress Edith,"
he said, addressing the young lady, "that the buck may grow
dangerous one of these days."

"What! Prince grow ill-natured! No, that I never will
believe," replied she.

"Still, an it should not displease you, I would fain keep by you, as you walk through the park; and if I be right in thinking that you be on the way to meet the young master's honour at the gates, why there's not much time to lose. He rides hard, and Master Henry told me he was to start at early morning from my Lord Falkland's."

"Woodruffe is right, Edith," said Henry, slowly rising to his knees. "Come, Lion! awake, shake yourself and prepare to meet your master."

"Valentine is not Lion's master," cried little Alice, as she clambered out of the coach, holding her baby fast in one arm. "I know Lion is thy dog, and so nurse says."

"But my pretty pet here is Valentine's," said Edith; "and he will say that his falcon looks well, and his feathers bright and smooth, I know."

"But when he comes to make him fly at a heron, I fear the cry will be 'Edith hath spoilt my falcon.' Over-much petting cools the courage. An he turns not tail and flies back to the fist, I am out in my reckoning."

"And if he do, Valentine hath plenty more."

"And so he hath, Edith; and if he be of my mind, he will give thee thy pretty falcon, to carry about daintily on thy finger, and not send him on any dangerous flights."

"I thank thee for thy good will, Henry, and believe thou wouldst; but now he must let me hood him again, and then we will move on as Woodruffe advises."

So this being done, they put themselves in motion. Henry and Lion taking the lead, Prince trotting by Edith, her little dog frisking about her, and the nurses, the coroach, the children, and Woodruffe, bringing up the rear. About a quarter of an hour's walk brought them to the avenue, with its welcome shade.

The avenue was of great length, with two rows of grand old oaks on either hand. On the bright green sward, beneath one of these shady alleys, overarched with cloister-like boughs and quivering green leaves, they went merrily on, enjoying the delicious coolness. Beyond the trees on one hand was a fine sheet of water, rippling and glancing in the sun, on the other were water meadows of emerald verdure, on which about twenty sleek cows were feeding. Beyond was a grove of tall elms containing a rookery, but the noisy inhabitants were away somewhere enjoying themselves in distant fields ; the ground then rose into slopes, and grassy hills dotted with sheep. Nothing could be more tranquil and peaceful. Only the tender cooing sound of the wood pigeon was heard through the air, and little Martin varied the song he had begun humming to himself as his coroach jolted over the ground, by imitating it.

The avenue ended in high iron gates leading into the chase, much ornamented with scrolls and leaves wrought in the metal, and having a tall stone pillar on each side, surmounted by the figure of an English mastiff, the family device, while the family motto, " Trustie and Trewe," cast in iron in old English characters, formed an arch over the gates.

A stone lodge on either side, belonged, the one to the under-keeper, Lawrence Leeson, and the other to Thomas Boult, the forester ; and the quiet was interrupted here by sounds of music which issued from the latter. It was not very harmonious music, however, for it consisted of the tuning of various instruments, and the discord was increased by a long loud howl from Lion, who never could bear music. At this noise there issued from the lodge the forester himself, in his green holiday suit, with a guitar in his hand.

" Why, Thomas," said Woodruffe, " art practising thy trills and jangling thy large fiddle so early i' the day ?"

After two or three low reverences to his honourable young masters and mistresses, Thomas explained that he and Lawrence had a mind to welcome the honourable Master Valentine as he entered the gates with something of a catch or madrigal ; and that, as Master Woodruffe knew, they had a pretty notion of a tenor and an alto, and they had gotten Michael Protheroe, with his good bass, to come and take a part, and he was sure to sing well, for he had a deal o' time to practise, as he sat at his loom, and had a good chance of being chosen for parish clerk, if so be his reverence the vicar was pleased to favour the notion, when old Archibald Simlet gave up, and withal they had a chance, he thought, to please the young master.

" But I heard a pipe besides your guitar," said Edith.

" Surely, my young lady, you did. Old Simon Dunkly it was you heard with his long pipe, and besides him, there's Christopher Knight with his quaint drum and tabor to mark the time."

" And what are you going to sing ?" asked Henry.

" A three-part glee it is to be," replied Thomas, " and out of Master Shakespere too, one that Master Russell taught us in the evenings, last winter time, and you shall hear what it be when the time comes. As our worshipful young master rides up to the gates, we shall come out, and stand as it may be just here, and strike up."

"But," said Henry, "we see only a little way along the road, because of its winding through the trees; he will be upon you before you have time to begin."

"Aha! Master Henry, but we have thought of that," said Thomas. "Abel, the verdurer's boy, is up on the high ground, quarter of a mile on, and he's to fire his piece first glimpse he gets, and so we be made aware."

"I should like to go up there too," said Henry.

"Here, Lawrence, bring out the gray nag for Master Henry," cried Woodruffe, "and he can ride up the hill and come back with Master Valentine."

"Now have a care what you do, Master Woodruffe," said Cicely. "My lady gave me the charge of the young masters and mistresses, and never said aught about the gray nag."

"Master Henry can ride just as well as Master Valentine himself," replied Woodruffe, rather offended, "and is to be taught the great horse soon."

"And him but thirteen," said Cicely, disdainfully; "I hope 'twill be long before they think o' training him for the wars, if ever they do."

"Well, he has rode his little nag since he was not much higher than my knee, and the gray nag many times, and I know my lady would trust me with him."

"It cannot be long before he sees Master Valentine and his company," said Cicely, softening. "For they will be a good company on the road. You all talk as if Master Valentine was riding his lonesome lone, like a pedlar with his pack."

"Very surely he is the one we think of the most, and so we talk most of him. But here's the nag, and make your mind easy, Cicely. More by token, I shall walk by him myself. There's plenty here now to take charge of the buck."

Henry, giving no heed at all to the altercation that was going on in the background, had already mounted, and was off with Lion by his side, and Woodruffe trudged after him, gradually recovering the effects of Cicely's tongue, which provoked him the more as he had sometimes entertained thoughts of elevating her to the rank of wife to the head keeper of Crewhurst, or at least of proposing that dignity to her, though he very well knew there were rivals in the field.

Old dame Leeson, the grandmother of Lawrence, who lived with him and his wife in the lodge, had come out to unlock the gates, and now invited her two young mistresses into her parlour to sit down and rest; they therefore took refuge there while the nurses and little Martin went into the other lodge to see Thomas Boult's young wife. She was newly-married, and had been one of the dairy-maids at the Hall, so they had plenty of gossip to talk over.

CHAPTER II.

THE ELDEST SON.

HENRY rode forward rather quietly at first, full of many
thoughts. He had none of the joyous feeling of one boy
meeting another. Valentine was so much older, so clever,
so tall and handsome, had such polished manners, was always
so admired and praised, that to Henry he was more like some
hero to be wondered at than a companion to be loved.   In
those days, too, the eldest son of a family of distinction was
made of more importance in comparison with the others than
even he is now.   He was sent to Eton or to Westminster, as
Valentine had been, the latter being preferred in his case
because the head master, Dr. Osbaldeston, was an honoured
friend of his father's, then to the University, and afterwards on his travels.   He was then, probably, introduced at
court in the train of some nobleman, and before his educa-
tion was considered complete, was entered at Lincoln's Inn
or the Temple to learn something of the laws of his country
before he became proprietor or legislator himself.   There
was no standing army, and the navy was a rough service.
The younger sons, on the other hand, were generally educated
at home, by the domestic chaplain, who though often a dull
pedagogue, punishing with a severity not now practised,

except in very rare instances, was sometimes, as in the case of Mr. Russell, better able to give them a sound training, which should fit them for pushing their way in the world, than a more showy course might have done.

Besides this inferior position as a younger son, Henry was, as we have said, apt to fall under the lash of Valentine's jeering moods, and had occasionally gone into violent passions when this happened. All this made him at first ride soberly on, sometimes wondering if Valentine had grown still taller; sometimes wondering if he wore a sword yet, sometimes trying to remember what Mr. Russell had said to himself about being good-humoured, and taking jokes as they were meant, and wondering if he should be able. At last he reached the high ground, very clear of trees for some distance, where Abel was posted with his gun, and looking out along the road over the open heath, distinctly saw a cloud of dust and the figures of six horsemen looming through it.

"Fire!" cried Henry, and forgetting, in a moment, everything but the pleasure of seeing Valentine again, dashed forward full gallop.

"Cicely indeed!" said Woodruffe to himself, smiling complacently. "Master Henry can ride with the best of them, and we want none of her wisdom. Now, Abel, that crack will do very well; run back and see that they all come out of their cottages and be ready to have a glimpse of him."

The space between Henry and the coming party was rapidly diminishing meanwhile. Very soon he could see them distinctly. There was Valentine again, and two young gallants with him, and behind them three grooms, with saddle bags, portmanteaus, and hat-cases strapped on their horses.

There were no railways then, nor even public coaches; no roads beyond bridle paths, except on the great thoroughfares to the north and west, and these very bad, so that in winter they were difficult for carriages; so instead of coming home from Oxford by the train, as young men do now, they had rode the whole way, resting one night at Lord Falkland's, whose hospitality to Oxonians was celebrated, and had been met at the distance of fifteen miles by Sir Arthur Carewe's servants and horses to bring them home.

The young masters, as well as their servants, were all armed with swords slung to a belt, and pistols in holsters, for there were frequent robberies on the road at that time, when distress and discontent were very general in consequence of the forced loans and irregular ways of raising money without consent of parliament; aggravated, too, by a late revival of the forest laws, and the extension of some of the royal forests, to the ejection of many inhabitants of cottages and houses which had gradually encroached upon the ancient forest land. The approaching party, however, seemed to have had no disagreeable adventures. They came gaily on, the summer wind playing among the feathers in their hats and their long curling hair, the spurs in their high riding boots and the silver ornaments on their bridles glancing in the sun, and their tight riding suits showing off their graceful riding. As they came near, Valentine, as if to show Henry his new dignity, drew his sword, and waving it over his head, cried—

"Stand! trusty and loyal squire! What tidings from our ancient hall?"

Henry was in the midst of the party in a moment, with joyous face and light heart, because Valentine was so kind

to him, and had answered several questions about home before
he was introduced to my lord of Morley and Master Henry
Wilmot, and then turning his pony, they all trotted along
together. It was a full month since there had been any
communication between them. We can hardly imagine such
a thing in these days of penny postage; but there was no
post then, except on the north road between London and
Edinburgh. The king had lately appointed a man on
horseback to carry the letters regularly between the two
places, to go and return in six days, a time which sounds
incredibly short, and which it appears was not actually kept
to. Everywhere else people had to send expresses riding, or
to trust to the carriers who traversed the country.

Before Valentine's questions were half ended, the tall
gates of his home appeared in sight, and he stopped to
exclaim with inward pride, " Welcome to Crewhurst, my
Lord Morley, and you our trusty and well-beloved cousin
and councillor, Harry Wilmot."

As he spoke, a hearty cheer sounded through the air, and
a crowd of the tenants and dependents of the family were
seen ranged on either side the entrance to greet their young
master. He took off his hat and thanked them with smiles
and kind words, and then threw himself from his horse and
ran forward; for inside the now opened gates he saw his
beautiful young sister Edith, with little Alice and Martin
by her side. She had never looked so beautiful in his eyes,
and he felt as proud when he introduced his friends to her
as he had done when he said, " Welcome to Crewhurst."
There she stood, under the soft shade of a spreading oak,
with the long avenue stretching into distance behind her,

the bright sunlight streaming across the velvet-like turf at each opening of the trees, and contrasting with the deep shadows they cast; her pretty hawk on her finger, her little greyhound at her feet, and the tame stag, a little startled by the shouts and bustle, careering lightly as the wind off into the park, and then returning to her side.

But now before Valentine had time to notice the children, he was startled in his turn by the music which suddenly

struck up, and had to stand and listen to the glee in three voices.

" Under the greenwood tree,
  Who loves to lie with me,
  And tune his merry note,
  Unto the sweet bird's throat,

Come hither, come hither, come hither:
Here shall he see
No enemy,
But winter and rough weather."

It was a gay scene; the children danced to the music; the crowd outside enjoyed it; Henry thought it was capitally performed, and Valentine was amused and pleased too; but his two young companions, assuming the airs of counoisseurs, rather shrugged their shoulders, and looked contemptuously from the one to the other, and he noticed it.

"What says Will Shakespere?" said he, addressing Lord Morley aside, but quite loud enough to be heard. "An a dog had howled thus, we had hanged him!"

"Ay," replied his lordship, in the same tone, "'tis no matter how it be in tune, so it makes noise enough."

Henry coloured and bit his lip. "They thought he would like it and be pleased, and now they will feel right vexed and troubled," he said inwardly.

There was a pause. A sort of gloom seemed to have fallen over the scene.

"So please you, sir," said one of the grooms, addressing Valentine very respectfully, "the horses are very warm, and Sir Arthur will not be best content if they stand about and catch cold."

"I know how to guide a horse as well as you, Sir Jackanapes," retorted Valentine, who was annoyed at what had been said about the singing, though he said the worst himself, and was therefore out of temper. "Fall back, and keep your place."

"Nay, but, Carewe," said Lord Morley, "the fellow is

right. Let us dismount and walk the rest of the way, if
Mistress Edith will permit us to keep her company so far.
It is but half-past ten, and though the avenue appears of
vast extent, we shall yet reach the Hall in time to prepare
for the dinner hour."

"So be it," said Valentine, assisting his friends to alight;
"and, as we have time, let us walk by the heronry,
Edith."

Henry had given back the gray nag to Lawrence, and the
three grooms were soon on the way up the avenue, each
with a led horse.

"Farewell, my masters, and many thanks for your warm
welcome and sweet music," said Valentine, as he took
Edith's hand to move on; but she slipped away from him
for a moment, and ran to the group of musicians. She had
observed that they heard her brother's words, and her
sweet nature could not bear to leave them with pained
feelings.

"They were only saying the words of a stage play," said
she. "All that is what is said in the play about quite other
songs. It does not mean yours. They were reminded of
the play by the song, and so they said the words. You
sang right well. I liked it much, and so did Master
Henry."

"Your young mistress says what is true," said a voice
behind her.

"Ah, Mr. Russell, were you here?" said Edith. "I saw
you not before."

"Edith, Edith! we are waiting," cried Valentine, and
she ran off to him. Henry and Mr. Russell were still by the

musicians. Old Protheroe looked very rueful and shook his head.

"I misdoubt about it very much," said he.

"And I know how it came about well enough," said Lawrence. "Lion there set up one of the very dismallest howls that ever came out of dog's throat, just as we started off; and what I believe is, that Master Valentine thought t was Thomas coming in with his tenor."

"Consider it not so deeply," said Mr. Russell; "your young master was pleased with what you all did to welcome him, and only said what he did to humour the mood of his friends. Your glee was well sung. Did I not teach you myself? We must have some more practice as the evenings lengthen."

The performers began to brighten up, but a good deal of whispering went on among them, which ended in an appeal o Master Henry.

"What think you, Master Henry?" said Thomas. "Shall we venture on a little masque, a sort of dance, as I may say, or the entertainment of our honourable young master while he dines?"

"A dance? a masque? Why, what sort of a thing do you mean?"

"'Tis more a sort of kind of mumming we mean, to make him merry," said old Simon Dunkly.

"Yes, come and do your mumming of a surety," said Henry. "He likes a laugh right well, and I shall be there o see, for I am to dine in the great chamber to-day beside Mr. Russell; so never doubt we shall laugh. Come, Lion!" and off they scoured together, round trees and up knolls,

c

following Mr. Russell, as he walked fast to overtake the rest of the party who had now reached the sheet of water.

Edith and Alice were throwing bread to the swans, which came in numbers to the banks to be fed, ruffling their feathers and arching their graceful necks. Valentine took a piece and broke it.

"What coarse stuff!" said he, as he did so.

"Old Dorothy at the lodge gave it to us that we might throw it to the swans," said Edith. "It is good and sweet, though it looks brown. Thou wouldst not have us feed the birds with manchet?"[1]

"I would," replied Valentine; "they ought to have it."

"Our mother says not," said Henry. "Our people eat brown bread, and when the poor beggars come she deals them out rye bread; she will not give to the birds better food than to men."

"But see how royally the birds comport themselves," said Valentine. "That magnificent one that sails so gracefully in front, and that all the rest follow, is a king. See now, he shall be called his majesty, and there is the beautiful queen by his side, and behind them come their train of courtiers, and the young princes and princesses."

"And," said Edith laughing, "the young princes and princesses have made their court dresses quite complete now, on purpose to please thee. They are as white and smooth as the very snow, instead of ugly and gray as they were at first."

"And see," said Lord Morley, "where comes the reigning

---

[1] The fine white bread made of wheat, and with some milk in it.

favourite to the water's edge to grace the pageant. Look at that painted peacock, with his jewelled train sweeping the grass, and his neck like the richest Genoa velvet dusted with gold. He minds me of our boyhood, Wilmot, when thou and I were Buckingham's pages, and saw many a gorgeous scene."

"Ay, his beauty may well recall our splendid master," replied Wilmot, "as he looked when he gave his last *fête* to their majesties, before his fatal visit to Portsmouth, when the villain Fenton took his life. He wore at that *fête* a suit that cost thirty thousand pounds, so precious were the pearls and diamonds that were broidered on it."

"'Tis said that his suit of uncut white velvet, and cloak set all over with diamonds, when he went to Paris to bring over her gracious majesty, was worth eighty thousand," said Lord Morley.

"I would rather be like that little brown falcon, and able to cleave the air, than a painted peacock," said Henry.

"No, no!" cried little Alice, "thou art wicked to say that, because thou wouldst kill the pretty little birds that sing in the trees, and our dear herons that build their nests so high and stand by the water so quaintly on one of their long legs."

"Ah, yes, Morley, we shall have some brave hawking," said Valentine, caressing his falcon, which he now held on his own finger. "Thou hast taken real care of him, Edith. And how are all the hawks, Henry? Is Ralph the falconer here still?"

"That is he; we should do ill without Ralph. Thou shalt see how well all the gentils look; and dost thou know of the pair of ger falcons from Norway?"

"Ay, my father told me of them in his last letter."

"Their wings measure five feet from point to point," said Henry; "so Ralph says."

"'Tis a great size; but I know not but I prefer to fly a good goshawk or gentil," said Wilmot.

"Thou shalt try all," said Valentine; "here is good store of herons, as thou mayst see;" and, indeed, numbers of Alice's quaint favourites might now be seen, for the party had reached the heronry. Some were standing, gravely looking into the water, on one long leg as she had described, but took flight when approached, heavily flapping their large wings, and giving their sharp wild cry as they rose; others were flying backwards and forwards between their usual haunt and the fish ponds not far off, where they found their food. "Shall we let the little falcon off for a flight even now?"

Alice began to cry.

"Why, what aileth thee, pretty little Mistress Alice?" asked Lord Morley.

"Mistress Alice cannot abide to hear of the herons being killed," said Cicely.

"She likes to look at them," said Edith, kissing and comforting the poor little girl; "and in spring, when they were sitting on their eggs, she would watch them and mark their long gray necks and crested heads as they showed against the blue sky at the top of the trees; and she saw when they brought food to their young, and watched the young take flight."

"Come to me, little Alice," said Valentine, taking her in his arms. "We will not harm thy herons now. Let me

carry thee. See, I will be thy palfrey all the way home," and
he set off bounding along with her, and she was soon laughing and playing with his curls, and telling him they smelled
as sweetly as the roses Goodwife Freeman was distilling ; and
then the stag let her pat and caress his sleek sides, and so
she was comforted.

"Is this fine buck our little pet of last year, Edith?"
asked Valentine.

"Surely he is. Hast thou forgotten our pretty Prince?
He is quite tame and gentle, but Woodruffe fears he may
grow dangerous."

"And thou shouldst be cautious, Edith. His horns
might do thee a mischief."

"Ah, that I cannot believe," she said, looking lovingly
at her favourite.

Little Martin must now be taken out of his coach ; Alice
must come down, and he must ride on Valentine's shoulder,
and so they walked on, Valentine and his burden in front.

"Thou hast store of bright creatures, Mistress Edith,"
said Lord Morley as they passed a little enclosure of wire-
work, where gold and silver pheasants were kept. "How
tame they are ! they come to thy hand."

"We have tamed them with care," she replied. "They
were brought home to our father by the young son of his
steward, who sails in a ship to and fro the Indies."

"And so thou hast deserted thy coach, Master Martin,"
said Wilmot. "Wouldst not like to see the brave coaches
in London with six horses in them?"

"I want to see them," said Martin. "Take me, Valentine!"

"Our mother has four in hers," said Henry, "and that is enough."

"'Twas Buckingham that first drove with six," said Lord Morley, "and well I remember how the crowd gaped and stared, though since that time we have seen eight in a coach."

"I would not sit cooped up in a coach to be dragged about like a dainty lady," said Henry, disdainfully.

"Why, how now, Master Henry? Thou art mighty scornful, methinks!" said Valentine.

"Henry is a country man," said Mr. Russell, "and hath not learnt the ways of the court and the city yet."

"I have been reading in the Chronicles of Master Speed and Master Stow," said Henry, "how in the time of Queen Elizabeth's majesty, a young gallant would as soon have been seen in the streets of London in a petticoat as in a coach."

"Ah, but those are old times now," said Wilmot. "There are scores, nay hundreds, of coaches to be seen in London now, and as many gallants as ladies in them. What wouldst say if thou sawest one carried in a sedan?"

"A sedan! what may that be?"

"A sort of chair, borne on poles by two men."

"I should hoot at him!"

"Then wouldst thou most likely get a good cudgelling for thy pains, for many a gallant is so carried," said Valentine.

"And was it the Duke of Buckingham that began this notable contrivance too?" asked Henry.

"Truly I believe it was."

"Lion! Lion!" cried Henry, and started off with his friend homewards, as if he could bear no more, followed by a laugh from the two courtiers at his rustic simplicity, in which Valentine joined. But Edith looked grave; she could have wished that Valentine disliked luxury and indolence too.

A sudden turn now brought them under a dark grove of cedars in sight of the Hall itself, with its many stone mullioned windows, its gables and pinnacles, and here and there the green ivy clothing the gray stone walls. Valentine set down his little brother, and hurried onwards, his eyes moistened with tears of affection and joy, for on the flight of stone steps that led up to the door, he saw a large group collected to receive him; the servants of the family were all there, and a few guests besides, but among them he saw only two faces. His father and mother stood in front of all, and now came quickly down to meet him. He was soon at their feet with uncovered head, after the reverential custom of the time, receiving their blessing, and then raised by their hands and fondly embraced and welcomed.

CHAPTER III.

AT HOME.

After the first moment of joy, Valentine presented his two friends to his parents. They were known to his father by name, and a slight cloud passed over his face, though he received them courteously. He had given Valentine permission to bring two of his college companions with him, and would fain those he had chosen had been steady students instead of young men of fashion, destined most likely to fill places about the court. But Valentine was such a favourite with his father, was so dearly loved and cherished by him, that any feeling of disapprobation was sure to pass off quickly. Sir Arthur held his son by the hand, while his face, usually grave even to melancholy, lighted up with pleasure. Lady Carewe, with her hand on his shoulder, looked long into his eyes, as if to read there the assurance she sought, that her boy had come back to her such as she would have him. Valentine interrupted this scrutiny by embracing her affectionately once more, and then turning round to make a low reverence to a gentleman who stood behind her with a lady on his arm.

" My Lord Willoughby, I am happy indeed and fortunate to find you here; and may I crave an introduction to your lady, of whom I have heard much?"

Lord Willoughby, after a hearty recognition, made the introduction.

Edith, Henry, and the children, with their nurses, had now come up the steps, and the entrance-hall, large as it was, could scarcely hold them all. Edith stood by her hand-some brother, and Henry, with his eyes beaming with joy, looked up at him as if he could not admire him enough.

" You may well be proud of your eldest son, Sir Arthur," whispered Lady Willoughby; "but I give not up my favourite, Orson, for all that."

The servants now greeted their young master with low bows, and reverences, and smiles, and began to move off; but when all had gone besides, there remained William Freeman, the butler, and Goodwife Freeman, the house-keeper, who were man and wife, and had been in the family for thirty years, and Nurse Crairy, all of whom remembered the day he was born, and had seen him grow up. He was declared by them to be grown taller by half the head, and broader across the shoulders also ; and nurse stroked his hair and blessed his goodly face, and told Master Henry he had four years to grow as tall in, and it was a deal to do, but yet she believed he'd do it, unless he was to be one of the short ones, and no matter if he was short in stature so he was great in grace.

After nurse's oration, they all began to ascend the wide oak staircase, and the travellers were conducted to their chambers to prepare for dinner, for the hour of twelve was

not far off, so that they had to hasten; but they succeeded
in being ready at the first summons of the bell, and were
ushered into the great chamber before it had ceased.

The great chamber, or dining-room, was not used when
the family was alone, but all meals were taken in a smaller
one called the parlour. This, however, was a festive occasion. The room was of great size, hung with tapestry and
finished with fine oak carving. The floor was of dark oak
and chiefly bare, but small Turkey carpets were placed at
different parts, before elbow chairs covered with purple cloth

embroidered with gold, of which there were several, though
the party at dinner sat on oak benches. It looked handsome,
even magnificent. There were many articles of massive
plate on the sideboard and in cupboards, or what we might
now call cabinets or chiffoniers. The table was covered

with a fine damask table cloth. The drinking cups and salt cellar were of silver.

The company took their seats before any of the dishes were placed on the table. A napkin of damask, to match the table cloth, was next handed to each. Freeman's voice was then heard proclaiming, " By your leaves, gentlemen, stand by," and at the signal, the cooks and serving-men entered with silver dishes containing profusion of fish, flesh, and fowl, and placed them on the table ; others followed, bearing the plates or trenchers, as they were called, also of silver. All then rose as Mr. Russell said grace, and then the feast began, with appetites to do honour to the good cheer, though it was only noon ; three of the party having ridden since seven in the morning, and all breakfasted at that early hour.

Henry could not attend to his dinner for continued watching in expectation of the mumming that Thomas had promised. Lion was lying under the table, with his head on his master's feet, and only now and then raised it to take a piece of bread or meat from his hand, and showed no sign of any approaching bustle ; but at last he did give a low growl, then a short howl, and music was heard in the gallery, together with a noise of feet and of suppressed laughter.

" Here they come !" thought Henry. Accordingly, when the door opened to admit the second course, there appeared Thomas, Lawrence, and Michael Protheroe, the three singers of the morning, dressed in the costume of the fools of the former reign, who performed a dance, with such preposterous antics, to the music that struck up outside, that Henry shouted with laughter, and the three Oxford students, though they tried to look grave and disdainful, caught the infection. When the dance was completed, the whole bevy of performers were furnished with cups of foaming ale to drink Master Valentine's health, which they did with right good will, and were then invited to go down to dinner in the servants' hall.

The ladies rose and retired to the withdrawing room soon after dinner was over, and here, in an oriel window, Lady Carewe and her daughter Edith sat at embroidery, while Lady Willoughby delighted them and herself by reading aloud the "Masque of Comus," which Mr. Russell had lately received from London from the author, his dear friend Mr. John Milton, as a parting gift before he went to Italy. Thus employed, time slipped away so fast that Edith had almost forgotten she had made Valentine promise to meet her in the garden at three. The great clock of the Hall striking the hour reminded her of it, and of her longing desire to talk with him, and find in him the same brother who had left her a year ago.

Having received her mother's permission, Edith went quickly down, entered the parlour, and stepped out to the bowling green, which was close to the house at that side. Here all the gentlemen, including her father, were engaged so ardently on a game at bowls, that after waiting a little while in the vain endeavour to catch Valentine's eye, she determined to go alone to the garden, knowing she should find nurse and the children there.

But Edith first walked up and down the broad terrace or alley that bounded the bowling green on the side opposite to the Hall for a little while, still hoping Valentine would join her. On each hand, the terrace had gilded balustrades, with obelisks, pyramids, and vases, at equal distances along its whole length. A flight of steps led down from it into the garden below, and she now leaned on the balustrade, looking down there, but as yet saw no one, though she had expected that the children would be out at this hour. The garden on which she looked was then considered perfection. It was square, and carpeted with turf so smooth and thick that the foot sank in it. On every side of this velvet-like lawn ran a broad straight walk. A small round pond, with a fountain in it, occupied the middle of the lawn. The fountain was in the form of a tree, made of copper, and was covered with numbers of little copper birds, which spouted the water from their bills, as did the leaves from their tips. On either side of the fountain was a yew tree, cut into quaint and curious forms, the top of one representing a gigantic peacock, and the other a pheasant. There were little flower-beds of formal shapes at each corner, but in them, though they were culti-vated with the greatest care, there were nothing like the variety of flowers we now possess. There were roses grow-ing on bushes of that good old exquisitely-scented kind, the cabbage rose, and pansies, and pinks, and stocks, or gilli-flowers, and a few others. Two smaller round ponds occu-pied the middle of each end of the lawn. A wall-like, high yew hedge, of extraordinary thickness, enclosed the whole garden, having at each corner an arbour, cut out in its thick-ness and furnished with seats.

While Edith stood thus, her thoughts had been filled with the beautiful poetry to which she had been listening, and wandering off to the tangled undergrowths and "alleys green" of the chase, as much more in harmony with it than the formal garden; but now they fixed on Valentine, and as they did so, she hardly knew why, the tears began to drop on the gilded balustrade on which she leaned. Yes, Valentine was changed. She had lost the dear companion, her playmate since childhood. He had become a young man, and preferred the companionship of young men to his sister, and she must prepare herself to see him leave home again, and even to see him go to foreign countries. In vain little Ariel, her pretty greyhound, bounded about her. She was too sad to look at him.

As she stood thus she felt a soft arm encircle her waist, and turning, saw her mother's face full of love and sympathy.

"What aileth thee, my Edith? Hath aught happened to pain thee, that thou weepest thus?" she asked.

Edith hid her face on her mother's shoulder, and only said, "Oh pardon me, my mother. It is nothing. I have no real cause of grief. Do not be troubled about me."

"Nay, but thou art not apt to shed tears for nothing, my daughter. I think thy mother hath divined thy secret. Thou thinkest our Valentine hath come home to us changed, and less loving than he used to be."

"It is so indeed, my mother. Neither doth he love me nor seek my company as he did before he left us."

"Have patience yet awhile, my Edith. Let us see what our love and his home will do. Think not more of it yet, but come with me to the herb garden. The merry voice of little Alice came on the air just now. We shall find nurse there and some of the maids, and see if they have gathered

good store of lavender and rosemary for Goodwife Freeman
to distil. The Lady Willoughby hath retired to her chamber to write, and I can enjoy an hour or two with my children."

Edith obeyed gladly, and they descended the flight of
steps together, and crossed the garden, and emerged through
an arch cut in the yew hedge into the other called the herb
garden. Here grew abundance of all those plants so much
used in medicine, in confections and syrups. There were
beds of camomiles, and of liquorice, and plantations of lavender and rosemary.

No sooner had Lady Carewe and Edith entered this fra-
grant garden, than a shout of joy was heard from Alice,
echoed by Martin, and both came running from among the
blooming lavender, carrying large bunches in their hands.
Two of the maids belonging to the still-room department
were busy cutting the long stalks from the plants, and the
task of the children was to hold them and carry them to the
baskets. Nurse was at work in a stone pavilion at the end
of the garden, and had many things to say to my lady, but
the children must first show her the large heaped baskets that
were ready to be carried in when Roger and John, the gardeners, came for them.

"No need to wait for the gardeners; let me take them,"
cried Henry out of breath with the haste he was in, and
already seizing on one.

"Have I not told thee, Master Henry," said nurse, "that
to bring the dog into the garden is a forbidden thing? See
now how he is treading down the thyme."

"Indeed, I had forgotten, nurse. Here, Lion, come away."

"Thou shouldst not forget, Henry; let it be the last time," said Lady Carewe.

"It shall, my mother; but wait for me while I take him away, if you will be so good. I am tired of running for their bowls, and want to come to you and Edith. Lion will wait at the gate."

Henry returned in a very little while, and began to assist vigorously in the work that was going on; and as soon as he was among them, there was sure to be laughter and merriment; though a little shy and quiet with strangers, he was always full of his jokes and fun with his sisters and brothers, and Edith quite forgot her heaviness while she sported about with the little ones. Lady Carewe had taken her seat by nurse, and was listening to her sad account of the state of Master Valentine's ruffles and collars, and giving her orders for repairs, and promising a supply of new linen and cambric.

When this important affair was concluded, and the baskets were quite filled, she dismissed nurse, and took charge of the children herself. This was the thing they liked better than anything in the world, and Henry gladly resigned the baskets to the gardeners, who now made their appearance, and followed her with Edith, as she walked between the two little ones. She took them first to the kitchen garden, where she wished to see the state of the vegetables, and where they had numbers of questions to ask. What especially interested her was the progress the potatoes were making. She had a small plot of those rare vegetables, and expected to succeed well in growing them. She also had a frame for raising melons, of which she was very proud. The peas were still bearing, and the cauliflowers and cabbages were good.

Outside the garden was an orchard of cherry and apple trees, among which were some golden pippins, and these were nearly all the fruit trees about the place.

Having walked through the kitchen garden, they went into the pretty flower garden with the lawn and the fountain again, and there, seated in one of the arbours with little Martin on her knee, and Alice and Edith one on each side, and Henry on the ground at her feet, she gave them a lesson about birds and flowers, their names and habits, and how to know each ; and if little Martin could not understand much of it, he was quite enough amused with arranging the rose leaves, that he had picked up on the grass, in pretty shapes on the round table before them.

They would never have been tired of listening to their mother, but Lord Willoughby and Sir Arthur interrupted them before an hour was out, and she joined them in a walk up and down the lawn. Edith then took charge of her little brother and sister, and sported about with them, but her heart was heavy ; she was longing for Valentine, and hurt at his neglect. She stole away from the children, therefore, when they were engrossed by some play Henry had contrived for them, and walked apart, her eye seeking her mother, as it always did when she was troubled. But here again she found no comfort. Her mother was listening to Lord Willoughby with an anxious face, and her father's countenance was heavy with care. What could be the matter? They could not have sad thoughts like hers.

As she passed them once more nearly, she heard the words "ship-money" and "Mr. Hampden." She could remember that the year before her father had appeared to suffer much anxiety on **Mr. Hampden's** account, and though she knew not the cause, she grieved that the anxiety had returned, and heaved a deep sigh.

"Sigh not, ladie, sigh not so," said a voice behind her, and at the same moment a hand was laid on her shoulder.

"Valentine! thou art come at last, then?"

"Thou knowest I must amuse these friends of mine. We have had a splendid game at bowls, and we have since been through the stables. Truly our father is rich in gallant steeds! Twenty stand there in stall such as the king's majesty might be proud of. I would I had one for mine own to ride in his service."

"Thou dost not still wish it, my brother? Thou wilt not really seek to go into foreign countries, and leave us for such dangers as thou mightest run into?"

Edith's eyes were brimful of tears, and they even began to trickle down her cheeks.

"Foolish girl! Nay, but do not let thy tears rain down like that. Thou wilt dim thy bright eyes and spoil thy pretty rounded cheeks."

"Speak not so foolishly, Valentine," she replied, dashing away her tears; "thou makest me feel angry with thee, and that is worse than feeling miserable."

"But listen to me, Edith. I long for change. I am tired of Oxford. Then our king! If thou hadst but seen him as I have: so stately, so grave, so proud, yet withal so courteous, thou wouldst burn to serve him as I do. And to think of the wrongs of his nephews, the Palatine and the brave impetuous-Rupert! The war lags for want of true hearts. Thou must help me with our father."

Edith shook her head mournfully, and they walked away together in deep talk, going up the steps to the terrace, and then out of sight.

The bell had rung for evening prayers, and the whole family had assembled in the chapel, when they entered together. The rays of the setting sun that fell through the painted glass sent not in sufficient light, or it would have been noticed by all that Edith's face was pale and melancholy; but the solemn tone of the organ under Mr. Russell's hands calmed her, and she joined in his thanksgiving that the family was once more united, and his prayer for a blessing on it, with something like a dawning hope that Valentine had been moved by her entreaties to think a little longer before he took any rash resolution. Yet Henry, who kneeled by her, observed her agitated state.

"Valentine hath not vexed thee?" he asked, with a face half of pity, half of anger, when the service was over.

"No, no. Good night, my brother. Thou hast a kind heart. Make him happy in his home all thou canst, and see that thou forwardest all his wishes to be merry with his friends."

CHAPTER IV.

THE CHASE.

A WEEK of continual festivities and sports had passed at Crewhurst. Hawking, fishing, boating, riding, visits in the neighbourhood, company at home, kept Valentine in a state of high spirits and excitement; and Sir Arthur was so happy in having his favourite son beside him, that he entered into all the amusements with zest, and seemed to have forgotten his cares, whatever they might have been.

But now on a fine August morning, when everything looks bright and peaceful in the park and avenue, what ails Valentine that he is so out of harmony with the scene? He is walking up and down the greensward by the roadway chafing with impatience. Sometimes stopping to look towards the Hall, as if expecting some one; then stamping, and muttering words that sound very like some of the fashionable oaths of the time. His hat is on the grass; beside it his gun; at last he flings himself down at full length, exclaiming, "We have lost the day now. I care not whether he comes or no. What time is there for aught like sport?"

While he thus fretted himself, his two friends lay lazily and in provoking contrast to his state of turmoil, each on one of the stone seats that were placed at intervals under the trees. Lord Morley had a smile of derision on his face, and Wilmot, placing his head on one side as a critic contemplates a picture, said:

"Most excellent Valentine, thy vassals are not so obedient to thy behests as thou didst fondly imagine."

"Thou shalt see soon how that will be," exclaimed Valentine, in a loud and angry tone, starting to his feet and seizing his hat. "Wait only till my return;" and so saying he set off at a quick pace homewards, a sort of dry cough from one of his friends, and a long, low whistle from the other, adding fuel to the flame of his passion as he hurried onwards.

The sport they were bent upon consisted in a kind of *battue* in the chase, which was often practised at that time of year, when it was too early to shoot game. A number of people were sent into the woods to beat the bushes and drive into a narrower and narrower circle all the wild creatures contained in them; foxes, squirrels, badgers, rabbits, hares— whatever, in short, was there; while the sportsmen stationed in the centre, armed with cross-bows, guns, or even stones and sticks, shot or knocked down whatever they pleased. This does not sound like very gentlemanly sport, but neither do bull-baiting, bear-baiting, and cock-fighting, which were still favourite amusements. We become, by little and little, less cruel as the stream of time flows on.

To enjoy this sport, the attendance of a large number of the servants would be required; and, indulged as Valentine was, he could not order this without his father's permission. He had intended to obtain it when the family assembled for prayers as usual at half-past six; but his father had already gone out on horseback, not to return for some hours. This was quite an unusual thing, and completely thwarted Valentine's wish to start for the chase immediately after breakfast. Still, if his father returned at nine o'clock there might be time, and Henry was ordered to be on the watch on the road by which he was expected, give Valentine's message, and bring the keepers and their assistants to the gates of the chase with all possible despatch. Here, therefore, the three young men waited; but nine o'clock came and passed and there were no tidings of Henry, and half-past nine came, and still there were no signs of him. Lord Morley now began to question the necessity of obtaining Sir Arthur's permission at all, arguing that it was certain to be granted, and that the accident of his absence was quite sufficient to excuse this deviation from accustomed rules. He reminded Valentine that, according to his own showing, he had perfect power to do whatever he liked, and could always make his doings appear right to his father if he managed well; and that, being the eldest son of the house, surely he could take it upon him to order so trifling an affair as this.

Valentine, though his conscience rather pricked him, determined to act upon this advice, and the three repaired to Woodruffe's cottage, which formed the very beginning of the village before mentioned. They scarcely expected to find him at home, but hoped to discover from his mother, who kept house for him, where he was. He was, however, at his cottage; but when Valentine made his request known to him, he shook his head. His master, Sir Arthur, had sent word that he should wait at home till further orders, and even if it had not been so, he could not go hunting in the chase without special leave. Valentine said that though Woodruffe waited at home himself, he might send for the under-keepers and foresters and their boys, and as to leave to go hunting in the chase, the word of his master's son was quite enough.

Woodruffe, however, made no move and sent no messages for his assistants. He stood leaning on his staff, looking troubled and puzzled, but evidently not intending to act on this sort of leave.

Valentine became very angry, especially as he saw a mocking expression on Lord Morley's face, and began to talk loudly and abusively to Woodruffe, in which his friends joined, but this made not the slightest impression on the keeper. He maintained a perfectly respectful manner, but continued firm in his resolution, not to order out the people without Sir Arthur's leave.

Valentine was obliged to give in—what could he do? but in order to issue one command that might be obeyed, he desired Woodruffe to go in search of Master Henry, who was watching on the road, and ask whether Sir Arthur had come back. Woodruffe said he was very sorry, but his orders were not to leave his cottage till Sir Arthur sent down to him, and to employ all his men on the upper plantations till dinner, so that he had no one about to go a message for him.

Thus baffled, the three young men returned to the avenue, after seeing Woodruffe shut himself in again, and another half hour slowly passed. It was now past ten; all the morning was lost; and Valentine was hurrying off home-wards, with he scarcely knew what purpose, when Henry at last appeared, walking slowly and heavily with Lion by his side and his usual oak stick in his hand. Valentine stopped short.

"Move thy legs faster, man!" he cried. "There's lead in thy feet surely. No wonder we wait so long if this be thy way of coming on."

But Henry made no better haste, and by the time the brothers met Valentine was in a fever of impatience. What then was his irritation, when he heard that his father had returned truly, but that when Henry, running to him as soon as he appeared, had made the request about the chase, his answer had been, "No member of my family, nor one of my servants, must enter the chase this day. Remember it is my command."

"The boy cannot have done his message well," said Lord Morley, who with Wilmot had come up to the place where the two brothers were standing silent, and looking at each other.

"Or he is making up a false tale," said Wilmot.

The blood rushed to Henry's face, and his eyes flashed with anger.

"Nay, Henry Wilmot, my brother was never known to speak what was false," replied Valentine.

Henry looked gratefully at him, and asked what he would like to do now, and if there was anything in which he could help. At this moment, the tame stag, seeing his friend Henry, came bounding from the herd and stood close by him to be caressed and patted.

"Where is my father? I will myself hear the meaning of this strange command," said Valentine.

"My father waited only while horses were prepared, and then set out for London, taking Ralph and William to attend him."

"For London! How is this?"

"He said nought to me. He spent all the time alone with our mother. I did but wait to see him go, and I heard him leave the same command with all at home about the chase."

"A strange fancy truly!" said Lord Morley.

"Sir Arthur meant surely that he would have no hunting there this day," said Wilmot. "He meant not that we should none of us go and wander among those old gnarled trees, and it may be take a shot at a rabbit. The paths look inviting to the last degree, and I mean to go in, so please you, Master Henry."

"So will not I," said Henry; "nor shalt thou if I can hinder thee."

"Thou art a proper young braggart, methinks!" said Wilmot. "Stand aside with thy dog and let me pass."

"Henry, thou art forgetting thyself strangely," said Valentine, "to stand thus in Master Wilmot's path. I take the same view of the matter with him. My father could not possibly mean that we should not go into the chase at all. What hurt can it do? He may have some wish about the vert or the game; but as for walking in the paths, that we may surely do."

"Our father said, 'No member of my family is to enter the chase this day,'" said the sturdy Henry.

"Ah! but he meant 'with an intention to hunt there.'"

"He did *not*," replied Henry.

"What! dost thou contradict me thus with thy rustical preciseness! I tell thee thou art a clown and a puritan to say so."

Henry's blood boiled. All the passions that Mr. Russell had been labouring to conquer began to rise in their fury. He neither spoke nor moved, however, but Lord Morley laughed scornfully at the "fearful scowl on brow and lip," as he said.

"We will go in, and he shall go with us, to cure him of his puritan notions," added his lordship.

Henry struck his stick so violently on the ground that it made a deep hole and planted itself there, and he leaned on it as much as to say, "Here I stand. Move me who can!"

"Ho, there! open the gates!" cried Valentine, knocking at the lodge door.

There was no one at home but Leeson's old mother, who came out smiling and curtseying to her young master with the key on her finger.

"Do not open the gates, Dame Leeson," said Henry in a firm voice.

The poor old woman stood looking from one to the other quite puzzled what to do.

"I tell thee to open the gates," cried Valentine. "What! are my commands to be disobeyed by every menial? Open instantly."

"Your master, Sir Arthur, has forbidden it," said Henry.

"He has not," retorted Valentine. "I will make short work with the matter," and seizing the key from the old dame he opened the gates himself, and as he did so, Prince bounded into the chase; Valentine, wishing to drive him back, ran after him, carrying the key and leaving the gates open.

No sooner was he out of sight, than Morley making a signal to Wilmot, the two seized on Henry, pinned his arms to his sides, and dragged him by main force towards the gates. He struggled with all his strength, and Lion gave a fierce growl and prepared to spring on Morley, who, seeing his danger, relinquished his hold on Henry, and pulling up the oak stick, aimed so furious a blow at the dog, that had not Henry broken its force by rushing in and stopping it, receiving in so doing a heavy blow himself, Lion would probably have been killed.

"Down, Lion," he cried, "down, sir!" and the obedient animal was quiet in a moment. Then the two combatants stood glaring at each other, Morley still wielding the club.

"You shall not dare to touch my dog," said Henry, gasping for breath.

"Walk forward with us, then," said Morley.

"I will not," replied Henry, violently; and he was instantly seized again by his two assailants. His strength, as he felt, was powerless against them, and his arm was almost disabled by the blow it had received, so he struggled less, but Lion growled again, and Morley kicked him.

"Stop!" cried Henry in such a tone that the two young men obeyed instinctively. "The dog will not see this ruffianly conduct and be quiet, and you shall not maul and kick him. Call him in, Dame Leeson, and keep him safe. Go in, Lion, go in!"

Lion obeyed very unwillingly, with his tail between his legs, and a low growl like distant thunder. Henry was then dragged on for ten minutes or so by his two tormentors, without resistance, for he found it was useless, and then they met Valentine returning, after an unsuccessful pursuit of Prince.

"Ah, I am glad to see Henry has come," he cried, as he walked smilingly towards them. "Is it not free and pleasant among the old trees?"

"Bid thy friends let me go, Valentine," said Henry. "I have come far enough to please them!"

"What, gentlemen!" said Valentine, flushing with anger. "This was going too far. I meant not to use unmannerly force. Take your hands off my brother, so please you."

They obeyed, and Lord Morley laughed. "It was but a jest," said he. "Here, give me thy hand, Master Henry, and thank me for a pleasant walk in this old wood, and for saving thy conscience; for if thou art chidden, thou canst put finger in eye and say, 'I did it on compulsion.'"

Henry held back his hand, but did not move. He was free to go now. Why, instead of going, did he rush forward further into the wood at his utmost speed?

"What can he mean?" asked Morley.

"I cannot tell," replied Valentine. "But hold! who are those two huntsmen I see among the trees? By heaven, they are hunting in our chase. See, they are even now starting their dogs after a stag."

"And the stag is thy pretty sister's pet, methinks," said Wilmot.

All three now followed Henry; but before any of them could reach the spot, the dogs had run down poor Prince,

THE KING'S HUNTSMAN.

and the huntsman had given him his death wound. He
was so tame that he had not taken alarm till too late. He
never imagined any harm was meant him.

Henry, first reaching the spot, knelt beside his poor dead
friend, gently stroking his dappled side, and at the thought
of Edith some tears fell on it. He was entirely out of breath
and could not speak, but he looked reproachfully at the men.
Valentine, however, rushing up, cried,

"Who are you that have presumed to enter my father's
chase and kill his deer?"

One of the men laughed insolently.

"And who are you, my young master, that calls this
ground thy father's, which is, in truth, the king's majesty's,
and belongs to the royal forest of Windsor? Be pleased to
return within thy bounds, and trespass not here where thou
hast no right."

"Thou liest like a villain and a thief, as thou art,"
returned Valentine, drawing his sword, "and if thou movest
not off, thou and thy mate and thy dogs, we are strong
enough to force thee."

"Carewe!" said Lord Morley, seizing his arm, "art thou
mad? These are huntsmen belonging to the royal household. Thou wilt get thyself into some serious danger by
thy violence. Dost not see the crest on their sleeves? 'Tis
the royal arms of England?"

Valentine was trembling with passion, but he lowered
his sword.

There was a rushing sound through the ferns, and
Lion, springing on the foremost huntsman, pinioned him
to the earth. The next instant, the other man had shot

the faithful dog in the side. He let go his hold, rolled over and gave one short howl. Henry started up, threw his clinched hands wildly above his head, and then fell beside his wounded friend, caressing him, begging him not to die, " Oh, not to die! but to look at him once more!"

Poor Lion did look at him, one last, loving look; licked the cheek that was laid close to him, and the hand that was fondling him; but the eyes became glazed; slower and slower moved the tongue; and then he stretched out his feet stiffly and died.

The cry that Henry uttered rang through the wood and went to Valentine's heart. To every one else there, it seemed childish folly to feel so much for a dog. Henry had shed tears for Prince, but none came now. He felt wild with mingled rage and grief, and he buried his face in the grass, clutching at the tree roots and tearing up the earth in his anguish. He heard contention around him, loud words, oaths, the clashing of swords. He never moved. If they killed him as he lay he did not care. At last he heard Valentine telling him they must go home, that he must stand up and come away, but he heeded nothing. Then he heard Valentine exacting promises that Lion should be carefully buried where he lay. This roused him at last.

"Nobody shall touch him!" he cried, standing upright. " I will take him home. He shall not be left here to be trampled on by robbers."

" You had best keep a civil tongue in your head, young master," said one of the men; and as he spoke he stooped as if to move the dog.

" Do not come near him," cried Henry. " I will kill any one that touches him."

There was a laugh at this boyish threat, which gave Henry double strength. He raised poor Lion in his arms. It was no slight weight, but the state of excitement in which Henry was made it seem like a feather. He walked fast on, his dog's honest face pressed against his breast, and the fine strong brown paws hanging stiff and cold over his arms. The three others followed silently. Henry, who had walked fast at first, began to stagger under his burden.

" Here, let me carry the old head!" said Lord Morley, in a bantering tone.

" No, no, do not dare to touch him!" cried Henry, and again he walked strongly on. Valentine never spoke, but looked dejected and miserable. At last they reached the gates, which were open. Henry passed through without stopping to look behind, and while the others delayed, locking the gates and giving up the key, hurried towards an old hollow oak which stood at a short distance in the midst of a thicket of holly and hawthorn. Through this he forced his way, laid his sad burden gently on the greensward, and then sat down on a root of the aged tree and buried his face in his hands.

Some one touched his shoulder soon. It was Valentine.

" Henry, Henry, leave him here and come home. The hour of noon is near. We must not excite observation by our absence."

Henry only shook off the hand.

" Come, Henry; do, pray, come. The dinner hour is near."

"I cannot go home."

"What shall I say? How shall I account for thy absence?"

"Say anything thou willest."

At this moment the bell was heard from the Hall, giving warning that it wanted but half-an-hour to the time when dinner would be served.

"I must go, Henry. Even now I shall scarcely be in time. Poor Lion! I would have carried him for thee gladly, oh, gladly; but—" He hurried away without saying more. Henry sat without moving till the sound of the footsteps was lost in the distance, then he looked up. He was alone at last. Then all the sorrow that had been pent up burst forth. Thick and fast fell his tears. Sobs, mingled with moans and broken words, burst from his aching heart. He threw his arms round his faithful dog; took the cold paws in his hands, and lay on the grass, feeling as if a black weight of misery had fallen over all the world.

It was not only this cruel death of his dog. Wretched thoughts of Edith and her stag, wretched thoughts about Valentine, about his father who had been so shamefully disobeyed, of his mother who would feel—Oh what would she not feel!—when she knew of the disobedience. Wherever he looked there was nothing but misery. Then came bewildered wonder as to the meaning of what had happened in the chase; the meaning of what those men had said. Could there be any connection between their claiming the chase for the king, and his father's command that no one should go into it? Was some misfortune hanging over his father? He raised his eyes from the ground, where

they had been fixed, and gazed up at the calm, blue summer
sky and the sunlight among the green leaves, as if to try
to find some help there. Among them, he saw the iron
tracery over the gates and the motto of his father's crest,
"Trustie and Trewe," and this made him look down again
at Lion.

"Thou shalt rest here," he said. "Trustie and trewe
thou wert, and in defence of thy master against wicked men
who would do him wrong thou didst meet thy death. I
cannot carry thee farther, and I will not leave thee here to
be seen by unfeeling people. Here shalt thou be buried,
and those words shall stand up above thy grave."

As he spoke he made his way out of the thicket, went
quickly to the lodge, and asked a little boy who opened the
door to his knock, if his father would lend him a spade and
pickaxe. The old woman came out at his voice, and seemed
surprised both to see him there still and at his request, and
inclined to question the meaning of it, but for this he had
no patience.

"Give me what I ask for," he said. "If you had attended to my words this morning, it had been better for
us all."

There was something in his tone that made her feel he
must be obeyed, so she brought the tools and he took them,
telling her he would return them soon, and went back to his
thicket.

Henry now began to dig a grave. His arm had become
very painful, but he did not care for that; the pain of body
even seemed a relief to him, it was so much less hard to
bear than his pain of mind. It took him a long time to

dig a hole that would be large enough. The ground was hard and mixed with tree roots, which required the pickaxe to get them out. Often he had to stop and sit down to rest, but the moment he had recovered his breath he began again, with an impatience that seemed to drive him on. When he had done, he tore some branches from the oak and laid them with their fresh leaves at the bottom and lined the sides with them. All was ready now. He had only to lay his dog in his grave. He began to raise poor Lion, but when, as he did so, the head drooped down and the legs dragged along the ground, strength and courage failed him all at once; he let his dog slide from his grasp, and sank down beside him on the heap of moist earth he had raised at the edge. He was in truth exhausted with fatigue, heat, grief, and all the passions he had gone through. At first he lay in a kind of stupor, but before long he fell fast asleep.

CHAPTER V.

VALENTINE'S TRIUMPH.

"Henry! my brother Henry!" these words awoke him. It was Valentine who had come. Henry stared round quite bewildered. There was a red light among the trees as if the sun were setting. Was that possible? He fixed his eyes on Valentine's face, which was full of sorrow and sympathy.

"Is there aught amiss, Valentine? What is it? Is my mother ill or unhappy?"

Valentine raised Henry's head from the ground and supported it on his shoulder. Then the boy saw his poor Lion lying cold and dead close beside him at the edge of the grave he had dug, and everything rushed back to his memory at once.

"Help me to lay him in, Valentine," said he slowly rising, but as he did so he turned sick and giddy and sank down again.

"Thou art ill, Henry. What can I do for thee?"

"Couldst thou get me a cup of cold water at the lodge? I am parched with thirst."

Valentine went and quickly returned with a flagon of pure water, which Henry took gratefully and drank with eagerness. As Valentine held it to his lips, the two

E

brothers looked into each other's eyes, a look full of sadness but full of love. Whatever had been wrong between them, was put right now.

"You will help me," said Henry rising. He took Lion's head tenderly in his hands, raised it from the grass, stroked the ears gently down, and kissed the fine broad forehead and put the paws straight. Valentine at the same time raised the hind legs and they lowered him gently down, and laid him on the branches, and covered him over with others. Then they threw in the earth. Many a tear from Henry's eyes glittered among the leaves before they were all covered, but he never stopped. He worked with feverish haste; Valentine, not so much used to such work, got tired and stood by, looking at him while he piled a mound over the grave.

"I shall not forget the place. But what is that in thy hand?"

"Thy oak stick. I found it on the path."

"Give it me," said Henry, and he planted it firmly in the mound. "I shall never carry it again."

Valentine offered to return the tools. When he had done so, they took their way homewards.

"I am very anxious to talk with thee, Henry," said Valentine as they walked, "about that which happened this morning, and how we should comport ourselves about it. Whatever be the meaning of the presence of those huntsmen in the chase and the words they said, there can be no need that we should mix ourselves up with the matter. Why should my father be still more vexed by hearing that we were there at all?"

"I do not understand thee, Valentine."

" I repeat, why should my father be troubled about it ? We were there only a few minutes actually. My going in at all was only to catch the stag, and yours a frolic of Morley's."

" Still we were there. We must surely tell him, or my mother, as he is from home, that we were there, and of the death of Edith's stag and of Lion, and of the conduct of those men."

" We must not tell either him or my mother. In fact, it is impossible now, for Morley and Wilmot (who is indeed the best romancer of the two) made up a most admirable story about thy absence, accounting for it in a very ingenious manner, while we dined, and gave a description of our morning's employments without saying a word about our short incursion into the chase."

" And didst not thou supply the truth which they concealed ?"

" Thou wouldst not have had me give the lie to my friends at our own board, especially when they only tried to shield me by their story?   It mattered little to them."

" Thou must go to them, and insist on their explaining to my mother this falsehood of theirs as well as they can. I know not how ; but explained and put right it must be."

" They have both left Crewhurst.   They took horse at two o'clock, and are gone on to London."

" I am right glad to hear it.   But it is strange : methought they were to stay a fortnight."

" They intended it, in truth ; but nothing could stop them.   I know not why they went."

" We shall be better for their absence.   Drive cowardly

thoughts away with them. Let us go straight to my mother and tell her the truth, cost what it may."

"It is very easy for thee, very easy indeed, to say that. There was no fault on thy part. Thou wert forced in. It is on me that all the evil consequences will fall. My father will not forgive the disobedience, and still less the deceit already practised on my mother, though neither was fault of mine. I made the old dame at the lodge promise not to tell any one of our going through the gates, and told her she should have a reward for her silence. When I took back the tools, she told me no one but herself knew it."

Henry now broke into passionate remonstrances: reminded Valentine of his father's love — his mother's tenderness; cast contempt on cowardly falsehoods, and entreated Valentine to shake himself free of them at once. But Valentine could not resolve to take this fearful step. He knew that his father, indulgent as he was, was a stern judge in cases of failure in the duty and reverence he considered his due, and would be disgusted and incensed at the deceit permitted at least, if not joined in, by himself, and he feared the punishment would be to send him back to Oxford, instead of letting him go into the service of the king, either abroad or at home, a thing he anxiously desired, and had already begun to hint at vaguely to his father. To keep Henry quiet, however, he pretended that he would only delay his confession, and that all he asked was that Henry would say nothing till he had made it. "It would be absolutely fatal to me and treacherous in thee if thou didst," said he; "see what an effect it would have if thou didst tell of this matter? It must come from me first."

" Surely it must. I will not speak of it till thou dost."
" Promise me that faithfully."
" I do promise it. But delay not thy confession, for till
it is made, I know not how to look at my mother, nor Edith,
nor Mr. Russell. To them all I ever tell everything that
concerns me or them. How can I talk with Edith as if all
was right with me, when I know her stag has been killed,
and my poor Lion is lying cold in his grave ? "
" Well, well, only remember that promise, and all shall
be right."
They had reached the Hall now. It was almost the hour
of evening prayers, and Henry, weak and faint for want of
food, as well as from the consequences of all he had gone
through, staggered up to his own room to try to compose
himself, and put his disordered dress into a better state, so
that he might make his appearance there without exciting
observation. His own impulse would have been to hurry
straight to his mother, and open his whole heart to her, and
lay his sorrows at her feet, and ask her to help Valentine,
and forgive the share he had had in causing them, and then
to have Edith's sympathy and give her his, while Mr. Russell
would counsel and strengthen him. This new plan of concealment and silence was misery to him, and actually seemed to
confuse his very senses.

When he opened his door, expecting to be quiet and alone,
he saw to his surprise that nurse was there, seated in a chair
by the window, fast asleep, with a little table by her, covered
with a cloth and some supper for him.

" My boy ! " she said, waking up as he went in, " what have
you been doing, and what have they been doing to you ? Come,

come, tell your old nurse. Why, what a face you have got! and here's a torn sleeve, and your brow is damp and cold, and look at your hands. Sit down, I say, and eat. I don't believe none of their tales and lies, those fellows. A row to Hampton Court to see the young princes in their coroach, and a walk back! Marry come up! Mighty fine! my boy has not been there. Ay, ay! old Dame Leeson, with her nods and groans, meant something more than that! Eat, I say, or drink some of this wine first, and then eat afterwards, and I will help thee to dress then.''

Happily for Henry, nurse talked so much herself, and then busied herself so earnestly finding another suit for him to wear, and getting him the water to wash his face and hands, and there was so much need for haste to be ready for prayers, that he was scarcely required to say a word himself; and poor kind nurse's supper did him good, though at first he did not feel as if he could touch it, and nurse's kindness did him good too. But when he heard the bell he crept down and entered the chapel like a guilty creature, unable to meet his mother's eye. The organ seemed to send forth a confused whirl of sounds, and he could not compose his thoughts so as to join in the prayers. When he went like the others to receive his mother's blessing, he never looked at her, and ran off and up to his room without speaking to Edith.

Next morning he awoke from uneasy dreams to still more uneasy thoughts, and got up with the determination to seek Valentine the moment that prayers were over, and force him to end this state of wretchedness at once; but Valentine began a lively talk with Edith as they walked away, and continued it throughout breakfast. Henry was perfectly astonished that Valentine could be so gay, but after vain attempts to catch his attention, saw that he was rising from table, and going out with their mother, and that she led him to the terrace.

"Now," thought Henry, "now he will tell her all," and he went to his lessons with Mr. Russell with a lighter heart.

Valentine, on the contrary, felt his heart sink as he followed his mother, fearing that by some means she had discovered his secret, and her first words confirmed his fears.

"I grieve, my son," she said, "that trouble should arise among us so soon after thy arrival. We had hoped thy stay might be passed in peace and joy, but, alas, it is not so."

"It has not been by any intention of mine, but by a a mistake," Valentine began.

"My son, thou art as innocent of the danger that threatens us, as I am myself. No, we share with others the sufferings of these evil times. The country cries out for a parliament, and the king grants it not. Meanwhile, he needs money, and the irregular levies oppress and anger the people."

"But the people should give willingly to so good a king."

"Thy father thinks not so. He thinks that by the ancient laws of England, it is only the Commons' House of Parliament that can levy moneys on the people. Remember the words of Mr. Hampden when he was committed to close custody in the Gatehouse five years ago, when our dear and lamented friend, Sir John Eliot, so soon to give up his life in the Tower, was still there. 'I would be content to lend as well as others,' these were Mr. Hampden's words, 'but I fear to draw on myself that curse in Magna Charta—which should be read twice a year—against those that infringe it.'"

"Yet, my mother, 'twas poor and pitiful in so rich a man to refuse so small a sum. Surely a niggard act!"

"Thou seest not, nor understandest the matter! But it is for no tax thy father is at this moment called in question. It is for his right to the chase."

"The chase!" echoed Valentine.

"Thou hast not perhaps heard how much the king, led on by evil counsellors, is enlarging his forests. He hath seized on the whole manor of Beaulieu, and taken it into the New Forest, whereby the Earl of Southampton is well nigh ruined. The forest of Rockingham is extended from six miles to sixty. In other places people have redeemed their land by heavy fines; many small landholders, and even cottagers, have had to pay sums according to their means; in this way money flows into the exchequer."

"Then these lands that they redeem have once been the king's?"

"It is true. They were in ancient times wild forest, but so was half England. No one could wish to see it return to that state."

"Still these are encroachments."

"Not always. Many landholders have titles granted by various sovereigns to the portions they hold. These, produced before the Forest Court, held at Stratford in Essex by my Lord Holland, are respected; the fines are levied on those who have them not. The blow hath now fallen on thy father. Only the night before last, at a late hour, he received intimation by an express from my Lord Holland, that his chase of right belongs to the royal forest of Windsor, and would yesterday be taken possession of by his majesty. It was to avoid any dispute between our people and those of the royal household that thy father forbade any member of his family, or any of his dependents, to enter it. He went to London to make his suit to the king in person, believing that he himself knows not nor intends this act of injustice."

Appalled to hear that the matter was so serious, and that he had caused, by his disobedience, the very mischief his father dreaded, Valentine turned pale and stood silent.

"Thou art shocked, my son, and no wonder; but we will do our utmost to save the land, were it only for thy sake. If it must go, we must bear the loss, but thy father will redeem the village, even though he pay a ruinous fine. Our poor people must not be turned out of the cottages they love as their own."

"But we are safe by our title; that cannot be disputed?"

"Not in justice; for that our charter was granted by King Henry is certain, and it was established before the commissioners in the time of Queen Elizabeth; but strange to say, it can nowhere be found."

"Lost!" said Valentine. "Surely so important a parchment should have been safely guarded."

"Thy father hath never had it in his possession," she replied. "Yet thy grandfather especially mentioned it in his last illness, and said it was safe. He died suddenly, and without saying much he meant to say to us, striving in vain to articulate words that would not come. He was in danger of his life in the troubled times of Queen Mary for conscience sake; the Carewes have ever been Reformers; and his papers were seized at that period. We believe

that he said in his illness rather what he wished than what
he knew, artd that our charter then fell into the hands of
the government of that day, and hath been found by the
present, and thus they know we are defenceless."

Valentine stood silent again.

"Thy melancholy grieves me to the heart, my son,"
said Lady Carewe. "How changed is thy face since only
a week since thou camest home to us with all the brightness of youth upon thee! Order thy favourite horse, and
take a groom to attend thee, and ride for an hour or two
this lovely morning. Thy father hath cherished that spirited
little horse, and many a time hath stroked down the white
star on his forehead, and longed to see thee mounted on
him. May it soon be so indeed."

Valentine was quite ready to agree to this proposal, and
was soon on his way.

With the careless lightness of his nature, he had soon
shaken off his melancholy. Putting his horse to a gallop,
he was miles away over heath and forest, by cultivated
land and green pasture, singing as he went, and casting
sorrow to the winds. All would be well. The king would
reverse the hateful order; his father would return in good
spirits; would never hear of the unlucky adventure of
yesterday; would have more festivities at the Hall; would
agree to his great wish for an introduction to the court.

Full of these pleasant imaginations, Valentine found
himself near the margin of a large mere, and heard the
barking of a dog, and saw overhead the bare branches of a
withered tree. Something in the sound and the sight
reminded him of Lion and of Henry. He drew up, left

off singing, and went on more slowly; then, turning a corner, came suddenly upon a lady and gentleman hawking, attended by a keeper with dogs. They were magnificently mounted, and were evidently people of distinction. Their falcon had, at the very moment of his approach, made its swoop on a heron, and the victim and his conqueror fell at their feet as he stopped. When the hawk had returned to his mistress's hand to be caressed, and to have his hood and jesses replaced, the lady said something in a low voice to her companion, who then looked hard at Valentine, and beckoned to him to approach.

"Pardon me, young gentleman," said he, "if I am mistaken, but it seems to me I speak to a son of Sir Arthur Carewe."

Valentine, respectfully taking off his hat, replied that he was right.

"Thy whole look and manner assures me," resumed the speaker, "that the Lord Morley has correctly estimated thy character; and that though thy father hath ever seemed ready to join the factious party, who would set up their vain conceits in opposition to the wise counsels and divinely-appointed rights of their king, whose will should be their law, yet thou hast a loyal and devoted heart, and art worthy of the honour I am now deputed to confer on thee. Our lovely mistress and queen extends her hand to thee, and permits thee the privilege of kissing it."

Valentine, intoxicated with joy, threw himself from his horse, flung his hat on the grass, and kneeling on one knee, fervently pressed his lips to the white and jewelled hand presented to him, vowing as he did so to devote his life to her service.

The queen smiled on him, and completed his conquest by a glance of her bright eyes.

"We are much beholden to my Lord Holland," she said, "for this introduction, and we hope to see thee again. Rise, now, and go on thy way. Thou mayst perchance hear from us ere long."

Valentine rose as he was commanded, and mounted his horse, riding away slowly and uncovered till he was out of sight of this royal vision of loveliness. Then careering off at full gallop, felt as if a glory was spread over earth and sky, and as if all nature did homage to him in his triumph.

He dashed up the avenue, through the park and into the court-yard, with his horse in a foam, and there saw the grooms busy over a number of dusty horses that had just come in. He saw at a glance that his father had returned.

CHAPTER VI.

HENRY'S DISGRACE.

WHILE Valentine was so pleasantly engaged, far differently had the hours passed with Henry. He was dull and distracted over his lessons, and quite unlike himself; so that Mr. Russell at last, shutting up the books they were attempting to study, looked him steadily in the face, and said to him, "This is but lost time, Henry. Thou hast something on thy mind."

Henry covered his face with his hands and did not speak.

"Tell me thy trouble, Henry. There is no grief so great but that a friend may lighten it. Surely I deserve thy confidence."

Henry sighed heavily. "You have indeed always been a true friend to me, Mr. Russell. Will you then, for this morning, cease to question me. I hope that before night, long before night comes again, I may tell you all that aileth me."

"Then I am right in thinking thou hast some secret sorrow?"

"Oh yes, oh yes, indeed! I am very miserable."

Mr. Russell looked at him with great concern. He loved Henry so much that to see this state of strange un-

usual silence and grief was truly painful, but he complied
with the request that had been so earnestly made, and dismissed his pupil immediately.

Henry, when lessons were over, had usually twenty things
to do, and was off to some active employment in a moment;
now he only used his liberty to run up to his own little
room, and shut himself in, anxious to avoid everybody till
he had heard from Valentine that his confession was made.

Lady Carewe, meanwhile, after spending an hour or two
over her many household cares and occupations, and reading
with Edith, went to the village, where she had been urgently
requested by Sir Arthur to prepare the inhabitants for the
possibility of their being ordered out of their cottages; while
at the same time she would soothe them with the hope that
he might prevent such a calamity, and with promises to protect them and establish them elsewhere if he were unable to
do so. It was a melancholy errand, and she felt very sad
herself. Edith, who had heard from her of the anxiety that
pressed so heavily, felt sad too, and missed her pretty stag,
who used always to gambol round her in the park. She often
looked round for him, and wondered where he was. As to
Lion, she wondered nothing about him; he was sure to be
with Henry wherever he was.

Everything about the village was outwardly peaceful, and
green, and pretty; but disquiet and fear had already got
among the inhabitants. Their lady's visit was much needed,
and brought much comfort. They had already heard of the
danger that hung over them, for a party of the king's guards
had come, and were quartered at the farm-house hard by.
Woodruffe had been there at the morning meal, and had

seen Farmer Rudd and his family with several of these men at their table, cutting into his beef and drinking his ale, and they had boasted that the ground his farm stood on would soon be the king's forest, as it once was and always ought to have been.

When the poor people heard that their honourable master, Sir Arthur, had gone to London to make his suit to the king about it, they seemed to feel as if everything was safe, for if Sir Arthur took it in hand he must succeed. Lady Carewe, wishing she could share in the confidence she had inspired, left them to return to the Hall. It seemed to her that even the heavy fine they might be prepared to pay would perhaps scarcely redeem the village, so determined seemed the purpose to take it, yet she felt ready to make any sacrifice that was in her power to save it.

The sound of horses' feet approaching rapidly was heard as she drew near, and Sir Arthur was soon seen far in advance of his servants and several other horsemen. She hurried on and met him as he alighted at the entrance, while the rest of his party turned off towards the court. Edith stood looking at her father, yet did not venture to speak to him, and Lady Carewe took his hand and gazed at him in silence, for on his face was an expression of sorrow so deep that she felt something worse than loss of property was hanging over them. He, also, spoke no word, but led Lady Carewe at once into his private room, where they remained together for a long while. Edith had seated herself in the corridor watching for her mother to come out, and when at last the door opened and she did come, her face was pale and her eyes red with weeping. Edith flew to her side.

"Things look very bad, my child," said Lady Carewe; " but I trust the worst will turn out to be a base calumny. Has Valentine returned?"

"No, my mother, I have but just inquired for him."

"Where is Henry ?"

"I know not. I have not seen him since he left the parlour after breakfast."

After a little inquiry, one of the servants said that Master Henry was up in his bed-room, John, the gardener, had seen him looking out of his window. Lady Carewe immediately went there, telling Edith she wished to see him alone.

Henry's room was so remote that he had heard no sound of his father's arrival. He still sat by his window, trying to learn the Latin lesson in which he had so grievously failed in the morning, and now and then looking out for Valentine, whose strange conduct in going out on his horse without telling him what had passed between their mother and him, had pained him very much, and left him in all the grief and perplexity of the morning. At his mother's gentle knock he opened his door, and his eyes fell before her.

"Henry !" she began, " never have I known deceit nor falsehood in thee. Tell me, wert thou and was Valentine in the chase yesterday ?"

The expected blow had fallen, then. Valentine had not made his confession. From others, not from themselves, had the events of yesterday come to the knowledge of his mother. Henry felt disgraced for ever in her eyes. He changed colour, he trembled, and his tongue clove to the roof of his mouth when he tried to speak. At last he stammered out, " Where is Valentine?"

"Is it possible ? art thou guilty then of disobedience, concealment, falsehood ? Oh, I could bear loss of fortune, loss of station, loss even of dear lives, better than this ! I trusted thee as myself."

Henry threw himself at her feet, clasping her dress, and drawing her back as she turned away from him. " Oh, my mother, pity me, and think the best of me thou canst!" These were all the words he could say. His voice was choked. By breaking his promise, and bringing Valentine to shame, he could have cleared himself in a moment, but neither was possible to him.

" Thou must come down with me to thy father."

" My father ! Has he returned ? Then there is no hope for us !"

" Henry, is it thus thou feelest at thy father's coming ? What a change!"

" Would he not wait till Valentine comes back ? Might I not see Valentine and talk with him first ?"

" Thy father will not wait. He requires thy instant attendance. In this, at least, show obedience."

She moved to the door, and Henry followed without another word.

Sir Arthur was seated at his table. Behind him stood Mr. Russell, and at his side the two huntsmen of the day before.

" That was the young gentleman," said one of them instantly, " who first ran up to us, and set his dog on us. Had not my comrade shot the brute I had been torn to pieces. It was the elder who drew on us."

" You may go for the present," said Sir Arthur ; " I will see you presently." The two men went from the room.

" Is this true, or a foul lie, Henry ?" said Sir Arthur, in a stern voice.

Henry did not speak.

" Dost thou remember my positive commands when I left home, and yet thou didst this thing ?"

Henry's anguish was almost past endurance. He stood before his father convicted of wilful disobedience, and of concealing his fault. But he could not break his promise, and he could not brand Valentine with the double disgrace of first causing all this wretchedness, and then flying from the consequences, and leaving everything to fall on his brother.

It was hard to bear, but Henry did not sink under the trial. He did not speak, but he looked steadfastly in his father's face. He was innocent, and he had a high and noble motive for his silence ; therefore, though he was very

pale, and though he trembled from head to foot, he could
meet his father's eye without quailing before it.

There was silence in the room for some time. Then
Sir Arthur, who usually preserved a perfect command
of himself, rose in extreme anger, his lips trembling with
passion.

"I will not endure this contemptuous silence," he
said. "A confession, a prayer for forgiveness, might have
moved me; but this stubbornness I cannot bear. Follow me."

Henry obeyed, and followed his father along many passages, and up several stairs, to an old and now uninhabited
part of the house, where there were some large rooms, either
totally unfurnished, or hung with faded tapestry, and containing a few old-fashioned chairs and tables, and such things.
Sir Arthur unlocked one of these, ordered Henry to go in,
locked the door on him, and left him without another
word.

It was at the very moment that Sir Arthur returned to
his room, leaving Henry a prisoner, that Valentine came in
from his ride, still under the excitement of the late meeting
with the queen. He went straight to welcome his father home,
meaning to keep up his plan of concealment, and bind Henry
strictly to it, for, now that his most ambitious hopes seemed
to be on the point of fulfilment, he was doubly anxious to
avoid giving offence. He appeared therefore with a smiling
face, flushed with his rapid ride, his eyes beaming with the
excitement of his feelings, and kneeled before his father of
receive his blessing, and say how rejoiced he was to receive
it again. Is it wonderful that his father, seeing this bright,

F

open, handsome face looking up respectfully and affectionately at his, and remembering that pale, trembling, silent boy
with his mournful but steady, and, as it appeared to him in
his anger, defiant gaze—is it wonderful that his father
said in his heart, "This, my eldest son, the son of my
love and my pride, is innocent; the fault has been the
other's. He alone is the guilty one." So deceitful are looks
sometimes !

Nevertheless he summoned the huntsmen back. He
could not doubt that Valentine had been in the chase. .
He now only had to discover why he had been there;
his own theory and partial conclusion was, that it had
been to save and protect his brother, who had gone first
alone.

"Do you know these men ?" said he to Valentine as
they entered, ushered in by Ralph, who remained without.

A thrill of fear shot through Valentine. He saw in a
moment that all was discovered, but the extremity of his position gave him power to meet it. "Unfortunately," said he,
in a tone of humility and grief, "I do know them. By a
total misapprehension of your wishes, as I have since learned
them from my mother, I went into the chase yesterday, and
finding these men had killed my sister's stag, I drew upon
them.

"Drew upon us, young sir !" said the man who spoke
before. "You wounded my companion, in revenge for his
saving me from your brother's dog; and had not Lord Morley
protected you, you would not have gone unscathed yourself."

"Valentine," said Sir Arthur, "as it does not appear

that you can throw any new light upon this unfortunate affair, by any further conference with the huntsmen, we have nothing more to say to them. Ralph, show these gentlemen to their horses."

There were a few moments of silence. Mr. Russell had remained throughout the whole of the proceedings, a mute but attentive observer of every thing that passed. He had now fixed his eyes steadily on Valentine. Lady Carewe had hidden her face in her handkerchief; she was completely overcome.

"You have to explain why you went into the chase, after my commands sent to you by Henry to the contrary," said Sir Arthur breaking the silence.

"Your command, sir, as I understood it, was, that we should not hunt in the chase. This we strictly obeyed. We neither took in gun nor cross-bow."

"My command was that you should not enter it," said Sir Arthur, raising his voice.

"I did not so understand Henry."

"Then he is guilty, as I thought. He could not, by possibility, mistake my words, which I even took the precaution to make him repeat after me. Yet, not only does he fail to deliver this message, but is himself, by the testimony of those two men, the first to disobey it."

Valentine's face flushed, and then became pale. Shame at his own base prevarications, shame at the injustice done to Henry, panic fear at the thought that a word from Henry might heap disgrace upon himself, by disclosing the truth, shook him to the soul.

"Thou feelest more deeply for thy brother than he de-

serves," said Sir Arthur, entirely mistaking the meaning of
the emotion he observed.

" Where is he ?" asked Valentine.

" Let us not think of him at present," replied Sir Arthur.
" His culpable disobedience, and thy rash behaviour in his
defence against these men, have cost us the chase."

" My father ! is it possible ?"

" The fine to redeem the chase I might have met, but
the ruinous sum I shall have to pay as penalty of thy rash-
ness, will render it impossible, without relinquishing other
and higher duties."

Valentine sank into a chair. He had been standing up
to this time, but this blow completely prostrated him.

" Far more painful to me than the loss of the chase, or
the loss of any amount of money," said Lady Carewe, looking up, " is the thought of my poor Henry. Nothing but
evidence I cannot gainsay, should make me believe this of
him. He hath faults, like all of us; but up to this time I
have never known him to be disobedient to his father, nor
guilty of untruth."

" Nor hath he now been guilty of untruth," said Mr.
Russell, speaking for the first time. " Henry hath neither to
you, my lady, nor to Sir Arthur, nor to me, denied going into
the chase.'

" But he hath not confessed it," rejoined Sir Arthur; " and
we know to a certainty that he was there before his brother.
To observe a disdainful silence, after the commission of a
fault, is next to a denial of it."

" There is a strange mystery about the matter," resumed
Mr. Russell. " Henry did not, as I well remember, appear

at dinner nor throughout the evening of yesterday. Where was he ?"

" He was burying Lion," answered Valentine.

" Poor Lion !" sighed Lady Carewe.

" Poor Henry !" said Mr. Russell, in a tone of deep feel·· ing. " Where did he bury Lion ?"

" Under the hollow oak near the gates," answered Valentine.

" My Lord Morley and Mr. Henry Wilmot gave a very different account ; and it seems strange to me, that you, Master Valentine, who were present at dinner, though Henry was not, did not contradict it."

" I have not time for these questionings now," said Sir Arthur rising impatiently. " I have most important affairs to arrange, which require the attendance of my steward, and couriers to despatch without an hour's delay."

" I can well believe it, Sir Arthur. Pardon me, sir, if my love for my young pupil, and, I may add, my confidence in him, have made me anxious to probe this business to the bottom. May I request to know if I keep the charge of him ?"

" Surely, surely, Mr. Russell. Let every attention be paid to his wants, but till I have time to think, keep him in confinement. The key I make over to you. He is in the wainscotted room in the east tower. My wife, thou wilt remain with me. I need thy counsel much."

" May I not see my brother ?" faltered Valentine.

" No. Until he confess his fault, no member of the family shall see him but Mr. Russell. I know his interest in his pupil will equally prevent weak indulgence and undue severity. To him I confide Henry. Let no one else, not even his mother, go near him."

From this sentence there was no appeal. Valentine, anxious to avoid Mr. Russell's eye, retired to his own room, and a short time afterwards went forth to walk alone on the terrace, and then into solitary parts of the grounds, to ponder over the tangled web of his affairs.

CHAPTER VII.

A MYSTERY.

EDITH sat alone towards evening in the pleasant summer room where she usually studied with her mother, feeling very dejected and unhappy. She was sure that something wrong had happened. Both her brothers seemed to have disappeared. Her father and mother had been shut up together for many hours, and had, she knew, sent for the steward and kept him for a long while with them. She had seen two couriers ride off post-haste with despatches. The usual customs of the family were suspended. There had been no gathering together at noon, but food had been carried to the private rooms of each. Nurse and the children were out, and the voices of little Alice and Martin, who alone of all the inhabitants in the house seemed like themselves, came in at the window; but only sounded sad in her ears.

Her melancholy thoughts were interrupted by the entrance of nurse Crairy, who, as if unable to stand, let herself drop into an arm-chair, where she rocked herself backwards and forwards, crying, wiping her eyes and constantly repeating, "Ah, well-a-day! Ah, woes the day! Ah, mercy on us!" till Edith was so frightened, that she could not ask what was the matter.

"I tell thee, my pretty love, my poor pretty ladybird—don't begin to cry and look at me so pitiful like that—I tell thee Master Valentine has broken some forest law or some of their laws, like Robin Hood and Little John, and killed a huntsman and one of the king's deer! Oh, well-a-day!"

"Killed a huntsman!"

"I tell thee it's true, and he'll be branded, or pilloried, or we can't see what, or it may be have his comely head cut off on Tower Hill."

"Nay, nurse, you must have made some complete mistake. What can Valentine have done?"

"I have not, I tell thee; and Master Henry's fault they say it is, and he's shut up in some lonesome old room. Master Henry disobedient, quotha! and tell lies, forsooth! Never tell me! They shall give me an account of my boy before another hour goes over my head, or I shall know the reason why. Marry come up! I say again."

"Oh nurse, do, pray, ask my mother if she would let me come to her for five minutes—only five minutes—that she might tell me really about it."

"I have been trying it myself, but it is of no avail, my pet. Nobody dares go and disturb her and Sir Arthur. He's not to be spoken to, as thou well knowest, when he's put out of the way, and it's not to be wondered at now, for they say all his houses and lands is forfeit, and so we're all ruined and undone!" And nurse began rocking again and crying and wringing her hands.

"What shall I do?" thought poor Edith. "Nurse, do listen to me! Go and try if thou can'st find Mr. Russell, and bring him to me to tell me what all this means."

Nurse obeyed, and returned after a few minutes with Mr. Russell, whom she found alone in his study. He calmed the worst of Edith's fears by assuring her that the greatest misfortunes that hung over the family were the loss of the chase, and a heavy fine, not death or imprisonment to any one she loved. Edith knew so little of the world or of hardships, that the loss of money did not seem anything terrible to her. She said she should be very sorry to lose the pretty chase, but then they could still see it through the gates, and the king's majesty perhaps would let them walk in it and pick the harebells and wood-sorrel in spring.

"Ah, well-a-day! but the Carewes have owned the chase hundreds of years afore the king or the king's majesty's father ever came out of Scotland to rule over us," said nurse. "Mayhap, if they'd staid where they was, it would have been none the worse for us. We did very well without them."

"But what hath Valentine done, and what is it I hear of Henry, Mr. Russell?"

He thought for a minute, and then, without giving his own impressions in any way, told her as simply as he could the events of the morning. She started up when he told her of what Henry was accused, and all her gentleness disappearing, declared that he was falsely accused; that he never would have disobeyed his father; and would never attempt to conceal the truth—no, never.

". As good a boy as ever trod on the earth," said nurse,

wiping her eyes. "A little hasty or so at a time, and wilful, and it may be forgetful and heedless; but him tell a lie! A mighty likely thing! Never! Marry and amen, say I."

Edith was struck dumb, however, by hearing of the undoubted evidence that he had been in the chase, and this brought out the sad story of her stag.

"Oh my pretty stag!" said she. "I loved thee so much. Thou wert so gentle and affectionate. I shall never stroke thy sleek sides again, and look in thy large wild eyes. Henry ran into the chase to save him! I know it has been so; but why does he not tell my father this?"

"Henry has had a severe loss himself. These huntsmen not only killed your poor stag, they killed Lion."

"Killed Lion! Is Lion dead? Oh my poor Henry! how much he must have suffered! Do, pray do, let me go to him and comfort him! After all he has had to bear, they have shut him up alone! I must go to him," cried Edith.

Mr. Russell told her Henry was not permitted to see any member of the family but himself.

"Let me go to my father and entreat him."

"No, we dare not interrupt Sir Arthur. He has heavy troubles to bear, and important affairs to arrange."

"Then, Mr. Russell, as you may go to Henry, and have been to him you say, go once again, and say to him from me, 'Edith trusts thee, dear Henry!'"

"Ay, ay! pretty pet! sweet heart, she trusts him," said nurse, still crying.

But when Mr. Russell had gone, charged with this mes-

THE SCARED VILLAGERS.

from a trencher that little Alice carried. As Edith
looked, the faces seemed all familiar to her. There were
Christopher Knight and old Dame Dunkly, and little
Amy Rudd, and Robert Hazeldine and his wife; she
knew them all. They all belonged to the village of the
chase.

What was the matter? Edith found it out but too soon,
by the words she heard her father say to them. He told
them that he had sent to London to beg for time. That he
would redeem the village by paying the fine the Forest Court
laid on, if it were possible for him to do it. That he had a
promise from the sheriff, "that till his answer came from
London no man should enter their cottages, if they behaved
quietly and made no quarrels or disturbances." Then her
mother spoke kind words to them and comforted them, and
bade them be of good cheer, for their lord would save the
village, if money would do it.

So now Edith understood that the whole of the chase,
even to the village, had been seized for the king.

There was no time for indulging in sorrow. The people,
frightened and disturbed out of their usual labours, had not
provided firing and food for the evening, and needed help.
The farmer, oppressed with so many men quartered on him,
was complaining bitterly. Lady Carewe set herself to the
task of smoothing away all these troubles with the energy
she always put into every good work. Food, and all that
was needed, was sent down to the village; Goodwife Rudd
at the farm found her larder filled with abundance in an
hour's time; Woodruffe was specially charged with the task
of seeing that all was properly distributed, and ordered to

remain on the watch through the night to guard against any mischief.

Distant thunder was heard while these preparations were made, and the poor people who had flocked up to the Hall in their panic, had scarcely got into the shelter of their cottages when heavy rain came on. The storm increased as night closed in, and the lightning flashed through the darkness; but Sir Arthur resolved to go to the gates of the chase and pass the night at the forester's himself, in order to see that the agreement made as to the cottages was faithfully kept. He could thus be on the spot in a few minutes, if any alarm occurred, so by ten o'clock he had settled himself in Thomas Boult's parlour, with two of the servants; and the poor people of the village, when they heard he was there, slept in peace, feeling sure they were safe under his protection.

It was nearly midnight before Lady Carewe felt that all was done, and that she might retire to rest. She went to her own room and looked out into the moonlight, with the most melancholy forebodings for the future, and most melancholy thoughts of the present, in which Henry's conduct gave her more pain than aught else. The storm had ceased, and a perfect calm had succeeded. There was a strange silence after the turmoil. It was interrupted by a low tap at her door. Having believed that every one was at rest, it startled her. She opened the door herself, and saw Mr. Russell with a lamp in his hand.

"I grieve, my honoured lady," he began, " knowing how many duties have pressed on you, and how great your fatigue must be, I deeply grieve to disturb your needful rest;

but something so strange and unaccountable has occurred,
that I cannot but acquaint you with it."

"Oh, does some new misfortune, then, hang over us ?"

"I trust it will not turn out so," said he; "but what to
think, I know not.   Henry has disappeared."

"Disappeared!"

"I went to his room, my lady, about ten o'clock—to give
him a message—a kind message it was, from Mistress Edith,
and to see after his bed for the night; both should have been
done sooner, but for the pressing need of my aid with the
poor people of the village; but he was gone; the room was
empty."

"His escape looks ill for him. It is rebellious, and looks
like guilt. Oh, my boy, I could not have believed this of thee."

"My lady, he could not escape."

"How! what mean you, then ?"

"I mean that his disappearance is an entire mystery to
me.   He could not possibly get out of that room."

"You speak riddles.   When had you seen him last ?"

"I visited him soon after Sir Arthur had given me permission to do so.   He immediately questioned me as to his
brother, and on my telling him what had passed, and how
Master Valentine replied to the questions put to him, he
buried his face in his hands, and never spoke again.
To all my words, which were sometimes severe, but were
often indeed kind, he replied nothing ; only when I told him
of the fatal consequences of the act of disobedience, he started
up, and looked at me with such a face of sorrow as deeply
affected me, and which, as I remember it now, affects me ;
then fell into his gloomy silence again."

Lady Carewe remained for a few minutes lost in thought, then asked to be conducted to the room where he had been. She followed Mr. Russell with trembling steps along the corridor, and through long passages, to the old part of the house, then up the stairs, and Mr. Russell having unlocked the door of the room, she entered with him.

"This," said he, "is the room. Here he was, but here he is no longer."

The room was of no great size; wainscotted throughout; and containing no furniture but a small bedstead, a wooden stool, a round table, and a box, which, on opening it, was found to hold a few old books. Lady Carewe, scarcely able to stand from fatigue and agitation, leaned against the bedstead.

"You see, my lady," said Mr. Russell, "that he could not escape from this room, even if he wished it, which I believe to be a thing he never would have done. The door was locked and bolted outside; the window is at a great height from the ground, and besides secured with thick iron bars. There is no second door, no tapestry to hide an outlet. I have wearied myself with vain attempts to find any sliding panel or other mode of getting out. There is no explanation but to suppose that some one has a second key, and has let him out, but that is unlikely in the extreme. The key, as you see, is a very peculiar one, and has always been in Sir Arthur's possession."

"This is most strange. My boy, my Henry, where art thou?"

"You are exhausted, my honoured lady. Suffer me to light you to your room. I will return and pass the night here. We can do no more."

"No more but trust in Him who orders all, and submit to His will."

Lady Carewe moved silently away, following Mr. Russell as he lighted her through the labyrinth of passages to the corridor; then they parted, and he returned to the mysterious room.

CHAPTER VIII.

MORE MYSTERIES.

Mr. Russell was right in telling Edith that he had left Henry in a painful and gloomy state in the morning, and indeed Mr. Russell knew not the extent of the pain. It was Valentine's baseness that rankled in Henry's heart. When he found himself alone again, he pushed away the table on which he had been leaning, got up from his seat, and began to roam about the room wildly, and struggling with passions that almost mastered him. "Was it possible that Valentine could be so mean, and cowardly, and false as this? Was it possible that he would persist in such a course? No, it should not be submitted to! He would insist on being confronted, face to face, with Valentine, and force him to tell the truth."

"But then, even then, when the truth was told, what a wretched state they were all in! His father half-ruined, Valentine disgraced, everybody made miserable." Again Henry's passion rose against Valentine and his two worthless companions, who had caused all these misfortunes, and he scarcely knew how to endure his own powerless condition when he remembered their violence and insolence.

G

A kind of reckless hardened feeling succeeded to all this, and he began to look about him at the room he was in, and examine what was in it. "If they choose to shut me up here," said he to himself, "and leave me all alone in this cold, proud way, let them! I don't care how long I stay here. I can do very well by myself. Let them pet and indulge their favourite Valentine, and be all very happy and comfortable with one another. Just as they please! No, I shall *not* bear it. Why should I have to suffer all this for a coward like Valentine?"

He tried to eat what Mr. Russell had brought, to prove to himself how very easy and unconcerned he was; but it would not do. The food seemed to choke him. It would not go down his throat; so he drank the water to the last drop, and then began to roam about the room again.

There was a box in the corner. This he opened, and found in it some old books. He knelt down and began examining them. One was an illuminated manuscript, containing legends of the Carewe family. After reading a few words, he became interested, and sat down at the table again and read the

VERY QUAINT AND CURIOUS HISTORIE OF PETER CAREWE.

Peter Carewe (as the legend told in strange old spelling, which is here altered,) was the youngest son of Sir William Carewe of Mahones Otrey, in the county of Devon, and was born in the year of grace 1526. He was ever a boy of high courage and stubborn will, and to bring him into order, his worshipful father resolved to send him to Exeter, there to attend the grammar school of the city.

For this purpose, Sir William Carewe sent a messenger to Thomas Hunte, draper and alderman of Exeter, who made known these his wishes and commands. That Master Hunte should receive the young Master Peter Carewe into his household to live in it, and must keep a close eye on him, that he went straight to school and played with no rude companions. If he be truant, flog him. This was what Sir William said by the messenger.

Then said Master Thomas Hunte, "Wife, this is a heavy charge. The boy, I am given to know, is pert and forward. He is the youngest son, and his father looketh to his learning to bring him some advancement. Sir William is a hard man."

Then said his wife in reply, "We must needs do Sir William's bidding. We cannot gainsay it."

And the next morning came the boy on horseback, with a single servant to attend him. "Here's sorry cheer, methinks!" said Master Peter, as he looked at the mean wooden building. "Nothing within but store of woollen stuffs."

Natheless, Master Peter must enter in. He went straight to school as ordered; but what then? He sits doggedly with book open before him. Syntaxis he will have none of. Every day he is flogged, for the master, whose name is Freer, is cruel; but 'tis all one to Peter. At Master Hunte's 'tis the same. He neglects noon-tide meals, and is off to pleasant fields, book of ballads in hand, in lieu of Latin, and reads actes and feats of chivalry, and deeds of knights and princesses. Is daily truant; but one whole day he never comes home.

Then was Master Hunte alarmed, and going in search of him, finds him hiding behind a buttress of the city wall. "Oh, varlet, have I caught thee?" cries Master Hunte.

"Not yet," says Master Peter, and he climbs to top of the highest turret, and then he cries—

"Let me be! keep down! If you press upon me, I will surely cast myself headlong down over the wall, and then shalt thou be hanged."

So Master Hunte wrote to Sir William Carewe. Then came Sir William riding to Exeter, with servants behind him, and Peter stands trembling before him.

Then crieth Sir William, "Bring the chain and the collar!" and they put the collar about his neck, and lead him by the chain through the streets; and he is taken home to Mahones Otrey, and coupled to a hound and lodged in a filthy kennel. In vain his mother kneels for pity.

But Sir William takes thought at last, and carries off his son to London, and places him at St. Paul's school. 'Tis all one. The schoolmaster can in nowise, whether by daily flogging or what it may be, get the young Peter to smell to a book, or to like of any schooling.

Then Sir William came again to London, and he walked musing as he went in Paul's-walk, and there he met a friend who was going to the French court, and told him his trouble; so this friend took Peter for his page.

Now was young Peter mightily pleased that he had done with syntaxis, and he was dressed in gay clothes, and fared well, and partook of courtly exercises; but what then? He had duties to perform; must keep to hours, must observe rules. He was ill at ease. He kept no time, he got into disgrace,

THE WORTHY KNIGHT, JOHN CAREWE.

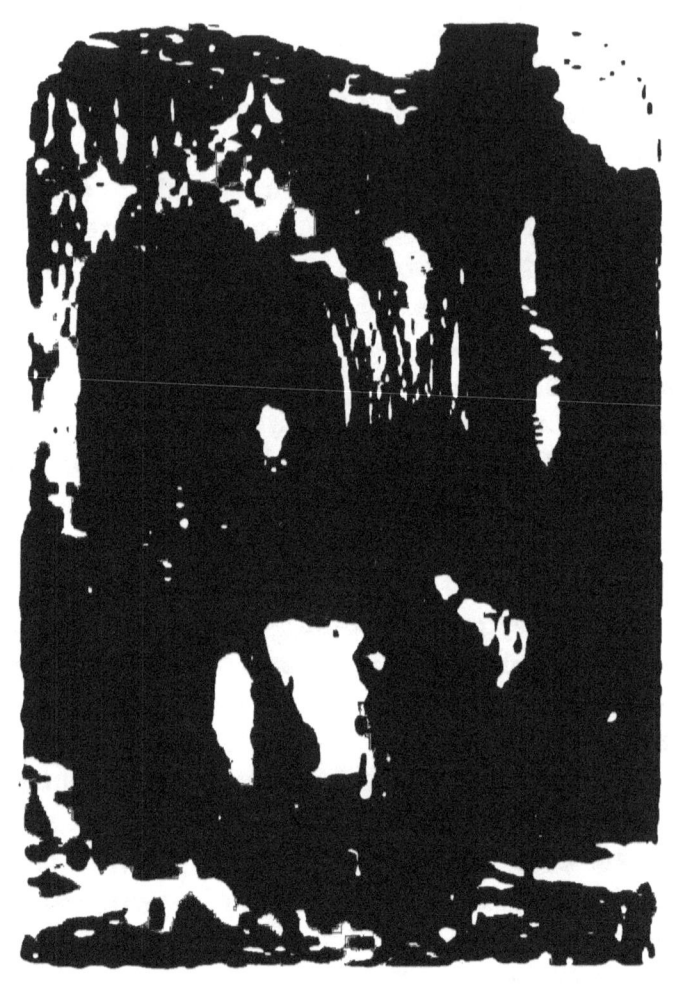

and sank to the stable, and became a mulet, with charge of the mules.

Now was Peter pleased with his liberty. His clothes were worn, but what then? He loved roystering, dancing, and virelays, and led a riotous, merry life.

But now Peter grows older, and he reads Froissart and Comines, and says to himself, " I am but a poor mulet!" and he drooped and was sad.

Then came the worthy knight John Carewe, from Henry the Eighth to Francis the First, and he drew up his steed at the gates of the monastery hard by, and the monks came out to do him reverence; and his steed was weary with long travel, and they besought him to enter in and rest. Then cried the horse boys, as they played about, " Carewe Anglays, Carewe Anglays, come see the knight with lance and plume!" Then said the knight, " Which is Carewe Anglays?" and they showed him Peter all in rags as he stood.

And the knight looked at Peter, and said, " Thou injured boy, I am thy father's brother! Thou shalt be to me as a son."

So Peter went with the knight, and got into favour at the French court, and at the Emperor's court, and he did deeds of valour at the battle of Pavia, and then he craved permission to go on a journey.

Sir William and Lady Carewe were seated in their hall, and a goodly company with them, when an armed knight craved permission to do them reverence. Then there stepped into their presence a tall young man of noble countenance in complete armour, and he doffed his plumed helmet and threw himself at their feet, and said, " My father, my mother! I am your son Peter Carewe."

Henry flung the book on the table when he had done. "It would suit Valentine more than me," he thought. "I am the poor mulct, and he will be the young knight of noble countenance that will kneel before father and mother and be forgiven."

His head had begun to ache, and the stifling heat of the coming storm affected him. He clambered up to the window and tried to open it, but it would not open, and his head ached more and more. To forget it he took up his book again, and now he read of noble deeds and acts of chivalry and self-devotion for honour's sake among his ancestors, and then he despised himself for having ever entertained such a thought as betraying his brother. He would die sooner! a Carewe should be ready to die rather than break his word.

The thunder began, the rain beat against the window, and it grew darker and darker. The storm increased. The lighting flashed through the window, which had neither curtain nor shutter, the thunder rolled overhead, and seemed to shake the tower. There was something in the storm that spoke to Henry's heart as he sat there alone. It was great and solemn. He became humbled before it, and suddenly found out that his proud, rebellious mood was very poor and pitiful.

But he felt more and more ill; and a craving for his mother, such as he never felt before, took possession of him. Mr. Russell had left him writing materials, and with the last glimmering light of day, aided by the lightning which now scarcely ever ceased, he wrote the few following words:—
"My dear and honoured master, Mr. Russell. I am very ill. My heads aches very badly. I am afraid I shall lose my

senses before you come again. Oh ask my mother to come ! Ask my mother to come to me ! HENRY."

Having finished this note, he staggered to the bedstead, and lay down with his eyes wide open staring at the lightning. At last the storm ceased. It became perfectly dark, inky dark, and as still and quiet as death. Not the smallest sound broke the silence. The strange calm made no change on Henry, except that he had taken his eyes away from the window, and fixed them on the opposite wall, where in his confused, half delirious state, it seemed to him the lightning had left a spark that still shone and returned his look.

What was that light that shone out of the dark wall ? Nay, as he looked he now saw there were two lights, bright, raying out into the darkness of his room. He tried to think ; tried to collect his senses and think. There was no opening in that wall. He had seen before it grew dark that it was a long wall of oak wainscot. And there was no room behind this that he was in. He knew this room was at the top of the old tower, and filled its whole space.

What could those lights be ? As he stared at them they no longer seemed lights, but two dreadful eyes. Yes, they were eyes glaring and flashing upon him. Some horrible creature was there.

He tried to recollect everything Mr. Russell had said to him about the folly and even crime of believing in spectres, witches, and the terrors that almost all the people about believed in. He tried to remember that everywhere we are in the presence, under the hand, of an almighty, all-good Father, who wills not that His children should be the sport of malignant spirits. Those were Mr. Russell's teachings.

But in spite of all he could do, dreadful images came crowding into his mind, and stories he had heard from nurse and from Woodruffe, who firmly believed in witchcraft, rose up one after another to his memory. Still, the effort he had made was not lost upon him. It gave him courage, and he was naturally brave, so he started up and walked fast towards those eyes, with a desperate resolution to find out what they were, and to end this state of horror which was worse than any certainty.

He knocked himself violently against the wall before he was aware, and the eyes vanished. He retreated a step and saw no longer the eyes, but two very small specks of bright light.

Were they glow-worms or some other luminous insect? He put his hands against the wall and could feel nothing, and yet he had covered up the lights. He removed his hands, and saw the lights again.

His headache had gone in his excitement, and now that his panic fear had vanished, he could think clearly. These lights must proceed from little holes in the wall, and there must be some hollow place behind it, though how it could be light there, it was impossible to conceive.

He took out his knife, and began to try to push it into one of the holes, but the knife was much too large to go in. Then he took out a small sharp-pointed tool that he used in carpentering and building little ships and boats, and found that he could push that in. He had a second of these tools. That also he took out and pushed into the other hole, and then began to work them up and down, screw them round, and drive them farther in.

Suddenly, as he was thus employed, he felt the floor give way under his feet; he broke through a wooden box or some structure that was too thin to bear his weight, and fell down a great depth; a whirring noise in his ears; flapping and beating of cold damp things, like bats' wings about his face; thumping and banging against projecting points to which he clung to save himself; still falling down, down, till at last he came with force to the ground, and found himself in dazzling light, and saw a man dressed in black who was pointing a large pistol at him, and who cried out in a thundering voice, " Stop ! whoever thou art. One movement towards me, and thou art a dead man !"

Henry lay gasping on the ground, half buried among those damp cold things that had fallen with him, and so bruised and shattered by his fall that he was quite unable to move, even if this fearful threat had not kept him as still as a stone. He lay there with his eyes fixed on the apparition before him, neither moving hand nor foot, and so dazzled by the light, and so giddy from his rapid descent, that this apparition seemed to wheel and quiver before his eyes, without his being able to see distinctly what it was like. He saw, however, to his comfort, that it lowered the pistol in half a minute, and then it spoke again, in quite a different voice.

" Eh ! what ! how ! In the name of mercy ! Poor boy ! Thou art hurt surely ! How cam'st thou here ? Is it possible ? Surely thou art little Henry Carewe !"

" And surely, sir," said Henry, greatly relieved, " you are Dr. Osbaldeston ? I saw you at Westminster school when Valentine was there."

" Have a care ! have a care ! art sure no one came

behind thee ? Hush ! say not my name again. Let me help
thee up. Why, what are all these papers and musty parch-
ments that fell with thee ? But no matter. Poor boy, thou
art greatly hurt. Why didst come ?"

" Oh, sir," said poor Henry, " I meant not to come. I
know not how I came or why ; but I am hurt in my arm
very much, and cannot move."

Dr. Osbaldeston, for he indeed it was, spake not another
word, but lifted Henry tenderly off the ground, taking the
utmost care so as to give him as little pain as possible, and
carried him to a couch which stood in the corner of what
Henry now perceived to be a comfortable small room, with a
bright fire of logs in a wide chimney, a lamp on the table,
and some books and papers by it. He would have wondered
very much at everything, but he had no time. The pain he
suffered as he was moved, added to all he had endured before,
made him turn suddenly sick and giddy, and he fainted dead
away.

The first feeling he had after this, was a cool hand laid
on his forehead, and another hand holding one of his and
gently pressing it. He had no pain, and it seemed so calm
and pleasant to lie so, that he did not open his eyes, but remained in a sort of doze. Thoughts and recollections then
began to press upon him : His father's anger, Valentine's
baseness, these came first, and he sighed deeply and opened
his eyes.

" My dear boy ! Henry ! you know me ? "

It was Mr. Russell's voice, and now Mr. Russell's face
was there, looking earnestly and very kindly at him. All
that about dreadful eyes, a heavy fall from a great height, a

man with a pistol, and Dr. Osbaldeston, was nothing but a dream, then!

Henry tried to move and look round, and instantly sharp pains that made him moan, they were so bad, came on.

" Keep quite still, my boy! " said Mr. Russell. " Thou art badly hurt, but all will be right soon, if thou keep still."

Mr. Russell moved to arrange something better for him, and then Henry saw what had been hidden before by his kind friend's bending over him, the little room, the bright fire, the lamp on the table, and Dr. Osbaldeston sitting at it turning over numbers of papers. It was not a dream, then.

" Jubilate! Io triumphe! " cried the doctor, and he held a parchment up in one hand, and beat it with the other.

" My good friend! Doctor! What is there to rejoice at ? "

" The charter! our excellent Sir Arthur's charter. Here it is! Henricus R——"

" Is it possible! " cried Mr. Russell rushing to the table. " Keep still, Henry! It is! it can be no other. This is wonderful! This is most fortunate! The trap through which Henry fell, was then the secret place in which his grandfather, Sir John Carewe, had hidden it, and which his sudden death prevented his revealing! To have found it at this moment is a thing we can never be too grateful for."

" My good young friend," said Dr. Osbaldeston addressing Henry, " if thou bruised thyself from head to foot, broke thy skin in various places, gave thyself a dangerous contusion on the head, and nearly frightened me to death, last night, it has been well worth while. Thou hast saved thy father's chase."

Henry was too weak and shattered to bear this joyful news. He became deadly pale again and closed his eyes. Mr Russell was by him in a moment bathing his forehead, soothing him, giving him some refreshing drink; and he soon opened his eyes again, and saw the doctor's face close to his, staring wildly and with wide-open mouth and so dismal an expression, that though it was very ungrateful of him, he could not help laughing.

"That is well! that is right! Now we shall do!" said the doctor. "You must take this to Sir Arthur immediately, Russell!"

"What is the hour?"

"Five in the morning. We have been up all night. When you have safely gone, I shall be glad to sleep. I grow tired, and our good young friend must sleep also again."

"I wish we could discover the egress into the room above by which Henry fell. I fear going out, now that it must be quite light, by our usual way, lest some one should see me. Give me the lamp."

Mr. Russell took the lamp, and standing on a stool, began to examine the roof of the room, continuing his search for some time.

"This trap is so admirably contrived," said he, "and the spring that works it must be so excellent, that I search in vain. After opening as it did last night everything has closed again as tightly as before. No! I think I have discovered it."

He pressed on a board where two square openings had at last struck his eyes, and a trap-door instantly opened downwards, disclosing a winding spiral staircase made of iron.

"Look up, doctor!" said he. "No wonder he was hurt!" They held the lamp and looked up. The stairs wound round like a screw, and ended close to a trap-door above.

"Let me light my lamp, and ascend," said Mr. Russell. "I may find the opening above. Tell me, Henry, how didst thou find it?"

Henry told him about the light he had seen, and how he had pushed the tools into two small holes, and that instantly it seemed to him as if the world was coming to an end and everything falling in ruins over his head. Mr. Russell then cautiously ascended, the doctor watching him anxiously.

"What art doing, Russell?" he said presently, in a low whisper. "Why dost thou come back?"

"I hear some one in the chamber above. We may be discovered if I open the trap. I see how to do it."

The doctor turned as pale as death. "We are already discovered perchance! Let me descend into the dungeon. I may yet escape and hide in the woods."

"I cannot think that any one is there but Lady Carewe, or it may be Sir Arthur himself; yet we must be cautious. I will ascend again very softly and listen."

Henry beckoned to Mr. Russell to come to him.

"If it be indeed my father and mother," he whispered, "pray of them to think the best of me they can. You trust me, Mr. Russell?"

"I do trust thee; and I had a message to thee from thy sister, Mistress Edith, who suffers bitter grief on thy account. 'Tell my dear Henry,' she said, 'that Edith trusts him.'"

Henry's tears were rolling over his cheeks. Mr. Russell wiped them away for him, kissed his forehead, said, "Bless thee, my dear boy! All will be well with us soon," and again went to the stairs, where the doctor was growing impatient, and evidently in a state of nervous agitation.

CHAPTER IX.

HENRY'S GENEROSITY.

WHEN Mr. Russell, creeping up the stairs as silently as possible, and without his shoes, reached the top, his head touched
the floor above. The stairs were constructed in a round shaft
of very narrow diameter, and the floor he touched with the top
of his head contained an iron bolt, no doubt communicating
by a spring with the holes above. If he withdrew it, he
doubted not the floor would open. There were the remains
of a small japanned cabinet adhering to it, which had probably contained the papers and the charter, and which Henry
had broked to pieces in his fall. He listened, and distinctly
heard Sir Arthur speaking in a low tone; and the voice
that replied was that of Lady Carewe. He hesitated not,
therefore, to tap gently on the floor above.

"Whoever thou art," replied Sir Arthur instantly,
"fear not to speak. There is no one in this room but Sir
Arthur Carewe and his wife, and the door is locked. No
harm shall happen to thee, on the honour of a gentleman."

"Sir Arthur!" replied Mr. Russell, "it is I—your chaplain; remove to a considerable distance, even as far as the
window, for the greater safety. I will then endeavour to
open a communication between us. All is safe, doctor!"

"We are both now standing by the window," said Sir Arthur's voice.

Mr. Russell touched the bolt. The effect was startling even to him, prepared as he was. The floor parted above his head with the same whirring sound as had happened when Henry fell through it, and having remained open about half a minute, closed again.

"Remain where you are, Sir Arthur," cried Mr. Russell; "I see that I must fasten the bolt back after touching it."

"We remain where we were," replied Sir Arthur immediately.

Mr. Russell now touched the bolt again. Again the floor opened, and he quickly clasped the iron work into a groove made to receive it. The hole above now continued open, and he raised himself with some difficulty sufficiently high to see into the room. The morning sun was shining through the bars of the window. Sir Arthur stood a little in advance of Lady Carewe, who, ghastly pale, leaned against the wall.

"Io triumphe!" shouted a voice, sounding hollow, from the depths below.

Lady Carewe started and trembled visibly, but her quivering lips were able to articulate the word "Henry!"

"Safe! I have left him but this moment," replied Mr. Russell, who was now in the room.

She pressed her hands on her heart and looked up, her pale face lighted with joy and gratitude.

"Now may Heaven be praised!" said Sir Arthur reverently. "What owe we not to thee, my friend? Pray, sit down, my dear wife. Thou art totally overcome."

"Sir Arthur," said Mr. Russell, "I have yet more to tell you. Look upon this parchment."

Sir Arthur took in his hand the parchment which Mr. Russell held out to him, and looked up absolutely speechless with amazement. Lady Carewe had seen it before he was able to command his voice. The lost charter! It seemed as though miracles had not indeed ceased.

"The accident which made Henry discover the secret place where doubtless your father, Sir John Carewe, had hidden it, shall be explained to you. It caused his fall down the stairs by which I ascended; but though the fall was from a great height, he is mercifully not seriously injured. No bones are broken. He is, however, wounded and bruised from head to foot, and requires extreme quiet to preserve him from any increase of fever."

"Let us go to him instantly," said Lady Carewe, hurrying to the opening; but when she saw the steep stairs which the light from below made visible, and thought of Henry's fall, she nearly fainted, and would have sunk on the floor had not Sir Arthur supported her.

She quickly recovered herself, however, but asked in a bewildered tone, "Tell me what dreadful voice I heard from down there. Who is with Henry, if indeed I am to find my boy there?"

"Vale, vale, amicus meus!" cried the doctor.

Lady Carewe with difficulty suppressed a shriek.

"No wonder thou art alarmed, my wife; thou who knowest not our secret. It is but our good friend Dr. Osbaldeston who speaks to us. He hath been concealed for a week in the safe room thou knowest of, between which and this, a

H

communication, totally unknown to me before, exists, as thou
seest, and with him thy boy is safe."

"Dr. Osbaldeston, the master of Westminster school,
concealed! For what reason?"

"He hath drawn on himself the vengeance of Archbishop
Laud, for some indiscreet expressions used in a letter, and
which have been betrayed by a servant. Being sentenced,
besides a fine, to branding and the pillory, he fled, and
happily reached this house, where but for adding to thy
already too great load of care, we would have told thee he
was received and sheltered. Mr. Russell alone knew of it
besides myself. He hath nightly visited him with food and
other necessaries, and thus doubtless he found Henry."

"It was just so," replied Mr. Russell; "I waited here
in vain for an hour before I went forth to make my way into
the secret chamber, intending to return. All I had found
was a note lying on the table, which I overlooked before."

"Ah, yes! It almost broke my heart," said Lady
Carewe.

"He sent a message to his father and mother even
now," said Mr. Russell. It was, "'Pray of them to think the
best of me they can.'"

"We do indeed! We have reason to believe some
fatal falseness is at the root of all this. I have heard of
things from Woodruffe this night during my watch that
have much shaken me, though as yet I know nothing.
Lead the way, Mr. Russell, and prepare Henry to see us."

A slow and careful descent into the strange room below,
Sir Arthur guiding and supporting Lady Carewe the whole
way, brought them into the presence of the triumphant

doctor, full of congratulations about the charter mixed with the deepest reverences to her ladyship, and lamentations that so lovely a lady should have to make a descent intó so dark a place, with something about Eurydice, in which he stopped suddenly, as if he could scarcely compare himself to Orpheus.

They had been so full of thoughts about Henry, that in truth they had almost forgotten the charter. But now Sir Arthur began to feel the greatness of his good fortune in having recovered it. Lady Carewe was already by Henry.

"Thy mother is come, my dear, dear boy!" she said, folding him in her arms so gently and carefully that even his poor wounded frame was not hurt by it. "She will not leave thee; thou shalt have her care and love by thee, day and night; but do not speak, keep very quiet, that thou mayst get well, to be a blessing to thy father and to me."

Sir Arthur was there now, blessing him, telling him to think no more of yesterday's sorrows, for though as yet he knew nothing, he believed and trusted the truth would be cleared up soon.

Henry could not utter a word for a good while. He only pressed the hands that were clasped in his, and looked at the two faces that beamed so lovingly at him, and felt very happy. But a trouble came into his heart soon.

"My father," he said, "can you indeed trust me?"

It was impossible to mistrust that open, sincere face. Sir Arthur assured Henry he did trust him, though nothing had been explained.

"Then, my father, if you would grant me this one request I should be so grateful, oh, so grateful to you! Do not try to have anything explained. Leave it all as it is.

It is done, and cannot be undone. Will you, indeed, not ask more questions of any one, and only think the best you can of me ?"

In his earnestness Henry's face had become flushed, and his eyes wild and bright. Mr. Russell laid his hand on Sir Arthur's arm, and said, "Promise him! We risk his life by this excitement."

"I promise what thou askest, and will faithfully keep my promise, my boy," said Sir Arthur.

Henry closed his eyes and smiled. His mother laid her hand on his forehead and put her finger on her lips. They were all perfectly quiet for some minutes, and then his regular breathing showed that he was asleep.

Mr. Russell now motioned to Sir Arthur and the doctor to ascend the stairs with him, leaving Lady Carewe in entire quiet by Henry. It was then settled among them that Sir Arthur must instantly take horse for London, carrying the precious charter with him, and lay his claim to have the chase restored to him before the Forest Court. Dr. Osbaldeston might make the agreeable change from the room below to the more airy one he was now in, and might immediately lie down on the bed that had been prepared for Henry, and take the needful sleep he had not yet been able to enjoy. Mr. Russell must, in the best way he could, explain to Edith, in the first place, that Henry was ill and nursed by her mother, and kept apart from every one else as yet, though her father would have patience and question no more now about the act of disobedience he had committed, and might also tell her the joyful news of the recovered charter. She was to be charged to acquaint Va-

lentine with all she knew ; but neither to her nor to Valentine must the secret of the room nor the presence of Dr.
Osbaldeston be revealed. With Edith these matters would
have been safe ; but the fewer who knew of them, the better.
To her was to be intrusted the care of the children, and
ordering of the household, which, with the assistance of
nurse, of Freeman and Goodwife Freeman, and Woodruffe,
would not be too difficult for her. Mr. Russell would bring
to Lady Carewe all that was needed for the patient. He
was a skilful physician and surgeon, having studied medicine
in his youth, and was accustomed to practise among the
poor. He had already bound up the wounds carefully.

"Thou must descend before thou doest aught else, my
young friend Russell ; thou must descend, and see that the
lovely lady below hath what such a place, grievously unfit
for her, though it was a palace of refuge for me, can afford
for her solace. See that a repast is spread for her. Remove,
I pray, those musty papers ; put on more logs ; it is ever
chilly there, though a pleasant warmth pervades the chamber
we are in, where Sol sheds his kindly beams ; trim the lamp ;
and above all endeavour to arrange for some seat formed of
the cushion thou didst so kindly bring to me that she may
repose." This speech was made by the doctor as he settled
himself in bed, having taken off his wig, and put on, in its
place, a knitted night cap, which he always kept in his
pocket. " Descend and obey my words, my young friend and
pupil of former days, and rejoice with me that our worthy
host's charter and my ears are safe."

Mr. Russell accompanied Sir Arthur to the door of the
chamber, and carefully securing it on the outside, went

below with him, and before long had returned with a repast
for the doctor himself, which, though he had quite forgotten that he needed it, he really did need so much that he
was unable to fall asleep for want of it.

"Ah, benedicite, my friend, as our kind archbishop of Canterbury might say, though haply he might fear thus to expose
his papist predilections; I wanted this! I wanted this!
But wait not till I finish. I can do very well. Go and
see to my lady, and all Sir Arthur spoke of. There is
much to do. Above all, be careful and risk no discoveries.
Till I be 'beyond Canterbury' there is no safety for me.
Ha! ha! a merry jest that! Eh! my young friend?"

And Mr. Russell, who was glad that the poor doctor could
in his precarious state be merry about anything, left him to
enjoy his repast, sitting up in bed in his nightcap.

The task of informing Edith of what had occurred, and
of what was expected of her, was very easy. She was too
full of thoughts of Henry and his illness to question about
aught else; and only said that she was sure, since her father
would have patience, and not wish to question more now,
that the truth would be discovered in time. The news of
the recovered charter made her very happy, but about it she
asked no questions, so no explanation was given to her. She
was trained to perfect obedience, and set about her duties
with cheerfulness. She had no difficulty in fulfilling them.
All the servants, from the highest to the lowest, would have
done anything in the world for sweet Mistress Edith, and her
little brother and sister were always good and happy with
her. The only person on whom her influence seemed quite
powerless was Valentine. He indeed expressed, as he felt,

the greatest joy at the recovery of the charter, and said he was delighted that his father would have patience and not question Henry now, though he blushed with shame as he said so. But for the kind message his father had left for him, with his blessing and farewell before starting for London, he would have been seriously alarmed lest his forbearance meant that something against himself had been discovered. A conflict of contradictory feelings was going on within him. One moment he was wretched about Henry, whose illness he believed to be owing to the violence of Morley and Wilmot in the chase, and the death of Lion, and all the sufferings of that wretched day, aggravated by the unjust suspicion and imprisonment in a lonely room to which the poor boy had submitted for his sake. The next, he was in a fit of excitement about the Queen ; impatience for the message from Windsor she had hinted at ; dread lest a discovery of the truth about that affair in the chase, should so irritate his father as to put a complete bar to the ambitious schemes he had in his head.

Unable to bear Edith's affectionate manner, and unable either to look or to feel at ease with her, he kept aloof therefore ; pretended he had studies for next term to attend to in his own room, and afterwards rode out alone. He dreaded also to meet Mr. Russell, who, it was easy to see, suspected the truth ; but Mr. Russell was much engaged with all his cares for the inhabitants of the secret chambers, and besides carefully avoided any questionings, remembering the promise made to Henry.

The day passed over in this manner, and the following morning arose bringing little change, except that Henry was better, and Lady Carewe able to leave him for a little while to overlook her household and comfort Edith with the hope of his speedy recovery. Valentine, as soon as he heard that she was in her own apartment, avoided her by walking away through the bowling-green, and wandering in the remote parts of the park, so guilty and suspicious of every one did he feel. In the afternoon of the next day, when Edith again expected her mother might leave Henry, he rode away, unconsciously taking the road towards Windsor.

He was going on at a slow pace, thinking sadly of all that had happened, and looking on the ground, when he was roused by hearing a horse's foot close behind him coming up at a brisk trot, and a voice cried,—

"This dull and gloomy mood scarcely befits a cavalier so lately honoured by the touch of the fairest and noblest hand in England."

"My Lord of Holland!" replied Valentine, starting from his reverie, "I have had much cause for sad thoughts since that bright moment in my life."

"Thy presumptuous arrogance in attacking his gracious Majesty's servants, has met with a rebuke, which, let us hope, has given thee a salutary lesson, young sir," rejoined Lord Holland.

"I knew not—how could I know, my lord?—that they were servants of our king and master. Had I known it, I would have respected them, hard as it might be to see my rights violated."

"Thy rights, as thou dost call them, are now restored through the gracious clemency of our sovereign ; who is ever but too ready to waive his prerogatives. The appeal made

to him is successful, and the Forest Court has reversed its
decree."

"Our eternal gratitude will be due to our sovereign for
this favour," said Valentine; forgetting it was simple justice.

"Alas! Master Carewe! gratitude to our sovereign
master is a rare virtue in England. Far readier are his
churlish subjects to deny him his clear rights as their
divinely-appointed lord and king, and to carp and cavil at
his decrees, haggling and bargaining over the petty subsidies
he demands, than to think of gratitude!"

Valentine felt that this was aimed at his father, and kept
an embarrassed silence.

"See, now, these forests," continued his lordship, "encroached upon in every direction; the ancient forest laws
nearly fallen into disuse, simply from fear of the mutinous
disposition of the common herd who now carry on their
squalid trades and mean occupations where once the game
roved free, and kings and nobles enjoyed the royal pleasures
of the chase. Yet because our king hath but resumed his
own in a few instances, there is a clamour as of a thousand
jackdaws."

"In some cases, there have been rights to the lands granted
by charter of earlier kings," said Valentine, trying to rally.

"In very few; and even in these few, small matter were
it to yield to him that which he asks. Such sports as these
compensate to him, in some degree, for the toils and cares of
government. Wert ever in France?"

"Never," said Valentine. "I have great wish to travel,
and above all, to see France, the country of our beautiful
queen."

"Ah! there thou wilt see what it is to be a king! There thou wilt see royal sport in good earnest! Ah, the grand hunts I have joined in there! the herds of deer, the fierce boars, roaming in those vast forests! 'Tis sport, indeed, to pierce the grisly monster, his tusks foaming and bloody, the dogs pinning him to the earth, while others that he has disabled lie howling out their lives."

"We have, indeed, no sport to match it here."

"Yet it might be tried. I see not why a few of the Westphalia breed might not be introduced; but I well believe the dastard cowardice of our English knaves would never stand it. They would attack a wild boar, that might seem to them to put the lives of their pitiful offspring in peril, with pitchforks and axes, spite of the law, do what we might. *Ma foi*, if the *canaille* in France were so to presume, the nearest tree would be the word. Ah, the king of France is a king indeed!"

"Often have I longed to see the French court," said Valentine.

"Thou shouldst see our own first. Then wouldst thou be able to compare the two, and see how circumscribed is the power of our king, and how vain the babblings of those men who grudge him even that poor measure of power he hath; forgetting that what they presume to call their privileges have arisen from his toleration, not from their right."

"The virtues of our king," said Valentine, blushing a little at his own tacit agreement in this fashionable doctrine of the time, which Lord Holland himself entirely deserted in a year or two, "will continually decrease the number of those who oppose his royal will, which, because he is

ROYAL HUNTING IN FRANCE.

virtuous, must needs be exercised for the good of his people."

"So may it prove ; and that thou wilt swell the ranks of those true and loyal hearts, I am well assured. I do indeed believe thee to be made of the true metal. Thou art intended to shine in a court ; to stand foremost among the foremost in loyalty and honour. The ancient chivalry of England, with its devotion to our church and our king, yet lives. It hath yet many a worthy representative. Among these thou wilt shine. It is thy destiny to redeem thy name and house from the blemish which hath fallen on it."

"I do, indeed, long to serve my king," said Valentine. "I have often burned to add my sword to those already drawn in the quarrel of his nephews."

"Why not first seek a place in his court ?"

"Above all things would it be my ambition ; but my hopes have scarcely, till that bright moment you began by rehearsing, mounted so high. Since that, indeed—"

"What wouldst say if I had permission from that queen of love and beauty to whom thou then didst homage, to enrol thee among her pages ?"

"Mock me not, my lord, with such words !"

"Yet is it true. Forgiving thy turbulent behaviour, of which she hath heard since that period, she wills it so to be. Meet me at this time, and in this place, two days hence, and the introduction shall be made. Till then, adieu !"

So saying, and without waiting for a reply, Lord Holland set spurs to his horse, and vanished down a glade of the forest, his two attendants, in their gay court liveries, at his heels.

The whole interview had been so sudden, so short, that Valentine remained stupified and bewildered, but in such a state of intoxicating joy that he forgot his father, his brother, and all else, except his own brilliant prospects, and the beautiful queen to whom his life should henceforth be devoted.

CHAPTER X.

VALENTINE'S CONFESSION.

LORD WILLOUGHBY came again to Crewhurst the following day. He had heard of the serious losses that threatened his friends, and had hastened to them immediately. He had found with pleasure that things looked much brighter than had been expected, in consequence of the recovery of the lost charter; but Lady Carewe was much depressed in spirits, having many anxieties on her mind, and was still in nearly constant attendance on Henry. It necessarily devolved, therefore, on Valentine to entertain their distinguished guest; but Valentine sank into long reveries, leading him far away from everything around.

"My father may not have returned before the hour of my appointment to-morrow," thought he. "What shall I do? I have never told him of my meeting with the queen, fearing he would scarcely like it ; and if he comes, and I tell him, how strange and sudden will this, my high fortune, seem to him? Then there is Henry. As yet he is confined to a lonely room and ill. I cannot see him ; indeed, I hardly wish it. What could I say to him, or he say to me, that would not perhaps agitate him and make him worse? It is miserable to go and leave him in this state ; but, on the other hand, if I tell my father the truth of that unlucky day in the chase, and if he is, as assuredly he will be, very much irritated against me, he will withhold his consent to my great appointment. That I could not bear."

While Valentine thus pondered, a courier had arrived bringing letters for Lord Willoughby, who was deeply engaged in reading and replying to them. Valentine, therefore, was left at liberty to muse continually over his position and prospects, and the same round of thoughts and struggles went on within him, with the addition of a fresh struggle, something that had never occurred to him before— the possibility of being so rebellious as to ask no consent of his father, but act for himself. When he looked up, after a long interval, in which he had been totally absorbed in himself, he was struck by Lord Willoughby's appearance, who strode up and down the room, his face agitated and pale.

Valentine rose astonished. "Is aught amiss, my lord? Have I been so unfortunate as to offend?"

"Would that were all, boy," replied Lord Willoughby. "That would be a small matter to move me thus. We live in evil days, Valentine. Mayst thou be worthy to take thy noble father's place, when he is summoned to leave this troubled world, wherein to be noble, and to have an English heart and spirit, means to be persecuted."

"But do not over many now seek to circumscribe our king's lawful power?" asked Valentine, echoing Lord Holland's words.

"Ah! is that thy feeling? Let me tell thee, Valentine, the king's power would be boundless over his subjects did he but use it lawfully. Never was a more loyal people than the English. They are not the king's friends, but his bitterest foes, who preach up his prerogative. They should be telling him of his people's sufferings and his people's rights instead, . and teaching him how to reign in their hearts, not how to tyrannise over their wills."

"But hath the king, in aught, shown this tyranny?"

"Hath he not even now permitted such power to his courts of High Commission and Star Chamber, that only for printing sentiments against stage plays, which have offended the queen, on the one hand, and arguments against episco-pacy, which have angered the archbishop, on the other, Mr. Prynne, a barrister, learned in the law, and of irreproachable life, Dr. Bastwick, a physician, and Dr. Burton, a popular preacher, have stood in the pillory, lost their ears, been scourged, and cast into jail!"

"Poor men!" said Valentine.

"Ay, and poor country! where such things are done. True, they were all Puritans; I like not their sour doctrines; but what then? they are sincere men. See, I will read thee the account I have here: 'When Dr. Bastwick mounted the scaffold, his wife, immediately following, came up to him, and like a loving spouse, saluted each ear with a kiss, and then his mouth; whose tender love, boldness, and cheerful-ness, so wrought upon the people's affections, that they gave a great shout for joy to behold it.' "

"And what did Bastwick?"

"I am advised that he replied, 'Farewell, my dearest; be of good comfort. I am not dismayed.' Ay, these things will raise a spirit in England that will not be laid. 'Tis said there were afterwards, among the people, great crying and lamenting when the cruel mutilations began, more especially in the case of Dr. Burton."

"But why must they print their sour, libellous words ?"

"See that words so pent up bear not fruit in worse deeds. Now must no man put forth aught without the censor's *imprimatur*. Besides these, here is Osbaldeston persecuted, condemned to pillory, and branding and loss of all his freehold."

"What! my good and honoured old master of Westminster ?"

"And only for indiscreet sayings in a letter."

"But my poor master! I loved him well."

"Thou art moved, then, for him ? He hath escaped, no man knows whither."

"I am right glad of that. I would not have had him injured."

"There is rumour, besides all I have told thee," continued Lord Willoughby, "that the Scots have risen in open rebellion, because the Liturgy hath been forced on them contrary to the promise made them. If it be so, we shall be forced into an unnatural war with them, or worse still, become a divided rebellious country ourselves. May I die before that day !"

Valentine stood amazed at the depth of feeling he witnessed. It was so unlike all he was conscious of in himself, and all he was accustomed to in his companions, that he could not understand it.

Lord Willoughby spoke again, in a more agitated tone. "But it was not this, not even all this, bad as it is, that had moved me so deeply when you spoke. It was a thing I have learned, almost too hateful for me to repeat; yet I do repeat it, for I would fain rouse thy spirit to stand in the ranks with those who try to stem the tide that sets so strong against our ancient liberties. Thou knowest that the long-pending trial of Hampden for refusal of ship-money will soon come on before the twelve judges. Hear what Lord Wentworth hath written of him : ' In truth, I still wish Mr. Hampden, and others to his likeness, were well whipped into their right senses. And if the rod be so used that it smart not, I am the more sorry.' And this is Wentworth, the king's prime counsellor, all powerful with him ! Whither are we tending ?"

"It was ill written," said Valentine, frowning. " Mr. Hampden is a noble gentleman, of great fortune and ancient descent, and my father's friend. It was shame so to write of him."

" But it is not because he is of fortune and high descent, though both claim honour from me ; and it is not because he is thy father's friend, that I would have thee feel indignant. It is that he is the friend of England; that his great qualities outweigh even his large possessions and his high descent ; that he hath stood forward a mark and martyr for liberty's sake, and to save our constitution from overthrow."

"But the tax he was asked for was so small, that, it seemeth to me, he might have paid and never felt it."

" The more noble he ! The tax was nothing to him, in mere money, but the rights of property, which its imposition would destroy, were much. Hampden refused it not on selfish grounds. It was for the cause of law and justice !"

I

Lord Willoughby left the room as he spoke these words, and Valentine remained in a strange maze of feeling. But he had soon forgotten Hampden. His thoughts were busy with the beautiful queen, splendid masques, court revels, and a life in London. He went out to walk alone again, to indulge these reveries, and his heart beat quick as he left the door, to hear the sound of horses' feet approaching. Was it his father?

He was soon relieved from the anxiety this idea had thrown him into. It was a courier bringing down the decree of the Forest Court for the restoration of the chase to Sir Arthur Carewe, and letters from his father announcing his return before the following night.

Lady Carewe's face grew joyous again, at the hope of seeing him so soon, and at the good news he sent. Henry, too, was better, and she looked forward to his being able to bear removal from his strange sick-room before many days were over. Many an anxious thought she had, of which she said nothing. The poor doctor had received secret intimation, through Mr. Russell, that he might be conveyed to Holland, could he reach Portsmouth in safety, and had left his hiding-place to try to accomplish this by walking through the woods and by-paths by night and hiding in them by day, Mr. Russell serving as guide, and they had set forth. Many a time she was, in fancy, far away with them in wild and remote places, dreading discovery, yet hoping the best.

Towards evening she invited Lord Willoughby to go with her, Valentine, and Edith, to visit the village and confirm the glad news of the morning, with very different feelings to those she had when last she went there. Already gladness was in every cottage. The guards were removed from the farm. The spinning-wheels were humming at the doors, or by the chimney corners, as the busy hands twisted the threads; the weavers were at their looms, and proud to show the strong linen cloth woven out of the yarn sent down from the Hall, that was spun by my lady's maidens the last year; and prouder still, to show the beautiful damask table-cloth, with the family arms and motto woven in it, that was nearly finished, and was all of the fine thread spun by my lady's own fingers the last winter. Not many could spin such thread as that!

Woodruffe came out of his cottage with cheerful face, but was occupied nearly all the time in asking questions about Master Henry. " Was he better? When was he to be out again? What ailed him? He was grieved for his dog, it might be! 'Twas pity Master Valentine would take no denial."

Woodruffe had got on such dangerous ground that Valentine hurried his mother on, under pretence of wanting to hear the music that was sounding from the farm. When they reached the door, and a serving maid opened to their knock, they saw a pleasant sight, very different to that which might lately have been seen when the rude soldiers· were quartered there. The farmer and all his family were assembled, and singing their evening hymn in parts; while Dame Rudd attended to the cooking of the supper, and joined her voice to the rest at the same time, with her youngest boy on her knee. Lady Carewe would not suffer the peaceful party to be disturbed, but stood reverently by, her heart joining in the devotion, with all the gratitude she felt for the blessings that had been granted, and the escape from so much evil and sorrow.

And she was followed by the blessings of the people on her way homewards.

"Yes, yes, bless her, and all the good family," said the farmer. "They do not desert us in distress, and they love to see us happy; they do. Bless and prosper them!"

Nurse was full of questions, as she waited on Edith at night, about the people, and whether they had fallen into their old ways again, and was pleased to hear how contented and industrious they looked. "Why, indeed and in truth," said nurse, "so they be, as good and orderly a set of people as any king would wish to have to rule over. What can he be thinking of, saving his grace and majesty that I should say so, to fancy that stoats and rabbits, squirrels and foxes, and such like goodly gear, can serve him, and fight for him and love him as his people can! He's thought better of it. Oh, he was sure when Sir Arthur went and spoke to him and showed him his errors; I knew Sir Arthur could right it, and so Woodruffe said. And now, good night, my sweet pet; and we're to have Master Henry soon, my lady says. He's safe, and well too, with my lady to take care of him, so his poor old nurse won't fret about him. Good night, my pretty love."

It was growing towards afternoon on the following day, when Valentine asked admittance to his mother's room. She was alone, and feeling happy in the prospect of the family being soon again united once more. But Valentine's agitated face disquieted her. He closed the door carefully; then kneeled at her feet and kissed her hand.

" Valentine! what hath moved thee thus? No ill news of thy father!" and she started up in terror.

"I have heard nothing of my father. It is of myself only I come to speak. Be seated again, my mother. I grieve to have alarmed you thus. I have a confession to make to you. Pity me, and say what you can to my father for me."

" Thy father is ever indulgent to thee, Valentine. Thou needest not any mediator with him; but speak all that is in thy mind. Oh what awaits me? What hast thou to confess?"

" I have wronged my brother by concealing the faults of my friends, and I cannot longer bear the weight of my discomfortable reflections on it. He is ill, and, it may be, will never recover while he pines under the suspicion that he did wrong, if, indeed, he hath not himself already told you of all that happened to him that unfortunate day."

" He hath told nothing. He ever preserves entire silence
on the events of that day—that unfortunate day, as thou
too truly dost name it. He hath even drawn a promise from
his father, not to inquire more or ask any questions about it
of any one, but leave it as it is, and think, our poor Henry
saith, ' the best you can of me.' "

Valentine's checks burned with shame at the contrast
between this conduct and his own. He might now have concealed the truth, and tried to lull his mother's suspicions
again, but he had caught a generous impulse from Henry,
and resolved to clear him at once.

" Henry did deliver my father's commands not to enter
the chase, resolutely, clearly, and resisted our disobedience
to the last. Morley and Wilmot dragged him in by main
force, and it was not till they had dragged him so far that
he saw Edith's stag the prey of the huntsmen, that he ran
forward with his own will. Then came his dog to his
rescue, and they killed poor Lion ! I have told you all, my
mother !"

" Ah yes ! ah yes ! All, indeed !" she said, in a voice
of anguish.

" I only went in to please my friends," Valentine went
on. " I cared not to have gone myself, and when I saw
them use unseemly violence to my brother, I was angry and
forbade it. I had gone on first in pursuit of the stag, and
saw them not begin it."

" Say no more ; no more."

" And canst thou forgive me ? Say thou dost forgive
me, my mother !"

" I pity thee, my son. I pity myself and thy father.

Ah, Valentine! It is not my forgiveness thou shouldst ask; thou shouldst cry to a Higher than I—' create in me a clean heart, and renew a right spirit within me.' Oh! how cowardly hast thou been!"

" Cowardly!" cried Valentine, reddening and starting to his feet. "Did I not draw in my brother's cause to avenge his dog, and risk my life for his sake?"

"Ay, but there is a courage thou knowest not of; a courage that is nought akin to brawls and violence. Oh that I could see that courage in thee!—I will say what I can to thy father for thee."

Valentine moved towards the door, but turned and looked at his mother, and seeing her in a passion of tears, rushed back to her, seized her hands, kissed them fervently again and again, then hurried away.

In ten minutes he was riding at a furious rate on the road to Windsor.

CHAPTER XI.

THREE DAYS AT CREWHURST.

THE great chamber is prepared as if for honoured guests.
Freeman, with important face, has spread the finest damask
table-cloth, set out the plate and the Venetian glasses, and
spread the carpets for the feet. The bell is sounding and the
company is ushered in. :

There walks in first, Lady Carewe, holding by each
hand little Alice and Martin, and followed by nurse, who
must wait upon them. The children look very happy, but
rather grave, impressed with the wonder of taking dinner in
the great chamber with their father and mother. Behind
comes Sir Arthur, who leads in one hand Edith and in the
other Henry. It is Henry's birthday, and the first day that he
has been sufficiently strong to leave his own room. This is the
festive occasion, for which the great chamber is prepared.

Sir Arthur presses Henry's hand, says kind words to
him, and looks lovingly in his pale face; but what a change
has come over Sir Arthur! It is but two weeks since he
returned from London, a strong man, of high and proud
bearing, prosperous with his recovered property. Those
two weeks have done on him the work of twenty years. His
head is bowed, his eye is heavy, a settled melancholy sits

on his face. The desertion of his eldest son, the darling of his heart, and worse still, the tardy confession that went before it, the conviction forced on him that his pride and confidence in that son were all misplaced; that there is no sympathy between them, that they have different principles, opposite aims, that a gulf has opened between them, with dark and dreary waters, ever to flow, ever to widen; all this has broken his heart. He is a strong man still—he will do his work and his duty; but the glory has passed away from his life.

How tenderly and sweetly Edith looks at him as he places her by his side, and how deep and full is Henry's love! If only his father could see into his heart, what consolation would he find there ! Henry has suffered so much since last he sat in that room, that on him too the weeks have done almost the work of years. He is but a boy, but he feels like a young man in his ardent desire to be to his father something approaching, at least, to that which Valentine was. When, in his illness, his mother told him of Valentine's confession, his pity and love for his brother became so strong, and his yearning to see him again and make all right with him so great, that the necessity to reveal Valentine's entrance into the queen's household, sooner than otherwise would have been necessary, followed. Henry had been educated in the strictest principles of reverence and obedience to parents. To him, therefore, Valentine's conduct appeared unnatural and dreadful, inspiring something like horror. Now that he had recovered his health, he had left off thinking so much of Valentine, and had fixed his thoughts on his father. If only he could behave so as to please him, to be a comfort to

him, make him look happier, that was Henry's great wish
and hope now. This day, his birthday, when he was restored
to health again, seemed the day to begin a new life.

Hardly had they taken their seats when the door opened
to admit another guest. Henry started up in joy. It was
the very friend he had longed for, his guide and helper in
the new course he was to begin—Mr. Russell. He had
returned that morning, and this pleasant surprise for Henry
had been determined on among them. The good doctor
was safe in Holland.

Mr. Russell had learned all that had happened from Lady
Carewe already; there were no painful explanations to go
through. Dinner passed in pleasant talk, and Henry's health
was drunk in heartfelt earnest love by every one. His little
brother and sister were enchanted to have him again with
them; Edith looked bright once more; his mother, who
knew so well what was in him, looked from him to his father
with eyes which, though they were tearful, were full of joy
too, because she knew that it could not be long before a true
affection, founded on mutual rectitude and sympathy of
character, would arise between them, and if she sighed for
her lost son, she ventured to say nothing of him yet. No
one dared even to mention his name to his offended father.

After this day, the autumn glided on very peace-
fully, and before winter there was a large addition to the
family. Sir Valentine Knightly and his lady, the father and
mother of Lady Carewe, had come out of Northampton-
shire on a visit, to spend Christmas at Crewhurst; and
with them their eldest daughter, the sister of Lady Carewe,
and her husband, Mr. and Mistress Cope, proprietors of

the ancient priory of Canons' Ashby. They brought a whole bevy of children, of all ages from five to fifteen, so that there was a great meeting of cousins, and many a merry laugh resounded through the hall.

Lady Carewe had hoped that this friendly gathering and the approach of the season that usually draws families together, would have softened Sir Arthur towards Valentine, and brought him an invitation to visit his home once more. But it was not so. Twice had Valentine written, humbly craving forgiveness, and begging to be allowed, if he could obtain leave from his royal mistress, to visit his home for a short time ; but Sir Arthur returned no answer. He did, however, though unknown to Valentine, maintain some watch over him, through Lord Falkland, who was much in London, and noticed and patronised the son out of friendship for the father. He sent good reports of Valentine's conduct at court. He was there observed for gentlemanly behaviour, and had not joined the set of reckless and extravagant courtiers, but rather the more orderly. The acquaintance with Lord Morley had been interrupted by that nobleman's absence in Paris.

Christmas-day was kept at Crewhurst with all the old hospitality and rejoicing. Great branches of holly, of yew, and laurel, not forgetting the mistletoe, were brought in the day before by the foresters, and with these the church first, then the little private chapel, and afterwards the great chamber, were decorated. Lady Carewe and Goodwife Freeman had been busy for a week providing abundance of good cheer. Every cottage in the village must have a substantial dinner on Christmas-day sent in, sufficient to make a feast for all its inhabitants. Not a beggar must be turned away from the door without a good meal. The tables in the servants' hall were laid for a party of fifty. The large nursery was to be filled with as noisy and merry a set as any of the others ; and the great chamber would be in all its glory. for the principal guests.

The weather was completely seasonable, the ground was covered with snow, and "icicles hung by the wall;" but merrily rang the bells from the church steeple on Christmas-eve, sounding clear through the frosty air, and the wassailers came and sang outside and the waits played at midnight. At six in the morning the bells rang again. Then all rose and dressed, and wished " Merry Christmas " each to the other ; and now they assembled in chapel, a large party, so large that the door must be left open, and far beyond it the worshippers joined in praise and thanksgiving for the return of the blessed day, and full swelled the Anthem to the organ.

Then as they sat down to breakfast there were voices without that struck up the old carol—

> " Was not Christ our Saviour,
>   Sent unto us from God above,
> Not for our good behaviour,
>   But only of His mercy and love?
> If this be true, as true it is,
>   Truly indeed,
> Great thanks to God to yield for this,
>   Then had we need.

> " This did our God for very troth,
>   To train to Him the soul of man,
> And justly to perform His oath
>   To Sarah and to Abraham,
> That through his seed, all nations should
>   Most blessed be,

THE WASSAIL BOWL.

As in due time performed, He would,
All flesh should see.

" Which wondrously is brought to pass,
And in our sight already done,
By sending, as His promise wa·,
To comfort us, His only Son.
For other gifts in many ways,
That God doth send,
Let us in Christ give God the praise,
Till life shall end."

Henry led the way, followed by a whole tribe of cousins, to see who the singers were, and invite them in to breakfast. There, be sure, was Thomas Boult, and there was Lawrence, and Michael Protheroe, and about ten more. They were highly applauded, ushered in, and then after a good bout of snow-balling, in which the young gentlemen pelted each other, they shook off their white peppering, and went up to breakfast with due order and decorum.

Now must all go to church, for the bells have begun again. The party from the hall was so large that the great pew which filled all one side of the gallery was full, and so were the two pews for the servants below ; and when service was over, the vicar joined them, for he must dine at the Hall to-day. The vicar is an elderly gentleman, and unmarried, and was not very friendly, because he belonged to the court party, and was a favourite of the archbishop ; but there must be no thought of cold politics and church parties to-day.

When dinner was over the games began. There was merry-making everywhere, in hall and bower, in cottage and farm, and an universal holiday. Nor at night was the old custom of burning the Yule-log forgotten. Woodruffe and

Thomas Boult dragged it to the chimney, assisted by Henry,
who pulled with all his might.

So passed Christmas. Then came the new year of 1638,
a year that began dismally in London, with a return of the
pestilence that had raged at the time of the king's accession.
The court was at Oatlands, and so Valentine was out of the
danger, and at Crewhurst all was peaceful; and in due time
the frost and snow vanished, and spring came round again.
  May-day came fresh, bright, and breezy. The nightin-
gales filled the air with their songs, the ground was gay with
wild flowers, and the blossoms of the hawthorn, though not
fully out, were yet to be found on sunny southern slopes, so

the tall May-pole on the green at the village was decked by early morning gay with streamers and garlands. Amy Rudd, the farmer's pretty little daughter, was to be queen of the May, and Edith was down at the village before the sports began, to deck her with a lovely crown of violets and primroses that she had made for her, and a sceptre all set thick with cowslips. There were two tents : one larger than the other, containing a feast sent down from the Hall. There were syllabubs, curds and whey, cheeses, cakes, and much more substantial fare. The smaller tent was for Sir Arthur and Lady Carewe, and some friends they expected. My Lord Falkland and a party of ladies and gentlemen were to rest that day at Crewhurst, on their way into Oxfordshire.

Henry, who entered into merry-makings with all his heart, dressed up as Robin Hood, and made his appearance with bow in hand and quiver at his back, and a train of his cousins and friends behind him, as Friar Tuck, Little John, and all his merry men ; Margaret Cope, the eldest of the family, was Maid Marian, and dressed with Edith's best skill ; Alice was a fairy all in green, with a white willow wand in her hand, and a wreath of lilies-of-the-valley in her hair ; and Martin was Puck. They hardly knew what he ought to look like, to be like Puck, so all they could do was to decorate him with the brightest colours they could think of, and he ran about among the rest, and laughed, and jumped, and rolled about, so that did very well. Edith had been too busy dressing every one else, to think of herself, but when she came down the avenue leading all the maids from the Hall, she looked the prettiest and loveliest there, as Woodruffe and nurse declared ; and when, retiring into the

tent, she was obliged by Robin Hood to put on a black
visor, because now a "merrie masque" must begin, they
complained of having lost the sight of her sweet face.

But the masquers were very merry. Two fiddlers hired
by my lady struck up, and there was dancing round the
May-pole, and plenty of laughter and fun. Robin Hood, of
course, had a trial at archery, and proved worthy of his
great name, being a first-rate marksman. Then was a great
game at prisoners'-bass, and when that was over, the procession of the May-pole began. Everybody present was collected; and then Edith, leading out the little May-queen, presented her to her loving subjects. She placed herself at
their head, and they, walking behind her in one long string,
went round and round the May-pole three times; then she
was throned on a seat made of dry moss, at the foot of the
May-pole, and there she sat looking on at the dancing for a
little while, till Robin Hood led her out, and she danced as
merrily as the rest.

The expected party was now seen approaching through
the chase. Among them were two or three young cavaliers,
who, catching the humour of the scene, drew up at a short
distance, sent a servant to borrow visors, then dismounted
and joined in the dance. Lord Falkland with the elder
members of the party, were received by Sir Arthur and Lady
Carewe in the tent; but among the ladies was one of whom
Henry was so fond, that he left the dances to hasten to her
side. Lady Willoughby had taken advantage of this pleasant
escort to come to Crewhurst; and the love between them
was mutual, as he was an especial favourite with her. They
were in full talk directly, and she soon asked him to lead her

among the revellers. He asked the names of the young gentlemen who had joined the dance.

"One is young Mr. Verney, another Mr. Gage."

"But who is the tall one, who stands aloof, or walks alone quite away from the crowd? See, he now stands near Edith. I guess that if I saw his visor off I should see his likeness to you, and then should I know his name."

"He is not my brother, and he is far handsomer than I."

"That I believe not."

"So thou art learning to flatter already, Henry?"

"No, I only say what I believe."

She smiled, but told him he would see his mistake when the visor was doffed. Edith came to her to greet her, led by the tall graceful cavalier.

Lady Willoughby spoke to him.

"I wait but for Lord Falkland's signal," he replied.

Henry started at the sound, and seized him nervously by the hand.

"Come away! come apart! here under the trees, and let me see thy face. Valentine! my brother, I know thee before I see thee, but let me look upon thy face again."

His face was uncovered, and Edith and Henry held him fast in their arms.

Oh, how handsome he was! He had grown taller and broader, and his features were more formed, his eyes more brilliant, his dress, air and manner, courtly and graceful, and he looked at them with a smiling face, as if half amused at their excitement, though there was trouble in his face too.

"Why, Henry!" he said, "thou art grown into a young gallant, instead of a rough boy. Thy woodland dress becomes thee, and thy chestnut curls suit thee well. Thou art not like a Puritan now, and I doubt much if I could put thee into a passion by nicknames, thou dost look so sage and manly. But my pretty Edith! prettier than ever. I must have thee at court; 'tis shame to leave thee to rusticise here."

"I will have none of the court," said she; "I love it not, for that it hath taken thee away from us."

"Far rather do thou come home to us, my brother," said Henry earnestly. "Our father will then look happy once again!"

At this moment Lord Falkland, issuing from the tent, held up his hand. Valentine faltered and turned pale. It was the signal that he might go to his father and mother. No one was present at that interview.

It lasted a long while. The dances were done; the guests had departed, some to their cottages, others to the hall, and the moon was rising in the evening sky, when they issued from the tent with their son. There were traces of tears on Lady Carewe's cheeks, and the settled melancholy on Sir Arthur's face remained unchanged. Valentine's was agitated, but whatever he felt was not deep. A court ball would smooth his brow again in a few hours. Now he walked silently, supporting his mother on his arm.

Before Henry went to rest that night, he was summoned to his father's private room, and there he found not only his father, but his mother, Lord Falkland, and Mr. Russell.

"This, my Lord Falkland," said his father, as he entered, "is my son of whom I have spoken to you. He is worthy, though so young, to hear the news you have brought us. Suffer me to present him to you. If, as I trust, his character as a man answers to the promise of his boyhood, he will serve his country on the like upright principles that the noble wife of Judge Croke has led her husband to follow; fearing nothing save to do that which his conscience disapproves."

Lord Falkland held out his hand, and received Henry kindly, and even affectionately, as he bent respectfully before him.

"The intelligence I have brought to thy father," said he, "concerns Mr. Hampden especially, but also greatly affects all who wish well to their country, its ancient monarchy, and liberties; and among all, none more nearly than our beloved king himself. I reckon it, although at the moment he will be angry at it, a great gain to him. For it must much import his majesty that his judges judge wisely and with integrity, and that the course of his affairs is so ordered that those who wish well to their country may see all differences healed, and liberty established under his peaceful sway. This trial of Mr. Hampden, which hath so long agitated men's minds, has now been decided."

"And is judgment then given in his favour?" asked Henry.

"Not so. That, alas! would be beyond our hopes. No. The majority of the judges have given judgment against my noble friend. But that which I have to tell thee hath greatly influenced the cause for which he hath stood forward, by showing the party, who by their evil counsels are dragging our king on to dangerous extremities, that there is strength in those who would stem the tide of tyranny. It appeared, at one time, as though an unanimous verdict

would be given against him, but Judge Croke hath made it
otherwise. He, like the rest, had resolved to deliver his
opinion for the king, and against Hampden, and to that end
had prepared his arguments, yet a few days before he was to
argue, he, on most serious thoughts and discourse with some
of his friends, did alter his mind on the matter. Then spoke
his lady, and heartened him, and said to him, that she hoped
he would do nothing against his conscience, for fear of any
danger or prejudice to him or his family, and that she would
be content to suffer want, or any misery with him, rather
than be an occasion for him to do or say anything against
his judgment and conscience. On this, he suddenly altered
his purpose and arguments."

"She was a noble lady to say so!" said Henry; "but it
seemeth to me a very strange thing that her husband should
need such words, and he a judge! How could he ever
think to argue that which seemed contrary to truth?"

"Thou knowest not the world, my young friend," replied
Lord Falkland. "Judge Croke hath, in delivering a judgment against the king's will, to face the consequences
thereof. They may be loss of place, or even a prison to himself, and want and poverty to his family!"

Henry looked very grave. "And is he the only judge
who hath given a judgment for Mr. Hampden?" he asked
presently.

"No; in this lieth the great importance of his resolution.
Inspired by his courage, Justice Hutton hath also given
judgment against the king; and Justice Jones, though not
going so far, hath much qualified his opinion; and Justice
Denham, being sick, hath sent a written judgment in favour

of Hampden.   These things will greatly shake the extreme
party in their course; and therein my friend, though he
loseth his cause, yet gaineth his purpose."

"And would all those judges, but for the example of
Justice Croke, have given judgment against conscience?"
asked Henry.

"Indeed it seemeth likely."

Henry looked, in his perplexity, towards Mr. Russell, to
whom he usually carried such difficulties.

"Thou art troubled, Henry, and no wonder," Mr. Russell
replied to his look.   "The times are evil, and tempt men to
do evil from want of courage to endure the suffering that
rectitude brings upon them.   Let it never be so with thee.
Keep firm in the narrow way, narrow as it now is, and enter
by the strait gate, let the consequences to thyself be what
they may.   Be truth ever thy guide; and walk in the thorny
path that leads to God.   Let me feel that when thou art a man,
thou wilt be true to the dream of thy youth; so shall I leave
thee with happy mind, deep as my sorrow is to leave thee."

"Leave me!"

"Yes, Henry.   It is even so," said his father.   "I have
for some time known that this blow was hanging over us,
but had hoped to avert it.   The order has gone forth against
keeping of private chaplains, which is thought to favour
separation from the church.   I have petitioned to be permitted to retain Mr. Russell, who is a friend so loved and
valued by us all, not as chaplain, but as my secretary and thy
tutor.   Lord Falkland has exerted himself much for me;
but in vain.   He will leave us early in the morning, in Lord
Falkland's company."

x

Henry was completely overcome. He rushed away, not being able to command himself. The bitter grief he felt was such that he could bear no comforting, and even the consciousness that Valentine was in the house, scarcely helped to lighten his load of sorrow. By morning he was calmer, and able to listen to Mr. Russell, who was in his room very early. He impressed on Henry that the duty he now had to perform was so important, that if he indulged in grief and sank into idleness, he would be criminal.

"Thy father loses his secretary in me," said he; "thou must supply my place. His melancholy in losing his eldest son, is even increased by the interview they have had; thou must cheer him and supply to him the place of two sons. He will be thy tutor; a better thou canst not have. His learning far exceeds mine. Give him the joy of finding a diligent pupil in thee. So shalt thou best console him, and make thy mother happy; and so best console me who suffer much—more than thou canst know."

"I promise to fulfil your words. I will never forget them. And whither do you go?"

"To Italy, to join that friend of whom you have heard me so often speak, and whose grand poetry you and I have read and enjoyed: Mr. Milton. God will bring us together again in His own good time."

They went down together. For the last time, the organ swelled through the chapel under Mr. Russell's hand; for the last time, his voice led the prayers; in an hour he was gone; and Valentine also went with the rest of the company.

CHAPTER XII.

WOODRUFFE.

A YEAR and a half has passed since that hurried and un-expected visit of Valentine to his home. There is a gray and stormy November sky, and the wind sways the branches of the tall trees in the avenue of Crewhurst, and howls among the ancient oaks of the chase, as Henry walks slowly towards the thicket where he buried his faithful dog, leaving marks of his footsteps in the thin covering of snow which had fallen in the night, a spade and pickaxe in his hands.

Outside the thicket Woodruffe is waiting for him, and they enter it together.

"I hope the stone is what you would have it, Master Henry," said Woodruffe, taking the canvas covering off a small tombstone that lay on the ground.

Henry examined it, and slowly read the inscription to see that it was right.

"This stone is Sette up,
Nov^er. I., MDCXXXIX,
To the Memory of my
Trustie and Trewe
Dog Lion,
Who died in defence of his Master
From cruel Men,
Aug^st. VII., MDCXXXVII.,
By me, Henry Carewe."

"It is well, and as I wished, Woodruffe. No; do not take the pickaxe. I buried him myself, and I would not other hands but mine should move the earth above him."

Henry, handling his tool with vigorous arms, had soon dug to a sufficient depth, and then he and Woodruffe fixed the stone in its place, he shovelled in the earth, replaced the turf, and stood silently leaning on his spade and looking at it.

"Thou wilt see that it do not get mossy nor overgrown, Woodruffe? Thou wilt look to it for me?"

"That you may be well assured of, Master Henry."

"Thou wilt also, I know well, take special care of the little falcon my sister loves, and thou wilt see when the heron that little Mistress Alice watched in spring on the tallest elm makes her nest, and take heed that no one harms nor disturbs her nor her nestlings."

"Very sure may you be of all that, Master Henry; but if you go on i' this strain, I shall soon play the woman with my eyes. Of a surety you and all the good family will return by spring. 'Twill be sad days with all hereabouts till they see them back; and there be not a man, woman, nor child in the village, nor about the place, that will not miss your kindly eye and cheery voice every hour o' the day, Master Henry; and this I know too, there's not a man nor woman that's kept in their service nor that's left in the hall that will not do the work and see to the property in doors and out as if the eye of the master and the lady was upon them. There's not one of us but will stand by your good family and serve them by day or by night. We love ye all, and among ye all, I don't know but what it's your very self, Master Henry, we love best of all."

Henry held out his hand and grasped Woodruffe's with a firm and long pressure. It was some time before he could master his voice.

"I hope we shall come back in spring, Woodruffe; and well I know thy words are true, and that all we leave here will be cared for, and safely kept for us. I must not stay longer, but thou wilt walk to the Hall with me. I know my father hath business for thee."

They emerged from the thicket, but Henry ran back for one minute alone. Then they walked at a quick pace up the avenue.

"And may I make bold to ask, Master Henry, if it seemeth to you, as a man may say, a likely thing that Master Valentine may come home with you in the spring?"

"Indeed we hope it will be so."

"It would be more pleasant and natural like, every way, Master Henry. When we down here heard from Will Scraply, as brought back the bay nag from Lunnon last March, (it was on Lady Day, as I remember well), that Master Valentine was going with my Lord Holland's cavalry to fight the Scotch, we none o' us liked it."

"Neither did I like it."

"It was not as we should ha' grudged our best blood i' the service o' king and country, nor yet that we wouldn't be no ways backward nor cowardly in a fair fight, but we none of us liked the notion o' fightin' the Scots. We'd no stomach to it. See here, now! There's old Duncan Carr as came in wi' King James, and settled i' these parts, there's not a quieter, honester, nor more hard-working man than he; and he's a Scotchman. He do speak outlandish a bit, but what

then ? He don't speak more outlandish than a Yorkshire-
man, and we seem brothers like, and don't like the fight no
how, and all the more because the king's majesty's a Scot
himself, and to go and try for to slay and harry his own
people, seems an unnatural thing."

"You're right not to like it. It's over now, and I hope
we shall hear no more of it."

" I promise you we don't like it, though, that way neither,"
said Woodruffe. "It's not right pleasant to think our lads
ran away."

" No, no, not quite so bad as that!"

" You see, Master Henry, Duncan Carr saith so ; and not
Will Scraply nor Ditchly, nor one that ever comes from
Lunnon, can say ought to gainsay it. Duncan saith that
when my Lord Holland showed his face at Kelso, and that was
Duncan's own country thereabouts, the canny Scots just tauld
him he'd best turn aboot and gae hame again, and he e'en
took their advice."

Henry could not help laughing at Woodruffe's imitation
of the Scotch "outlandish" language.

" And then what's it all about ? Duncan, ye see, he gets
budgets o' news by the carriers wi' their pack horses as come
by Carlisle, and he laughs, and we don't like it. What's
it all about ? I say again. If the Scots don't like bishops,
and do very well without them, what then ? The king
knows very well, so Duncan saith, that they never did hold
by bishops. They're his own people, and who should know
if he don't? It don't look well to go and fight with his own
people. It won't thrive."

" They have made an agreement now without fighting,"

said Henry; "and I hope they will keep to it. The Scots
have got the king's promise to leave them to worship God in
their own way, and the Scotch have given him back his castles,
and forts, and ships."

"But then they had taken them away! There must
have been fighting some time or other."

"No, the lords that manage their matters made haste
and took possession before the king had time to prevent them,
directly they heard he was coming."

"I don't think the king gets properly served," said
Woodruffe. "That be not the way I should look after *my*
master's rights. What were those about as looks after *his*
matters? I'm sure he pays them well, to judge by the mort
o' money he's always wantin'. No end o' loans, and ship-
money, and fines. The country's harried wi' them, and I'm
sick o' hearing o' them, for my part."

Henry sighed. He was sick of hearing of them too.

"But, after all, it was about Master Valentine I began,
and it's about him I want to hear the rights o' the thing.
You see, Sir Arthur would raise no troop himself."

"No, the war was against his conscience."

"And a heavy fine he had to pay, and so, they say, had
many an other."

"Yes, my Lord Brooke, and Lord Say and Sele, and many
others."

"But, for all that, Master Valentine goes to the war with
my Lord Holland. That's what we cannot make right no
how."

Henry was troubled at this speech, but after a few minutes'
silence, he spoke, resolving to try to put this point at rest if

he could, and feeling that he ought not to be angry with this old and faithful servant for putting it.

"My father," said he, "is not one that will force any one to think as he does. My brother likes to serve in the court, and to take arms at the king's bidding. My father, therefore, though it would please him better that it were not so, lays no force upon him to prevent it."

"Just so. But if you will not be angry with me, Master Henry, I have only one more question to ask. Is it true, as the story goes in the country now, that going to the war has not thriven with Master Valentine, no more than with the king?"

"What story is going in the country?" asked Henry.

"Why, you know, Master Henry, that many a gentle-man and nobleman hereabouts furnished troops for the war, though Sir Arthur did not, and since they're disbanded, they told us here many stories about it; and some o' them say how Master Valentine turned among the first, and rode post to Carlisle, and so to Lunnon. But others, and far the most, say how my Lord Morley called my Lord Holland to task because he turned, and how Master Valentine had a regular stand-up fight with one Colonel Lunsford, that's a mighty favourite with the king's majesty, thereupon, and called him coward. However that be, they say my Lord Holland was in a regular towering tip-top passion, and dismissed Master Valentine from the service."

Henry bit his lip. He was vexed that this story had got abroad. Full of mistakes as it was, it was so far true, as to be one of the chief causes that took Sir Arthur to London. It was quite true that Lord Holland, who had originally

favoured Valentine so much, had now become his enemy,
and that the wish to secure the heir of the Carewes to the
court had become indifferent to him now, as he was himself
veering towards the liberal party; and it was quite true that
Valentine had insulted Colonel Lunsford. To remove Valentine from the post he held, now that he had lost his friend
and protector, before farther quarrels or any evil consequences resulting from the hatred of a man like Colonel Lunsford, was important.

" You must contradict flatly all they say about deserting
his colours," said Henry. "My brother would never do
that. As to a fight, they have got that all wrong too, but
it's too long to put right. You may say, if you like, that my
brother has quarrelled with Colonel Lunsford, with very good
reason, and is very likely to come home soon. If you add,
that his father and his brother are very glad of both, you
will only say the truth."

" Thank you, Master Henry. I see how it has been, I
think. We are getting nigh the Hall now. Would you
mind coming round by the stables to see how forward the
grooms are with their horses for the mornin' ?"

Henry consented, and they went straight to the court-
yard, which they found full of the bustle of preparation for
an early departure next morning. A waggon stood ready
packed with furniture, boxes, and hampers. Two waggons
had already been sent on. The coach was in like manner
packed with many of the smaller things. Straw, canvas,
and ropes were strewed about. It might have looked
melancholy to some eyes, but it raised Henry's spirits.
He liked the change, he liked going to London, which he
had only seen on short visits, and he longed to see Valentine

again ; so he felt light and gay at heart, and went into the stables and patted and stroked the horses as they ate their corn.

There was many an empty stall now. There were only the four coach horses, and four saddle horses, and Valentine's bay, which was to be led to London for his use. "To-morrow the stables will be empty," said Woodruffe, sadly, as they walked away.

"But thou must come and visit us in London, Woodruffe," said Henry. "There are brave sights there. My father has hired a house by the river, and we shall see the barges and boats, and many a gallant pageant, so they tell me. And then there is the king's palace of Whitehall, and the Palace of Westminster, and St. Paul's, and the Abbey. Thou shalt come and see them all."

"Thank you, Master Henry, and if I can think it right to leave all here in charge of Leeson and Boult, I should like it right well. Shall you see Mr. Russell in Lunnon now?"

"Oh no! no such good fortune. He's far away in a country called Italy, with a dear friend of his."

"Is that a good country, that Italy?"

"It's a beautiful country, with rare and grand cities, and marble palaces, and beautiful pictures, and great riches, but they cannot be good men there."

"And why so, Master Henry?"

"Why, Mr. Russell told me in a letter he wrote to me, that he and Mr. Milton—that's his friend, you know—had just been to visit a good old man in prison ; a very clever, great man ; kept there only for speaking the truth."

"That's bad. And what was that good man's name?"

"Galileo."

" A quaint name too ! Not one I ever heard afore. And what was the truth he told them and they didn't like ? I suppose he told them o' their sins now, or the like o' that ?"

" No. He only told them that the sun stood still, and the earth we live on moved round him."

Woodruffe clapped his hands to his sides, and laughed till the echoes rang again.

" Ah ! you may laugh," said Henry, " but it's no laugh - ing matter to him."

" To think, now," said Woodruffe, suddenly turning grave and almost angry, " what devices men may be for contriving ! The earth going round ! the sun standing still ! Don't I feel the steady ground under my feet? It don't run away from under me. Don't I see the sun run his daily course? Mustn't I believe my own eyes? They'll tell one next this holly bough I pick up with its red berries is a birch broom, fit for a witch to ride on!"

"But, Woodruffe, Galileo knows the truth of what he says."

"You think so, perhaps, Master Henry; but for my part, I think that same Master Gallio, or whatever his name may be, don't know the moon from green-cheese. Belike he never got up to breakfast, else he'd have seen the sun rise o' one side, and travel round and set o' th' other."

"For all that," said Henry, "Mr. Russell has taught me the other way."

"Ay, ay," said Woodruffe, "you're young, and will believe anything Mr. Russell says; and Mr. Russell he goes on a studyin' and a studyin' of indoors, and a worritin' and a worritin' of outdoors, visitin' sick people and dying people, and one thing or another, till his brains is wellnigh addled, it may be. But don't tell me! I wouldn't put that poor Gallio in prison. What's the use on't? I would bid him get up o' mornin's and look about him, and he'd soon know better. He would see the sky grow red and then golden i' the east, and then up comes the sun, and mounts i' the sky, and then stands most overhead at noon, and by evenin' sinks i' the west in gold and crimson, like unto his state when he rose. Where be that Master Gallio's eyes?"

"Now, Woodruffe, listen to me. This great stone shall be the—"

"No; if that poor good man could tell us now what the

sun does wi' himself all night now, and how he gets round to
th' other corner o' the world, ready for mornin' again, that
would be something like."

"Mr. Russell could tell you all about that."

Woodruffe smiled, and patted Henry gently on the back.

"You think so, I dare to say, Master Henry; but wait till
you're as old as me, and you'll know better. Mr. Russell,
now, was great i' teaching us the Gospel, that I will say.
Many a time I've listened to him when he was talkin' to old
Dame Leeson. She never could fancy the new translation
o' the Scriptures ordered by King James. She quarrelled
mightily wi' it, and never went to church wi' good will because the vicar read out of it. 'Twas his orders, you know.
What could he do? 'Appointed to be read in all churches,'
that's the orders. So Mr. Russell he used to say to her, says
he—I can't go for to pretend I can go for to say it just in
his exact words, but says he, 'What matters for a word here
and a word there? Do as well as you can what you think
the words really mean,' says he; and 'I think that will
serve,' says he. In that, I thought Mr. Russell spoke well;
but as to that other matter o' the sun and the world going
round"—and Woodruffe shook his head and smiled again
contemptuously.

"Well, I will not say any more about it now. Some
day, if Mr. Russell comes back, he will tell you himself."

"No, no. In teaching the Gospel, as I have said, and in
putting down fanatics now, there he was great. That last
Christmas time he was here, comes a preacher from Norwich,
and stands on th' green, and reproaches us for the holly
boughs and misletoe, and for singing of our carols, after the

good beef and ale my lady sent, and Mr. Russell talked well
to him.   I warrant he beat him dead at his arguments, and
brings him in to my cottage after, and seats him by the fire,
and gives a look to my old mother, and she brings out as
good a slice o' beef and as foaming a tankard o' ale for him,
and he enjoys it as well as ever fanatic did.   And Mr. Russell's no papist neither, not he.   But besides that matter of
the earth slipping from under our feet, he's mightily behind
about witchcraft.   No use to tell him of a witch.   See if he
wouldn't go to the stake himself, sooner than some arrant old
witch should burn!"

"Here we are at the door.   I must go in, and your
supper must have been ready this half hour.   But come in
and sup at the Hall."

"No, thank you kindly, Master Henry.   I must be home.
Mr. Russell won't meet wi' the Pope in any of those foreign
parts, will he?"

"If he do, never fear," replied Henry laughing.   "He
will not turn papist.   I will be answerable for him."

"Good night, then, Master Henry."

"Good night, Woodruffe.   I shall see you, I know, before we mount in the morning."

"Of that you may make sure.   Good night, and bless
you, and all the good family, wherever you be."

CHAPTER XIII.

LONDON IN 1639.

BEFORE the sun had been an hour up on the following morning, the family of Crewhurst Hall were some miles on their way to London. Lady Carewe had had a sore parting to go through. She had left her little Martin behind, under the charge of nurse, whom she could trust as herself. She would not risk taking him at his tender age into the un-healthy air of London, nor into danger of small-pox, which was the terror of all mothers, and which the rest of her family had happily gone through. But she would not brood over sorrows. Her task now was to do her part to reclaim Valentine, and bring him back to his family.

In the coach were Lady Carewe, Edith, and Alice, and Mistress Cicely, as she was now called, because she was promoted to the rank of my lady's own woman, and waited also on Mistress Edith. Without sat Alice's nurserymaid Mary, and one of the housemaids : Goodwife Freeman and another had gone by the waggon before, to see the house made ready, and get all the furniture and goods that were sent in properly placed, for with themselves the family moved all they should require. Freeman, and William the serving man, sat behind ; the horses were driven by postilions. Sir Arthur and Henry rode, followed by two grooms; all, including Freeman, well armed.

A party so strong as this was in no danger from robbers. But it was not in their power to escape bad roads. It was very late in the season for a journey. Nothing but the sudden change in Valentine's position would have made Sir Arthur resolve on taking it now. He had intended, however, to go in spring, when all men now looked for a Parliament; and this journey in November had been hastily resolved on, because to manage Valentine's retirement well would not be easy, and would require time. The roads then were very bad, the more as the snow had melted and left them soft and muddy. On Sir Arthur's own property, and in his immediate neighbourhood, they were tolerable, and the coach got on at the rate of six miles an hour; but there was a swamp between Crewhurst and Windsor, where the ruts were so deep that Sir Arthur had directed Farmer Rudd to send two of his strong plough horses and two men to wait there and help the coach on. Lucky it was he did so.

As soon as the heavy coach got into the narrow track that ended in this swamp, the men made their appearance from a little roadside posting-house, and yoked their good powerful horses in front, one mounting his horse, the other, with a long pole, walking to push behind, or to one side, or to lift up, or whatever the case might require. The jolting and rocking of the coach were so great that the ladies would gladly have got out, for they were shaken terribly, but the mud was so deep they could not possibly walk, and had to bear it as well as they could. Alice, who cared little for being shaken, was constantly laughing, but Cicely was very frightened, and, but for her lady's presence, which kept her quiet, would have shrieked and exclaimed continually. Sir Arthur and Henry, floundering through as well as they could, their horses sinking sometimes nearly to the knees, had enough to do to get through themselves. The whole party were therefore very glad when they reached the town of Windsor, and put up for an hour to rest the horses.

The road between Windsor and London was one of the best in England, so that their worst troubles were now over, and as they rested one night at Hounslow, at the house of their friends, Mr. and Mrs. Bellasis, they made an easy journey on the second day, though not without much jolting and some very bad passes, and came within sight of London early in the afternoon. The weather was bright and fine for November, and there lay not then over the city such a cloud of smoke as now we see ; besides that the extent of London, and the number of its inhabitants, have so immensely increased since that time, there was very little coal used then. There was a prejudice against it for domestic purposes, and wood and charcoal were the common fuel.

Sir Arthur and Henry rode by the windows of the coach, pointing out all the objects of interest to Edith, who had never been to London before, and Alice, who was full of life and questions.

They were travelling along a road between fields and hedgerows, and were admiring the beautiful wooded hills of Hampstead and Highgate to the north ; and now they turned down a winding lane, now called Park Lane, and saw a long line of road before them, with grass fields of the finest green, dotted with cattle and sheep.

"Now, look out, Edith, and you will see the distant roofs of Westminster Abbey and Westminster Hall."

"I see them. They are beautiful. That is the abbey. I should know it by the picture Henry made of it for me when he went to London with my father last year. But what is that dark, gloomy, large house beyond the field, where the sheep are feeding, and nearer to us than the abbey and hall of Westminster?"

"That is the palace of St. James's," said Henry. "Thou dost not describe it very royally, methinks."

"It is not pretty at all," said Alice. "Methought palaces were all of gold and marble, not ugly dark houses."

"Wait a little while, Alice," said Henry; "you shall see Whitehall soon. Then thou wilt see a palace."

"To-morrow she shall see Whitehall," said Lady Carewe. "To-day we shall not pass it."

They went on through fields till they reached a village of some size, which Sir Arthur told them was the village of St. Giles's, and he said there seemed to be so much building going on about it since last year even, that it would soon become a part of the town if so it went on. The houses were mostly of wood, and the road here was very bad, jolting them as much as any road they had passed through that day.

Now they came to St. Martin's Lane, and a hum and bustle was round them. There were houses all the way on one side, and a quickset hedge on the other, bordering the fields. Many people were walking to and fro on the causeway. Carts jumbled along, and coaches, drawn by two lean shabby horses, and in shape very like our omnibuses, but even more like bathing-machines. These, Sir Arthur told Lady Carewe, were hackney coaches, and plied for hire, taking passengers about at a certain sum per mile. It was a new invention since she had been in London.

They came then to the village of Charing, and turned into the Strand. There was but one solitary house between Charing and St. James's Palace; but when they turned into the Strand, they had left the country behind them.'

"Oh, now I like London," cried Alice. "It is pretty now."

"Thou dost not see London yet, but thou hast seen Westminster. The Strand lies between them, and that is where we are," said Lady Carewe.

The number of riders, and of coaches and foot passengers, had prevented farther talk at the window by this time. Sir Arthur and Henry were obliged to fall behind, and the postilions had to guide their horses carefully to avoid running against the many vehicles of all kinds they met, besides that the road was very bad, and dirty and muddy in the extreme.

But the scene was lively and beautiful. On the right hand, as they drove along, was the river Thames, no longer the narrow though lovely river they knew it at Windsor, but wide and full, and sparkling under the rays of the setting sun, and glimpses of it were seen between the large houses and palaces of the nobility, with fine gardens that stretched down to its banks. The river was gay, too, with numbers of boats, some of them wherries, shooting along under the vigorous strokes of the watermen, others gliding under white sails. They drove on, meeting many riders, on spirited

L

horses, generally dressed in a style of show and expense which astonished the country visitors, and though Edith and Alice were quite unaware of it, their bright complexions equally astonished these London gallants. They passed many coaches filled with ladies, dressed also in rich garments, sometimes of Genoa velvet trimmed with furs, for the weather was cold enough to require warm clothing. These coaches were drawn by four, sometimes by six horses, and the hackney coaches that drove about in the throng looked very shabby beside them. But the coaches did not go fast, even with their six horses, because of the holes and ruts full of black mud of which the road was full. Even on this November day, therefore, many people, and even many fine ladies, preferred the river to the road, and several boats might be seen conveying them on their way from one part of the town to another.

But now the way was stopped by a handsome carriage standing at one of the grandest of the noblemen's palaces, and a train of courtiers and ladies richly dressed, to attend a banquet at Whitehall, issued from the door, and descended the steps to set forth in it. Edith and Alice did not lose the opportunity to examine the jewels and satins, and all the bravery of this party; but it pained them, and made Alice cry, to see that while one footman stood at the carriage-door with long cane in hand, another used his to beat away a crowd of miserable beggars who had beset the carriage.

Lady Carewe soon called attention to Temple Bar, saying, that was one of the gates of the city of London, and that the large building just within it was the Temple, that Mr.

...... dressed in a style of show and expen-... .... the country visitors, and though .... of it, their bright complexion...... London gallants. They passed ...... in rich garments ...... of ...... for the weather ...... enough to require warm clothing. These coaches were drawn by four, sometimes by six horses, and the horsemen that drove about in the throng looked very shabby beside them. But the coaches did not go fast, e... with their six horses, because of the holes and ruts full ... black mud of which the road was full. Even on the November day, however, many people, and even many fine ladies, preferred the river to the road, and several boats ...... carrying them ...... from one part ...

But ...... was ...... by a luxurious carriage standing at one of the grandest of the noblemen's palaces and a train of ...... and ladies richly dressed, to attend ...... in Whitehall, ... from the river and descended ...... Edith and Alice did not lose ...... counting the jewels and ...... and all ...... as they ...... a ...... down and much ...... to ...... down with bags ...... to hand, coaches ...... and his ...... away a crowd of miserable beggars who had b... ...... carriage.

Lady Oarewe soon called attention to Templ Bar, ... ing, that was one of the gates of the city of London and ...... the large building just within it was the Temple Bar...

A LONDON COACH.

Henry Vane had told them about, where the lawyers studied and lived.

"But now, why are we stopping? Why do we not drive through the gate and go into London?" asked little Alice.

"Ah, Valentine, my dear brother!" This exclamation came from Edith. They had stopped at a handsome house. The door was open, and Valentine on the steps. Henry had jumped from his horse, given it to the groom, and had hurried to him as he handed out his mother. They had arrived at their home for the winter.

Used to the spacious entrance-hall and wide oak staircase at Crowhurst, it looked very mean and little to them at first in this London home; but no matter. It was London: and from the windows of the withdrawing-room, to which the servants ushered them immediately, there was a view of the river. A small garden, with green grass and some trees, only separated them from it.

There, in the afternoon, after they had had time for rest and refreshment, did the whole family assemble on a balcony that projected beyond the house, and looked out on the wonders below, with Valentine as showman. Valentine did not look so happy nor so well as he did when he came to Crowhurst on that bright May-day; but whatever sadness had got into his life, he soon shook it off, and, delighted with the wonder and admiration of Edith, Henry, and Alice, became as gay as ever. His melancholy moods never lasted long. At first Alice thought his face was not so "lovely and so sweet as it used to be," because he had a dark moustache on the upper lip; but when he took her on his knee, and she found this moustache was perfumed as sweetly as his hair, she became reconciled to it. And then she told him she liked his blue and silver suit; it was very pretty; and she liked his ruffles and large white lace collar, with its sweet points, and Henry must have one too.

Alice would have gone on longer admiring Valentine in a strain which even made Sir Arthur laugh, but for the questions that Edith and Henry were beginning to ask, which drew her to the window.

" What was that crowd of people about, and where were all the boats going ? There must be a hundred boats. What were so many wanted for ?"

" That is Temple Bridge."

" But a bridge goes across a river; this place only juts out a little way into it. You have shown us London Bridge. There it is a good long way off to the left. It goes all across the river, and has houses on it, and boats go under its arches, and there is no other like it."

" Ah yes! this is called Temple Bridge, but it might just as well have been called Temple Stairs, or Temple Wharf. It is a place where people take boat, and land, and all those boats you see, are waiting to be hired; and the numbers of men standing about are watermen."

" What numbers of them there are !"

" I believe there are forty thousand of them in London, including the private watermen belonging to the court and the nobility."

" Oh what a number !" cried Alice.

" Dost see that grave gentleman, Alice ?" said Valentine. " He has just called a boat, and is handing his respectable lady wife to the steps to get in."

" And see, there is another waterman wants them to get into his boat; and they are pushing so, the lady looks quite frightened."

" Now they are beginning to fight, I believe," said Henry.

" Oh, they will hurt one another—they will tumble into the water !" This exclamation came from Alice.

" But now," said Henry, " the old gentleman and lady are rowing off in a third boat with another waterman, and laughing as they go."

" Look to the right, and you will see Essex Stairs. There are again many people and boats; and further on is West-minster Gate ; that is another landing place, and Whitehall Stairs. There are boats and people at all these."

" I see. How many people there are ! How busy they all seem !"

" Then see the stairs besides that belong to the gardens of the great houses. There is no crowd on them, only a few watermen in handsome liveries, and a few gaily-painted wherries and barges. The nearest to us belongs to my Lord of Essex; farther on lies the Duke of Buckingham's, and beyond the Earl of Northumberland's. One of my Lord of Northumberland's barges is passing even now. I know his liveries."

" How beautiful is the river !" said Edith, " with all these palaces on its banks, on either side, with their turrets and pinnacles among the lofty trees. The grandest are on this side, but there are some very fine too on the other. All who live on the other side, must then cross to London by London Bridge or in a boat ?"

" Surely yes, but either way is easy. There are many stairs, as you see, on the other side."

"Oh look upon the lovely swans!" cried Alice. "I can count twenty, thirty, forty. What numbers!"

"Now you must turn the other way. You can see that fine cathedral rising above all the houses near it? That is St. Paul's. And what is that in the far distance beyond, thinkest thou, Edith?"

"I know well, if thou meanest that with the four turret tops. That is the Tower of London. Henry brought me a drawing of that. Ah, how much we have to see! But here comes Mary to take away Alice to rest, and I am well assured the little girl needs it."

Alice indeed had begun to grow sleepy, but the two brothers and Edith continued to sit at the window, after she was gone and after their father and mother had retired to their private room, and as darkness fell over the scene, Valentine remembered the splendours of former days and recounted them.

"It is dull now in town," said he. "This season men are thinking over-much of the troubles with the Scots and of the disaffected at home; but last summer had you seen the entrance of the queen's mother, Queen Mary de, Medici! That was a brave sight: our king, who went to meet her, to do all honour to the mother of his consort, seated by her side in one of his coaches with eight of his beautiful horses to draw it; the streets lined with his guards and the people crowding to see the sight. She was magnificently entertained. Men say that her allowance from our king was a hundred pounds a day!"

"Her large attendance of Jesuits and priests has not been pleasing to the people," said Henry; "so my father hath told me."

"No, and, 'tis said, not to the king neither. But I would thou hadst seen a braver sight yet than this of her entrance. It was a masque given to her majesty our queen by the gentlemen of the Inner Temple and Gray's Inn at court. Hadst seen how they took barge at Winchester Stairs, and landed at Whitehall in most triumphant manner, with torches and wax lights, and how the queen danced with some of them !"

"I thought a queen was too lofty in station to dance with the young lawyers of the inns of court!" said Henry.

"Ah, thou hast still some of thy precisian notions about thee. It hath been much objected to our queen ; but in truth she cares little for that. She must have her way and her will, whatever that be, and will bate none of it. She loves gay revels, and above all, dancing, and will not be restrained in it ; and why should she ? In her own country, no man dares to object to that which at court they please to do, and she is too proud and hath too high a spirit to permit it in England ! "

Whatever argument might now have commenced between the brothers, was interrupted by a loud knocking at the outer door. Edith started up and turned pale.

The noise was indeed enough to startle any one, but Edith's alarm only made Valentine laugh, so that he could not speak for some time.

"It is but the watch ordering us to light up," said he at last. " Come to the windows facing the roadway and you shall see."

Another loud and impatient knock sounded as they

opened a window over the house door and looked out, and
then they heard besides a loud ringing, and saw the watchman with his lanthorn and bell. The servants had now
opened the door, and the watchman called out in a loud
monotonous sort of song—

> "Lanthorn and a whole candle light!
> Hang out your lights! Hear!"

Valentine ran down to explain the matter to the country
servants, and set his own serving man, who was in attendance on him, to show them what they must do, and accordingly a lanthorn with a whole wick candle in it was speedily
hung at each side of the door, and the watchman proceeded
to the next house, and so on to one after another, repeating at
each his loud knock, the ringing of his bell, and his monotonous song—

> "Lanthorn and a whole candle light!
> Hang out your lights! Hear!"

At the summons, the inhabitants of one house after
another hung out their lanthorns, some only one, the larger
houses two, and thus all along the Strand a poor glimmering
light, like darkness visible, was by degrees thrown on the
causeway.

" And what when these candles are burned out?" asked
Henry.

" Oh, by that time the darkness may have its way. The
order is only that from All-hallows to Candlemas, the lights
must be hung out from six to eleven ; when it is not moonlight."

" It must be dark enough in London streets after eleven
then ! "

" Dark enough ! and I would advise thee never to be out then nor even after nine. 'Tis not safe, I promise thee. Robberies and murders have ever been frequent in the streets, and methinks are on the increase."

" That is dreadful, Valentine !" said Edith. " I would we were safely back at Crewhurst. Thou goest not forth to-night ?"

No, this night Valentine had leave to remain at his father's house.

¯ . " Even were it not for the gangs of robbers," continued Valentine, " and of riotous drunkards who mean no harm, but may much annoy an unaccustomed stranger, the way is too foul to walk in without light to assist in avoiding the pits and sloughs, very perilous and noyous to foot passengers. In this fashionable quarter of the Strand thou knowest but little of it, though even here, thou didst cry out upon the mud in coming. But in quarters which also are very favourite and frequented by many of the nobles and gentry, such as Covent Garden and Drury Lane, the streets are narrow, and many of the houses, built of wood, project over the causeway, and the wind hath little power to dry up that which is cast there."

" Truly," said Henry, laughing, " thou needst say no more. I will on no account venture to tread those streets in darkness."

" What bright lights are these I see rapidly advancing ?" asked Edith.

" 'Tis a coach with two footmen behind carrying flambeaux."

" It comes very near and stops at the next house. Look

at the pretty lady so bravely dressed, who gets out and goes up the steps."

"She has been at some party, or it may be the theatre and has come home. See the footmen put out their flambeaux in the iron extinguishers by the door and follow her in, and the coach drives away."

Our party were now summoned to supper, and left the window.

CHAPTER XIV.

THE CITY AND THE COURT.

On the following morning, because the weather continued bright and clear, and because Valentine was still with them to act as guide, Sir Arthur proposed for his family a drive about the town, and first into the city, whither he himself had business, and was about to ride on horseback. It was fixed that they should meet him by waiting at the portico of St. Paul's, where he would be found by Valentine or Henry in Paul's Walk; this Paul's Walk, as the middle aisle of the cathedral was called, being a place of common resort, both before and after noon, for lords, merchants, and men of all professions.

They therefore set forth in the coach, which was of ample size for all five, and passed at once into the city through Temple Bar, driving up Fleet Street and Ludgate Hill, busy and populous quarters, containing many houses of the principal merchants, as substantial and large as those of the aristocracy. As they drove on, they began to pass various shops, but these were not, as they now are in those streets, splendidly set out with rich goods of all kinds. They were generally low, and without any show in their windows; and to make up for this want of attraction, the master of the shop walked up and down before his door, crying, "What d'ye lack? What d'ye lack?" and proclaiming, in a loud voice, all the articles he had to sell. When he was tired, his apprentices came out and supplied his place, calling out quite as loudly as he, though sometimes in a shriller tone, "What d'ye lack?" and occasionally, when they thought they might venture it, stopping passers-by and trying to get them into the shop and persuade them to buy. The bustle and noise of the streets were considerably increased by these 'prentices, and they afforded immense amusement to Alice as the coach slowly jolted along.

At last it came completely to a stand still, and there was such a noise and tumult in front, that even Lady Carewe would have been alarmed had not Valentine, who alighted to see what was the matter, assured her it was only occasioned by a party of courtiers, who had just landed at Paul's wharf, probably from Greenwich, having insisted on taking the wall of a worshipful city magistrate, followed by six of his 'prentices, and pushed him into the mud. The cry of "'Prentices! clubs!" was indeed heard resounding along the streets, and crowds came running up to the scene of action. A fight between the 'prentices and the servants who attended on the young gallants had begun, but some of the city constables coming up soon ended the fray, and the passage became clear again.

Soon afterwards they stopped at the splendid portico of St. Paul's, as it existed before the fire of London, and Sir Arthur, who had been watching for them, came out to them, and made them admire the beautiful Corinthian columns, though, as he said, he could not admire the taste which had been shown in adding such a portico to a gothic cathedral; but Lady Carewe reminded him that as Inigo Jones had done it, we must suppose it was right.

He mounted his horse and rode along Cheapside with them. This was a street of noble substantial houses, now inhabited by the great merchants, but until lately very much liked by the people of degree, who had now gone farther west to such places as Covent Garden. Here the din and Babel of tongues, mixed with the throng of passengers and of carts and coaches, quite bewildered the country party. On every side, the masters and 'prentices were crying, "What d'ye lack, sir, or madam," bells were ringing, hackney coachmen were trying to persuade city madams "to ride," instead of walking through the mud, and among all, the merchants, with grave faces full of business, were thronging to be on 'Change at twelve o'clock.

The postilions were directed to drive homewards by Holborn and Bloomsbury, which was a quieter quarter, and then once again passing down St. Martin's Lane, they drove by Charing down Whitehall to see the palace. Even little Alice, high as her expectations had been, said it was very beautiful. She saw no gold nor marble, but still it was like a palace. The finest part of it was the banqueting house, built by Inigo Jones, and the only part that now remains.

Before a week was over, London had become tolerably familiar to our party. They had visited the Tower, and had rowed down to Greenwich; had been to Westminster Abbey and seen Westminster Hall, and the outside of the deserted Houses of Parliament, and the dreaded Court of Star Chamber; and now they began to feel settled and at home, and received frequent visits from Valentine. Sir Arthur was much engrossed by business, and often rode away in the morning and did not return till evening. At last his face became less anxious. Towards the beginning of December, he succeeded in securing his son's retirement from court without giving offence, and made arrangements to place him in the suite of Lord Arundel, who was shortly to depart for the Continent. He knew that Valentine would not be contented at home, and was anxious, while he removed him from a place that had now become dangerous for him, to give him the advantage of seeing other countries and other customs under favourable circumstances.

This prospect was so agreeable to Valentine, that he ceased to regret giving up his life at court, with all its attractions, and began to long for the time when he should begin his new career. But the last evening of his service at Whitehall, there was to be a court ball, and he wished that Henry should see something of it. He proposed, therefore, to take him in and station him in one of the galleries, or ante-chambers, and afterwards bring him into the state apartments, if if he should find it practicable.

Henry was well pleased to see the grandeur and bravery of which Valentine had talked so much, and having obtained his father's consent, prepared to take advantage of the offer. Early in the afternoon, therefore, dressed quite to Alice's satisfaction, having on a suit of green silk slashed with white, and one of those lovely pointed collars which she admired so much, he was conveyed in the coach, in this new character of a young courtier, to Whitehall, his mother and sisters accompanying him there and setting him down. Henry had already learned "to sit in a coach like a daintie ladye," but this was the first time he had been dressed like a courtier, and he joined very heartily in the laughs and jokes that his companions in the coach made on his splendid appearance. Valentine was in waiting for him, as they had agreed that he should be, in the outer court, and as the coach drove away the two brothers, standing side by side, with uncovered heads, made in sport low reverences to their mother, bowing almost to the ground, then turned and entered the palace.

"Our Henry grows tall, and, to my thinking, handsome too," said Edith.

"He will never have the regular features of Valentine," replied her mother. "But I can well believe there may be many who, like our dear Lady Willoughby, even prefer his stronger and more marked cast of face ; and for sincere and earnest expression of eye, none can exceed him."

"And his expression tells the truth, my mother."

"He well deserves thy love, Edith. It joys me to see what a comfort he is to his father, and what love has grown up between them. Thou knowest how, when he was a boy, I often grieved to see how little thy father cared for him, and how completely Valentine had all his affection. It is different now. He loves Henry and knows his worth, but yet he yearns after Valentine, and well I know the sacrifice he makes in sending him abroad. But thy father thinks only of the good of others, never of his own pleasure."

"We must all do our utmost to make my father cheerful, and make his home happy to him."

"Thou art never wanting, my daughter. Thy sweetness

is thy mother's joy and stay; and with thee and Henry, I
were wicked to repine."

"Dear mother, you make me happy by saying so; and
there is little Alice, besides, to cheer you."

Thus happy in each other, they returned home, while
Henry was initiated by Valentine into the pomp and splendour
of the court.

It was nearly the hour of the evening banquet or supper
before the ball, and Henry, after waiting for some time in a
gallery, was brought into the grand hall, and stationed near
the door, by Valentine, who then returned to his place in
attendance upon the queen.   It was a splendid sight.

The king and queen were seated at table, with their lords
and ladies in waiting, and pages behind their chairs, while
the young princes stood opposite.   Some guests of distinction were seated at other tables.   A concert of exqui-
site music was going on all the time.   The walls were hung
with some of those magnificent pictures with which Charles
the First enriched his palaces.   Henry was not a judge of
art; and on him the wonderful Titians, Correggios, and
Raffaelles, and the master-pieces of Rubens, were lost in
great degree; but the grand picture of his present majesty
on horseback, by Vandyke, caught his eye.   He looked from
the head in the picture to the king as he sat in his place,
and saw the accuracy of the likeness, and the remarkable
manner in which the painter had caught the very spirit of
his subject.   As he looked, he felt a glow of loyalty arising
within him.   That proud, melancholy face, the whole bearing and manner, seemed to him suited to a king.   He could
understand now why Valentine was devoted to King Charles,

—why he seemed ready to forget injuries done to himself and his family, and loved to serve the king better than any other service. The queen did not please Henry so much. To his eye she was not even handsome, though she was generally reckoned a beauty. Her jewels sparkled and her eyes sparkled too ; but there was an expression in them that he did not like, and her manner was imperious and haughty, not dignified, or such as he fancied a queen's should be.

He saw Lord Falkland at one of the tables, but he knew no one else. Many ladies there were, but he did not admire any of them. The colour in their cheeks was bright, but fixed ; it did not come and go like Edith's. He felt sure they were painted, as he had heard fine ladies often were. Then the little black patches on their faces troubled him; never having seen the fashion before, he disliked it extremely.

Still the whole scene was gay and gorgeous, and for the moment Henry was delighted with it, and began to regret that Valentine was so soon to leave it.

The banquet being nearly over, Henry stood aside among the throng, having observed a signal from Valentine that he should do so, and was soon obliged to follow in the train with the rest. He now remained for a time in a corridor, and saw the company begin to arrive. Numbers were in sedan chairs. It seemed very appropriate for ladies to be carried so, and set down in the very corridors leading to the rooms of state, in warmth and light, when the door was opened, instead of being exposed to the cold air, as those who came in coaches must be ; but his disgust was great whenever a chair, being set down by its two sturdy porters, a young gallant appeared seated in it, and daintily stepped forth, smoothing down his

M

curls, and spreading perfumes of musk and ambergris through the air, carrying in his hand his jewelled gloves, much too fine for use. To Henry's farther disgust, several of these gentlemen had the fixed red colour in their cheeks, and the little black patches that he had disliked so much in the ladies. He decided that he would much rather be one of the porters than one of these gentlemen, whose great aim seemed to be to look as like affected fine ladies as possible.

While he was fuming inwardly at the sight of these fops, a party of a very different order entered the corridor. They were a group of three or four men, with high intellectual countenances, whom he at once set down as some of those artists or authors whom the present king patronised and liked to have about him. If Henry had had any one to tell him their names, he would have heard that he had seen among them the great painter Rubens. Three men with blustering manners and martial air, dressed in military uniform, came next. They walked along with a swaggering gait, jingling their swords, and making all the noise and bustle they could. They wore on their faces, not little round black patches like ladies, but large ones, some square, some lozenge-shaped, some like half-moons.

While Henry was looking after them, half-laughing at the absurd appearance they made, a young gentleman addressed him by name, and said he was deputed by his brother, Mr. Carewe, to conduct him into the ante-room, whence they would shortly be admitted to the ball-room.

" You are amused," said he, " at the appearance of those worthies."

" Who are they ?" asked Henry, " and what makes them

decorate their faces in so strange a fashion? They seem
to have been in the wars."

"Ay, or they would have us think so; but their patches
would in that case be wanted for their backs, not for their
faces. As to who they are, Colonel Lunsford knows better
than I. He took them to Kelso, and finds them useful as a
sort of reformados, or, to speak more plainly, bullies and
bravoes."

"Colonel Lunsford! He is little better than a re-
formado himself, if report speaks true. Was he not out-
lawed, or am I mistaken?"

"Hush, there he is!"

"In the uniform of an officer?"

"Ay; he has passed on now. Shall we follow to the
ante-room?"

An officer of state here presided while the company
assembled. Again Henry was struck with the splendour of
the room, hung, like the large hall, with fine pictures, and
brilliantly lighted and decorated with evergreens, in honour
of approaching Christmas.

"Surely that is Lord Morley," said Henry.

"It is. He has not appeared at court before since the
campaign in Scotland."

Henry had never seen him since that day, the very recol-
lection of which made him shudder.

Scarcely had Lord Morley passed up the room, when a
tumult arose in the direction in which he had disappeared.
There were loud voices and the clashing of swords; and a
sudden rush of all the company backwards, almost drove
Henry on to the staircase. But he caught a glimpse of

three or four men struggling at the spot whence the sounds came, and among them he fancied he saw Valentine.

He pushed his way therefore into the room again, through the retreating crowd, and found the tumult increasing. There were loud cries of "The king!" "Make way!" "Shame! In the very presence of their majesties!"

Amidst these cries, still went on the angry voices and clashing of swords, and again, in the midst of the swaying and struggling mass, who now occupied the entire end of the ante-room, for every one else had fled, he saw Valentine distinctly.

Henry rushed madly into the very midst of this struggling throng, and saw Lord Morley standing above some one whom he had knocked down; while Valentine, with drawn sword, kept at bay two of those patched warlike blusterers whom Henry had noticed before. It was the third who lay on the floor.

In a moment a number of the guard had rushed in. Lord Morley and Valentine were seized, disarmed, and hurried down the room towards the stairs, and Henry, following, cried madly upon Valentine, and besought the guard to release him.

No one heeded him, till, as he continued to run after the guards, one of them seized him, and told him to stay where he was, and mind his own affairs.

"Let me go! I *will* see what they are going to do with him. Let me go with my brother, I say," cried Henry, struggling with the man.

"Why not let the poor boy go?" said a very handsome gentleman who had just come up the staircase. "Who is he?"

"He must be a son of Sir Arthur Carewe," said an officer of the guard, in reply, "as he calls the prisoner his brother. Young Carewe has got into a brawl in the very presence of their majesties."

"Let the boy go, then! His face speaks for him."

"No man ought to know more about faces than yourself, Sir Anthony. Loose the young gentleman!"

"Let him have my coach," said Henry's advocate. "Sir Anthony Vandyke's coach for Master Carewe."

"Sir Anthony Vandyke's coach!" was shouted from lacquey to lacquey. "Sir Anthony Vandyke's coach for Master Carewe!"

But Henry thought not of coach nor lacqueys. All his soul was occupied with Valentine, and the danger into which he had fallen. He continued to seek among the throng at the outer entrance till he saw, by the light of the flambeaux, a party of soldiers of the guard, with Lord Morley and Valentine in the midst of them. Two hackney coaches drove up directly. He saw Lord Morley thrust into the first, with two men of the guard inside and two outside, and into the second Valentine was forced.

"Take me! Let me go with him!" cried Henry.

In vain! He was pushed back and knocked down among the crowd. It was raining, and he was covered with mud from head to foot; but that he cared nothing for, so that he could keep sight of Valentine. He scrambled up again; forced his way through the people, crawled under the horses' legs, and got clear into the middle of the road. Then he ran with all his speed after the coach, caught it, and hung by the back, as it went on, much as boys often do now. In time he worked and coiled himself up so as to sit on the bar at the back, without being perceived, as jolting, splashing, and rolling, the clumsy coach drove on.

CHAPTER XV.

A NIGHT'S ADVENTURES.

THE way was very long. The rain and wind beat against Henry, and the mud splashed up over him. His court dress, little fitted for such work as this, was wet through, his head was uncovered, and his hair dripping with water, but the anguish of his mind was such that he was quite unconscious of his woful plight. All he wished was that he could make Valentine aware that a friend was near him; that he was not totally alone in this extremity. But it was vain to wish. The back of the crazy, jumbling coach as effectually separated them as if they had been miles apart.

They passed along the Strand. He could see his home with the two lanthorns by the door. It was about half past eight o'clock now. If his mother had known how near to her, and in what a wretched condition, her sons were, what would she have felt? He thought of her, of his father, and sisters, but no thought of getting off the back of the coach, and getting safe in, entered his head. He could not leave Valentine in his danger.

The coach jumbled on, passed through Temple Bar, and drove along Fleet Street. Then turned into a narrow winding street where mud and holes and noisome odours were worse

than ever, and stopped at last. They were at the gates of a
large stone building.

One of the guards got down and rang the bell by the
gates. It was opened instantly, and Henry saw within a
court dimly lighted. He got down, crept quietly round to
the window, and said in a distinct voice, "Henry is here!"

He thought he heard an exclamation, but was instantly
pushed aside so rudely that he was not sure.

There was scarcely any delay. The door of the coach
was opened. Valentine was made to get out, and a guard
seizing him by each arm, he was hurried within the gate.
Henry then heard bolts, bars, and the clank of chains; the
guards laughed, talked, and got into the coach to escape the
rain ; it drove off, and he was left standing alone.

Never in all Henry's life, perhaps, and he had many a
rough day in it, did he feel so desolate and wretched as at that
moment. In his despair, he went up to the gate and rang
the bell. A small grating was opened in a door, and a face
appeared at it. Then a harsh voice asked "Who is there?"

"I am the brother of the prisoner, and claim to be admitted to him."

The grating was closed instantly, without a word. In
his rage at this insolence, Henry rang again and again loudly.
The grating was opened again at last.

"If thou dost not begone and let me go to sleep in peace,"
said the same harsh voice with a brutal oath, "thou shalt
have the best flogging thou ever hadst in thy life. The prisoner hath quite enough to do to mind his own matters
without being plagued with a cheating, lubberly beggar like
thee !"

The words brought Henry to his senses. He became aware that he could look like nothing else but a wretched beggar, and that to claim to be the brother of Valentine in his splendid court dress must appear nothing but imposition. Besides, what good would it do to be shut up in this prison too? for prison it was, without a doubt. The only thing to be done was to find his way home, and see if his father could get Valentine free. His father! That name brought with it all home fears and anxieties. By this time he had been expected there for an hour.

Yes, he would find his way home. But how? Beyond the prison walls, against which a few lanthorns burned, everything was perfectly dark. The order to "light up" was imperfectly obeyed in that and most other poor and neglected neighbourhoods, and whatever lanthorns had been there had burned out. To attempt to walk on was like running against a black wall, or groping into a hollow cavern. He knew only the direction in which the coach had driven off, and that way he walked slowly and cautiously, feeling before him with outstretched hands.

If he met any one he would give some money to be shown the way. He put his hand to his pocket. It was turned inside out. Purse, everything was gone. That hope was vain. Happily, Henry had a stout heart of his own, or he would have been ill off now.

Straining his eyes through the darkness, he caught the glimmer of a light, and then he heard a bell. It was a watchman. He would stand quite still till this man came up. But while he determined this, a door opened close behind him; fumes of tobacco and strong drink flew out, and a disorderly crew rushed forth pell-mell. Many of them could not stand, and rolling over in the mud, were left behind. Others separated in different directions, some disappearing down neighbouring courts and alleys. Some held on their way, singing, shouting, and pushing each other into the kennel as they quarrelled for the wall. With this rabble rout, who had just issued from a tavern, Henry would have been carried away or knocked down, but that the light of the door showed him an iron railing by its side, and he clung to it so closely that they all passed him. Fortunately for him, he had lost every appearance of a well-dressed young gentleman, and only appeared to them like a beggar hoping for alms. One of the men, even, in a drunken voice, asked him if he would have a cup of arrack, and began fumbling in his pocket for money, but forgot what he wanted before he found any, and reeled on with the others.

These people carried lighted torches, and choosing the party that went the way he knew would lead to Fleet Street, Henry followed it. As to the watchman, he had prudently hidden himself in some safe nook till the crowd passed by, and was seen no more.

Having reached the corner of Fleet Street, after long delays and many stoppages, the drunken party disappeared down a lane, but Henry was now in a straight line with his home. No lanthorns, however, glimmered even here. He had heard the clock of St. Bride's strike eleven some minutes since.

He stopped again, holding by the wall, and looking into the black darkness the way he wanted to go. At a distance he saw a red light close to the ground, and smoke rising. What it might mean he could not imagine, but it served as a beacon to him. Groping his way slowly, often stumbling over rough places in the causeway and knocking his head and grazing his hands against inequalities in the wall, he made towards the light, but he presently heard the tread of many feet, though he saw no light, and heard no voices. He again took his plan of clinging to the wall, but this time he was pushed away from it, and hurried in the direction he had come from for some distance, by a body of silent men, before he could extricate himself. Whatever these people were going to do, they seemed to know their way without any light. But the darkness that shielded their purpose also shielded him, and he managed to get out of their company by dashing into the middle of the roadway, wading in mud. Here he could see the red light distinctly; but for it he should have been utterly bewildered and lost his way. There were no carts nor coaches at that hour.

At last he saw that the light was caused by a bonfire in the middle of the road, and that there were many dark figures moving about round it. When he came up he could distinguish a watchman, and a congregation of wretched, ragged beggars trying to warm themselves at the fire. The watchman's duty seemed to be to heap it up with wood, but he had to be on the alert to prevent all his wood being stolen. Henry recollected having heard that it was considered useful as a precaution against the plague to light bonfires in the streets at night. The light helped him on a great way. When he lost it he still held on, and only had one more alarm. He was horrified by shrieks of "Thieves! Murder!" and then saw several watchmen with their lanthorns come out of corners and nooks where they had been concealed. The mob dis-

persed when they saw the lanthorns, and Henry caught fast
hold of one of the watchmen by the arm ; but all he got by
this was a volley of oaths and abuse, and threats of the
stocks and a good flogging for a sturdy beggar, as he was.

Baffled in this last attempt at finding a protector and
guide, he began again as he had hitherto done to grope on
alone, following the glimmer of the watchman's lanthorn at
a distance. His eyes, now used to darkness, could just
distinguish the old archway of Temple Bar standing up black
against the murky air beyond. The watchman passed through,
and he followed, and saw to his relief the two lanthorns by
his father's door raying out into the night. They had been
replenished with fresh candles for his sake.

He mounted the steps and rang, and then for the first
time felt that he was exhausted and faint.

The door was opened instantly by Freeman. He must
have been on the watch.

"Master Henry! in the name of Heaven! You must
have been robbed and murdered !"

A pale face behind Freeman brought back Henry's
strength at once.

"My mother ! Fear not ! Valentine is safe, and I am
not hurt." She could not speak, but laid her trembling
hand on his shoulder.

"My father !"

"He is ill ; very ill. Thank Heaven ! thy ring woke
him not ; and Edith watches by him. He knows not of thy
absence. My boy ! thou art hurt ! thou art dying !"

"No ! It is only that I am tired and cold."

She led him in and made Freeman get him into bed, only

sending word to the anxious Edith that her brothers were
safe. They had suffered terrible anxiety, the coach, when
sent for him, having returned empty, and the servants having been unable to get any account of their young masters,
probably in consequence of orders of secrecy. Lady Carewe
busied herself about him, bringing him food and cordials, and
wrapping him up warmly. He quickly recovered under this
care. Such a night's adventures would have killed a fine
gentleman about town, but he was a sturdy countryman with
good old English strength and courage to support him, so he
soon begged his mother to think no more of him, but to come
and sit by him while he told her about Valentine. Then as
cautiously and gently as he could he told her what had
happened.

She was dreadfully alarmed, evidently, but she controlled
herself for his sake, knowing his need of rest.

"Try to sleep now, my son—my dear son," she said at
last. "In the morning thy father may have recovered
sufficiently to aid us with his counsel. His fever is greatly
abated. Thou must be strong to help in the morning;
therefore sleep now. Thou dost deserve to sleep in peace.
But for all thy sufferings and exertions this night, we should
not have known where thy brother was, and I have been
like the mother of young Mr. Gage, who was shut into the
Bastille, and she heard no tidings of him for months. Ah!
it is not come to that in England yet, but we know not how
soon it will be."

She kissed his forehead as she left him, and, utterly
exhausted as he was, he was soon asleep.

It was late the next morning before he awoke from a

sleep so sound that he had forgotten everything; but the sight
of his father by his bedside brought all the heavy truth to his
memory at once. Sir Arthur looked ill, but to Henry's anxious
inquiries he replied that he was sufficiently well in health,
and wished to hear every particular of the events of the night
before. As Henry obeyed, he listened attentively, and taking
out his tablets noted all down, especially the fact of what the
young gentleman whom Valentine had introduced had said
of those swaggering men, probably, as he observed, a set of
bravoes expressly employed by Colonel Lunsford to raise the
brawl. He also expressly noted Sir Anthony Vandyke's
interposition. When Henry had described the site and
appearance of the prison to which Valentine was committed, he said it could be no other than the Fleet Prison,
to which offenders against the Court of Star Chamber were
committed.

Having taken notes of all these things, Sir Arthur, after
a short silence, said—

"My son, thou art young in years, yet I feel so much
trust in thy discretion and courage, that I will make thee
acquainted with my present anxious position. So shalt thou
see best how to serve me. Art thou able to rise and dress?"

"Quite able, my father. I am only a little stiff and sore,
but that will soon go off."

"Come to me, then, in an hour, in my study, and we
will confer together on this sad matter."

The hour had scarcely passed, when Henry knocked at
the door of his father's study, and there found both his
father and mother.

"We are going to trust thee, my son, with all our

anxieties," said Sir Arthur; "but it is in strictest confidence. I do not doubt that Valentine will be brought before the Star Chamber, and will incur a heavy fine. The necessities of the king are so great, in this his last struggle to avert a Parliament, that fines are laid on heavily. While I feel thus assured, I am totally unable to pay it. Only yesterday, I learned that, as far as the means to raise money at this moment are concerned, I am totally ruined."

Sir Arthur, calm and firm as he usually was, seemed unable to go on. His lips quivered, and he was silent for some minutes. Lady Carewe took his hand, and held it in both hers.

"It is not the loss of money, as thou well knowest, my dear wife, that moves me thus," he said at last; "it is the effect on our unhappy son. To what rigours they may expose him, or to what lengthened imprisonment, in default of payment, I know not."

"Oh, my brother!" said Henry, in a low voice of terror. "But ruined! How is it so?" he added.

"Only yesterday, I heard in the city that Herbert, the great goldsmith, with whom I lodged my rents, and from whom I ever drew my money, has, with some others, lost so large a sum in the mint that he is bankrupt. The king hath seized, under the name of a loan, money lodged there by the merchants and goldsmiths to the amount of £200,000, and by this is Herbert bankrupt."

There was again a silence.

"I trust to thee to mention to no one this matter, as far as it concerns me; the public will soon know of the fact itself."

"I promise faithfully," said Henry.

"That we, that thy mother and we all, can cheerfully face such privations as our circumstances require, I know well. It is Valentine for whom I fear; and until his examination is over, and sentence passed, I would fain keep my necessities secret, lest the knowledge that they cannot raise money from me should drive his judges to greater rigours; and yet I think they dare not practise them!"

Sir Arthur rose in excitement, and his cheeks flushed with a sudden colour, which quickly faded away.

"I will do all your bidding, my father."

"I must not lose a moment in making what interest I can for him; the means to raise money must be an after consideration. The information thou hast given me this morning directs me well how to begin. Lord Falkland will assist me to resist the malice of Colonel Lunsford, and Sir Anthony Vandyke may befriend Valentine. It is also most important that we know where Valentine is. While I do my utmost in the quarters I have named, thou must go to him in his prison. I have sent to endeavour to obtain an order for thee, and expect it every minute. Without telling him my misfortunes, for I dare not trust his discretion, work on his mind so as to make him so comport himself before the Star Chamber as to co-operate with me in conciliating enemies and making friends. I would have no dishonouring concessions. Simply a quiet bearing, and an acknowledgment that a brawl in the presence of their majesties was an outrage requiring an apology. Thou understandest me?"

"I think I do, my father. I will do my best."

"Order thy horse, then, and take a groom to attend thee, and God speed and bless thee, my son."

Henry was on his way, furnished with an order of admittance to the governor of the Fleet Prison, before half-an-hour had passed.

CHAPTER XVI.

THE PRISONER.

THE Fleet Prison has now entirely disappeared; but it
existed as a prison for debtors from the date of the abolition
of the Star Chamber by the Long Parliament till a few years
ago, though the building itself was not the same as that
before which Henry dismounted on his father's mission.
That dismal structure was destroyed in the great fire of
London. It consisted of five storeys of cells, besides an
underground one, and was therefore of great height, and also
of great length and strength; and seen by daylight, with the
dismal feeling that within it his brother was confined, it
naturally appalled poor Henry. He rang, and producing
his order, met with a reception very different to that of the
night before. After a little delay he was admitted.

It was Henry's first visit to a prison, and the gloom, as
well as the confined, unwholesome air, affected him deeply.
He was led up a staircase, and found himself in a passage so
dark that he could scarcely see the jailer before him, who led
the way jingling his keys. The passage seemed of intermin-
able length, running, indeed, the whole length of the prison,
and only seven feet wide, and lighted solely by a window at
each end. There were doors on either hand throughout the

whole length, numbered outside. At No. 50, the jailer stopped, and before unlocking the door, said—

" You will find the gentleman rather sulky. They be so at first, generally. But he may have what food he wants, or drink, or what it liketh him to say." He then unlocked the door, and telling Henry that only an hour would be allowed him, admitted him and locked him in.

" Valentine! I am come to see thee, from my father!"

Valentine, dressed exactly as he was in the brilliant rooms of Whitehall, started up from a miserable bed on which he had been lying, and the two brothers stood face to face, holding each other by both hands. Valentine was completely prostrated by his misfortune. He had thrown himself on the bed when he was first locked in, and there he had lain, taking no heed of the jailer, who had already been in this morning with hopes of extorting money for some wretched comforts he offered. The high-grated window admitted little light, but Henry could see that he looked ill and most dejected. The taint of the prison was upon him, and the court suit he wore made him look the more wretched, as it recalled the far different scene in which he had so lately worn it; the sumptuous rooms, the blaze of light, the beautiful works of art on every side, the perfumes, the music. What a contrast!

It was some time before Henry could produce any effect on him. His senses seemed stunned. At last he broke into passionate exclamations against Morley for dragging him into this senseless quarrel, and against the bullies who had trepanned them both. From rage he passed into bitter grief at the ruin of his prospects in going abroad with Lord

N

Arundel.   At last he thought of his father, and the disgrace
and expense and trouble to him, and then consented to listen
to Henry.

The jailer returned at that moment, but on Henry re-
monstrating that the time could not be up, it was found that
the man had come again to bargain about food, feeling sure
that money was to be had.   Henry ordered breakfast for
his brother, and a fire to be lighted in the grate, to take off
the damp and chill.   All these cells contained chimneys,
and were comfortable places in comparison with the cells in
some other prisons, being usually occupied by persons of
some position in the world.   Sir Arthur had sent money to
supply all necessaries.

Somewhat cheered in spite of himself, Valentine now
listened to Henry, but would give but little assurance of any
wise conduct on his own part.   He had been shamefully used !
To throw him into this dungeon for such a trifling offence,
into which he was inveigled unawares, was cruelty.   They
would fine him.   He was grieved about it; but his father
would not grudge the money to redeem him from an imprisonment into which he had been cast by no fault of his own.
Henry left him when summoned away, with a feeling that
nothing but telling him the real state of affairs would sufficiently impress him to make him cautious.

A week of anxieties and delays had passed.   No access
to the prisoner had been allowed again, and Sir Arthur could
get but little aid in settling the affair.   Lord Morley was
tried without delay, and sentenced to a fine of £10,000, and
a year's imprisonment.   It was natural to suppose that
Valentine's punishment would be lighter, only that his

father's name was obnoxious to government; if it approached this large sum, the difficulty would be very great.

Of all to whom Sir Arthur applied, he found Sir Anthony Vandyke the kindest and most courteous. He was really fond of Valentine, who had often been in his studio, and listened with so much interest, and expressed so much sympathy for the poor young prisoner, as well as the younger brother " who had shown such indomitable will" the night of the arrest, that to him Sir Arthur confided his heavy losses and his consequent inability, at the present moment at least, till he could sell some of his property, to meet the demands of the Star Chamber. Sir Anthony seemed so alarmed and distressed by this disclosure, that while Sir Arthur was gratified at the kind feeling, he was himself more alarmed for Valentine than he had been before.

There was little delay in the Court of Star Chamber. Valentine was brought before it a few days before Christmas, and after a short examination was punished as heavily as Lord Morley. He was sentenced to a fine of £10,000, with imprisonment during the king's pleasure, in default of payment.

Henry, who was always on the watch, was waiting at the door of the Old Star Chamber Court in Westminster to hear the result. His father was in court and present at the trial.

A stranger accosted him.

" Master Carewe, I think?"

"You are right, Sir."

" You will be permitted," said the stranger speaking rapidly, and in an under tone, " to go in the coach with your brother. Keep eye and ear open, and act promptly." He

put a paper into Henry's hand; moved away among a number of people standing about, and disappeared.

Valentine, guarded, was brought out immediately afterwards, with complexion heightened by the taunts to which
he had been exposed. As he stepped into the coach that
was ready to take him back to prison, Henry pressed· after
him, simply saying "By permission," and was allowed to get in.

There were no guards inside, but two behind and two
in front outside. When the flush went off Valentine's face,
Henry saw the effects of the prison in his sallow, anxious
countenance, and with beating heart looked at the paper
he still held in his hand, to see if there were hope or help
there.

"Read, Valentine! It is for thee!"

He read, "Thy father is a ruined man, and cannot redeem
thee. Be ready!"

"What lie is this?" asked Valentine.

"It is the truth."

Valentine sank back almost fainting. Henry, remembering the words of the stranger, kept eye and ear open, and
was ready for what might happen.

It was evening and growing dark, and snow fell at intervals. There was a stoppage in Fleet Street, owing to a large
cart containing beer barrels, which were being delivered into
a tavern, having been drawn across the way, and the road
was so bad, it was impossible to pass by going round it. The
driver of the coach swore at the carter, and he returned the
oaths with interest. A crowd began to gather.

"Keep off!" cried one of the guards. "Move your cart,
or you shall be forced. We are on the king's business."

Heavily and slowly the cart was turned and left just room enough for the coach to go on again.

They turned into the narrow street that led to the prison. A waggon had broken down and its contents and its wheels and other heavy gear were strewed about. They came to a stand again. There was fresh shouting, swearing and threatening. It was impossible to pass. It grew darker and darker.

"There's a lane to the right," said a voice in the crowd, "that leads out again into the end of this street." Henry thought he knew the voice again.

"Take that lane to the right," said the guard.

The driver obeyed. It was very narrow in the lane. As they went on, another coach came driving towards them at a furious rate. There was not width for two coaches. A noisy quarrel began between the drivers, and a great crowd collected. Some came to the horses' heads. The guard declared with a furious oath that it was a rescue—jumped down, and fired; the horses plunged, kicked, and broke the shafts. Valentine was alive again.

"Now, Carewe," said the same voice at the window.

Henry burst open the coach-door with a violent kick, after a vain attempt to open it, and only saying, "Follow!" jumped out, and crawled under the coach to the opposite side; saw there at a glance that Valentine was close to him, and they both got on their feet, and ran at full speed through a whole net-work of courts and alleys. All sound of the tumult they had left had ceased, and not a soul was near them when they stopped.

"Where are we?"

"Close to the Thames, as I think,"

And, indeed, dark under the snow, which now fell thickly, they saw the river flowing. They were near Paul's Wharf. They made for it and looked for a boat. There were only two watermen still there. It was too late, and the weather too bad to expect fares.

"A guinea to row us a mile or two down the river!" cried Valentine.

"Get in, sir," said one. "Up the river, you meant, my honourable young gentleman," he added, when they were seated. "We can never shoot the bridge in this tide, and the wind blowing like that."

"Very well. Up, then!"

The wind increased; the boat tossed as if in the sea. The waterman said he must land them at the nearest stairs. They were now close to Whitehall.

"Another guinea to pull us up higher," said Valentine.

The waterman pulled away. Henry, who was a strong and skilful rower, took one of the oars, and they got on faster. But again the man protested against going on.

"Keep across to the Surrey side, then," said Valentine.

The man obeyed, but stopped at the first stairs, saying he would not attempt Chelsea Reach for ten guineas.

They landed. It was so dark and lonely they felt as if they had nothing to fear.

"Are we at Lambeth stairs?"

"Yes, my master."

"Ah. Here are two guineas for thee."

"Two more would not be over-much to keep a quiet tongue in my mouth."

"What matters a quiet tongue to us!" said Valentine, proudly. "On, Henry! No bribe we can give can buy him." They dashed off into the darkness.

A large building, brilliantly lighted, was before them.

"The archbishop's palace!" said Valentine. "We have run into the lion's mouth."

"The lion cannot see into his mouth," said Henry.

"Right well suggested. No man could think we were such fools as to come here."

They now found themselves getting into the midst of a crowd of people; beggars and cripples were mixed with a number of decent, respectable, but mostly poor people, some of them with an air of decayed gentility, but all were streaming one way, towards the open door leading to the servants' offices in the palace. It was Christmas time, and charity was administered in this way.

Acting on the principle that it was good policy for them to run into the lion's mouth, Valentine proposed to follow with the rest. They had both large cloaks on. Their hats were so battered and soaked by the wind and snow, which had now changed to sleet, and their whole dress so splashed and disordered, that they looked sufficiently shabby to pass muster. Henry, however, gave Valentine especial charge to hide his face as much as possible, and to keep quiet. This caution was necessary; for Valentine, true to his volatile nature, and delighted with his freedom, was in high spirits. Henry also took a warm cravat off his own throat and tied it round Valentine's, covering up his long curls entirely.

In this manner they entered the archbishop's palace,

among the throng of his pensioners, and seated themselves in
as remote and quiet a corner as possible.

There was abundance of good cheer serving out. Great
rounds of beef, brawn, and chines of pork, and plenty of
strong ale. They both, Valentine especially, enjoyed it
extremely. He whispered to Henry that the air of the river
was mightily more appetising than the Fleet. Henry actually turned pale at his mentioning the word, and gave him a
kick under the table.

"Rough weather, my master!" said an old man, who sat
next Valentine. "Sad it is for us poor folks that has to go
through it. 'Tis well for them as can live in palaces!"

"Ay, ay, 'tis well for them!" returned Valentine, in a
whimpering voice. "But they give us good brawn and ale."

"Hold thy peace!" whispered Henry.

Just then a sound of drums, trumpets, and clarions was
heard, and a voice proclaimed—

"Stand by and uncover! His Grace's meat is served."

and a whole train of cooks and serving men passed through
from the kitchen and up the wide staircase, carrying up the
feast.

In the midst of the noise and confusion, Henry had a
minute to whisper, without fear of being overheard—

" I have a wonderful scheme in my head. Nurse's son,
the waterman of Vauxhall, married our pretty Cicely. They
would be true to us through fire and water. We cannot be
far off. Can you find the way?"

" Surely I can. A good idea."

They moved to the door ; a crowd was passing.

" Best let the crowd pass by," said a lame old man to
Valentine. " 'Tis a hue and cry after two gentlemen running
from the bailiffs, they say !"

Henry's blood ran cold.

" Ah !" said Valentine. " Roystering, ill-living fellows,
that have cheated their tailors, I make bold to say. I have
a mighty feeling for those poor tailors."

" Ha, ha ! I thought as much," laughed the old man.
" I thought thou hadst a smack o' the goose about thee."

" Which way did they run ?" asked Henry, while Valentine tried to swallow this not very flattering remark.

" Putney way, so I heard tell. I think we may go on
now, my masters, and thou mayest back to thy board. The
good cheer hath made me mighty merry, ha, ha !"

Well pleased to hear the pursuit was in the opposite
direction, they turned towards Vauxhall. It was only seven
o'clock yet, so rapidly had their flight been made. There
were plenty of people about in the low neighbourhood they
sought, and lights in taverns to help them through the maze

of lanes towards the stairs. Crairy the waterman was well
known, and a little inquiry brought them to his door. His
house was more substantial than the common, and his
mother's good lessons, and Cicely's savings and management,
were visible both outside and in. The waterman was seated
by a good bright fire, after his day's work, with a baby of a
year old on his knee, and the pan of fried meat that Cicely
had been cooking for his supper hissed and sputtered, and
filled the little room with a savoury smell. She opened the
door herself, and Henry, instantly uncovering his head, to
show her who he was, put his finger on his lips, pressed in
with Valentine, and bolted the door inside.

He need not have bespoke silence. She was so astonished
that her voice utterly failed her, and, for a wonder, Cicely
had no words. But words soon came, and wonder gave place
to horror, both in her and her husband, at the words,
"Star Chamber," which Henry told them was Valentine's
danger, in order to show them the necessity of secrecy. To
be "Star Chambered" was dreaded in those days like
death.

The earnestness to serve their young masters shown
both by man and wife, was boundless. They should be as
safe as if they were over the seas. They must sit down by
the fire and dry their wet clothes. They must eat and drink
only what was good enough for them !

Thanks to the archbishop they wanted nothing but
warmth and rest. There was time to think now. In the
first whirl of the escape, the excitement and danger had prevented all thought, but now Valentine's despondency had returned. He had escaped from prison, it was true, but even

if he succeeded in avoiding recapture, how unfortunate he was! Where were his hopes and prospects flown? What did those words mean, "Thy father is a ruined man!" Henry, on his part, had anxious thoughts also. "What would his father think of this flight? Would he not perhaps condemn it? If Valentine were retaken, would not all be worse than ever? Oh that must not be; He *must* not be retaken."

They longed to be alone and to talk over their difficult circumstances, and Cicely was already preparing a small upper room for them, in which she made up a bed with all the best bedding and linen in her small establishment. Thither they retired, not to sleep, but to think what to do next. They knew that Crairy and Cicely would be true to them, but to remain long in this small house was impossible, without discovery. Henry's wish was to get to Crewhurst and hide Valentine in the secret room, the access to which from without he knew. But how to get there, through a neighbourhood where their faces were so well known? Another anxiety pressed on him; the thoughts of home and the fears and sorrows there. How to calm these without danger to Valentine, he had not resolved when sleep overcame him.

He awoke with the first stir of the noisy neighbourhood in the morning, and now his head was much clearer. The river afforded an easy access to the neighbourhood of Crewhurst. The last part of the transit there, between Windsor and his father's property, would be the most dangerous. Scarcely could he see how to manage that, but it must be attempted. Before day-break he had despatched Crairy in his boat to Temple Stairs, with directions to see Sir Arthur himself, and deliver to his own ear the following message: "We go whither thou and Osbaldeston wot of." He would venture no more, nor would he send any written words.

The anxious thought now was how to disguise themselves.

"I could buy worsted stockings, stout shoes, and a freize coat, dye my face, and look like a country lout well enough," said Henry; "but thou art so completely like a fine gentleman, it would never do with thee! We might sooner make thee like a lovely young lady, if only thou wert not so tall, than like a farmer."

"If I might make bold," said Cicely, who was waiting on them at breakfast, "to give my advice, I think Master Valentine might do well for a buxom dame; say now, your mother, Master Henry."

Valentine threw himself back in his chair, and laughed immoderately.

"I hold by my plan," said Cicely again. "He must let me dress his hair like a woman's. Not like mine, but in rustic fashion. I know how 'tis done; and we must shave off his mustaches—that's a matter of necessity. Then, if he would let me buy him a proper suit—though how to get a petticoat long enough! Well, I must lengthen it myself; but I make certain sure I'm right when I say that if he wore a high-crowned hat, a good gray cloak, with a hood to draw over his hat, because o' the cold, or it may be the rheumatis in his head, and would let me paint his face like a ruddy country dame, he would do well; he would look, for all the world, like one. Tall and buxom, to be sure, but what then ? I have seen some such i' the country; yes, quite as tall as he!"

Valentine continued to laugh, but would not consent to this scheme at all. "How could he ride like a woman?"

"But we would get Crairy to pull us up to Windsor in his boat. Thou couldst sit in a boat like a woman. Only how to land at Windsor? 'Twould be too dangerous."

"Once i' the town, if you could but get safe in," said Cicely, "you could go to Jacob Grindlay's hostelrie; him as married Woodruffe's sister."

"Surely we could. They would help us on and be true to us in any strait. I know Jacob well, and any one belonging to Woodruffe is sure."

"But I dread Master Valentine striding on in's petticoats. He must not have a chance to walk. He ought to step out o' the boat on to his horse."

Henry thought of one place after another. There was Walton-on-Thames, Weybridge, Shepperton. A good posting-house at Shepperton, close to the stairs. There he might hire horses. He must consult Crairy. Meanwhile, Crairy did not return. Possibly Sir Arthur was out, or, sad to think, he might be ill. As time went on, Valentine said he would consent to any plan likely to get them off, for the danger of remaining in this little place, in that crowded neighbourhood, became more and more evident. Somehow or other, they must be on their way to a safer hiding-place before another day broke.

"But if he's caught," said Dame Grindlay. "Oh, the powers, what then? They'll pillory him, and, it may be, cut off his handsome ears!"

"Never speak o' the like," said her husband, angrily; "I tell thee, dame, the Star Chamber, bad as 'tis, do not do these things to gentlemen like him."

"I warrant thee, then, and wasn't Master Prynne a learned gentleman?"

"And who ever said Master Valentine was a learned gentleman, dame? I tell thee they will not do those things to Sir Arthur's son; but 'tis a sore thing to think how they may coop him up in the Tower, it may be to die there, like Sir John Eliot. He's safe here to-night though, anyhow, and let 'em have the best beds, dame."

Henry thanked him, but begged no change might be made in the order as to their beds. Let them have the two little rooms they had chosen, and in the morning they would tell their wishes farther.

They were very quiet all the morning, and in the afternoon they were on the road again, as before, with Jacob Grindlay for company, mounted on his old gray mare. They took the road to Crewhurst; skirted the chase, and entered it by the road from Oxford. When safe under the trees, in a very lonely place, they dismounted, and Valentine took off his woman's dress, and appeared in one of the same description as Henry's. His long hair, tightly rolled up on the top of his head, was concealed under his hat. Then they made up the dress into a bundle, and filled it with heavy stones; took off the saddle and pillion and tied stones to them; went to a large deep pond near, broke the ice on it, and sank

them. Jacob then took the nag in hand, bade them a hasty
farewell, prayed God bless and preserve them, and rode off
while they continued their way through the chase.

"We cannot be traced, I think," said Henry, "if he
sells the nag at Reading."

"And that he's sure to do, as we charged him to hold
straight on there, and take anything he could get for it."

The sky was perfectly clear of clouds. The moon rose
and threw her silver light through the bare boughs, covering
the snowy ground with a network of shadows. They went
off the wide bridle track, through narrow paths that wound
among thickets of holly and ivy, under the gnarled and
knotted tree-trunks. They knew every foot of the ground,
and could thread their way anywhere in safety.

Suddenly they stopped in alarm. They heard a whistle
distinctly, and then a loud voice calling "Wolf!"

"That is Leeson!" said Valentine. "He would never
betray us!"

"We need not his help, and the fewer we trust the better. Things are whispered unawares from one to another.
Keep close!"

"I will, King Solomon! But Wolf scents us, and will
find us, do what you will."

Such shouting, whistling, and cracking of a whip followed
as showed how hard Leeson had found it to call in his dog,
and poor Wolf had to bear a punishment for it, as they heard.

They went on again; climbed the park wall, and walked
by the heronry. There were no herons now; all had migrated
long ago; the swans were sheltering among the reeds on the
brink; the water was frozen, and the cold moonbeams glim-

mered across it. All was very still and desolate. They
stopped and looked at the scene. They had halted on the
very spot where, little more than two years ago, Valentine
came home so gay and happy with his friends, and showed
them the beauties and glories of Crewhurst so proudly.
What a change there was now! The cold desolation of the
scene was but a type of their altered fortunes.

It was very silent in the park. The deer had gathered
under their sheds; the cows and sheep were housed; only
the owls hooted from time to time from some old ivied
wall.

At last they came within sight of the Hall, passing by
the stables. All was silent there, too. Not a steed stood
in stall now.

They were winding round behind the stables, to get to
the secret opening which Henry knew, when he held back
Valentine with a strong grasp, saying, in a whisper—

"We are watched! Climb up after me!" and in a
minute they were high up among the branches of one of the
old cedars, and completely hidden from below by its thick
foliage.

Valentine now saw to his dismay, as distinctly as Henry
had done, a number of people silently moving among the
trees. They passed on beyond the entrance to the court of
offices, and continued to move towards the Hall.

"What can it mean?" whispered Valentine. "I see
two women and a boy with them. They cannot be bailiffs
or sheriffs' officers!"

"The foremost man carries a drum. Can it be a party
of soldiers?"

A NIGHT ALARM.

"But how then about these women?"

"Hush, they are coming under this tree!"

"What did the man say?"

"He said, 'There's not a light in a single window.'"

"Ah! they know of our plans somehow. Some one has betrayed us. These women are showing them the way. They are scouts, and have a strong party concealed."

"What are they doing now?"

As Henry whispered these words, the drum began to sound. A signal doubtless to the concealed party! After a pause it sounded again, their hearts beating time to it. The party had stopped in front of the tree. It was an awful pause.

A great coughing and clearing of throats now began below; doubtless another signal!

"They must have seen us, I fear!" whispered Henry; "but keep still and silent for your life!"

The drum now, accompanied by a pipe, sounded again, and the two performed the symphony to a well-known carol; then all the party, raising their voices, sang the words, the women and boys taking the high parts. The words were lost in the distance, but after the music came a loud voice, which they recognised as Thomas Boult's.

"God bless the good family, and send them home to us! and we've sang their wassail to the empty house. A cheer for Sir Arthur Carewe and all his noble family!"

Then came a good hearty cheer.

"It is worth while to be in adversity to make one know what good hearts there are in the world," said Henry, and he had to dash away a tear as he spoke.

o

"It is very dismal, though, and a great trouble, to be in adversity. I do not like it at all," said Valentine.

The party below began to move away again; but now a light appeared in a window of the Hall. It was opened, and old nurse's head, well wrapped up in a handkerchief, was put out. The party upon this moved towards the house, and a short conference began. The two brothers in the tree could hear nurse's shrill voice, but could not catch her words, but as it ended in the light disappearing from the window, and an opening of the door, and as after a short stay the wassailers took their departure, and all became perfectly quiet again, it was natural to infer that nurse had regaled them with some good ale, wished them merry Christmas, and they had gone home.

"Now we may slide down and get into our hiding place," said Henry.

"Sorry cheer we shall find there, I expect."

"I would I saw thee safe in it, for all its sorry cheer."

They were on the ground again now, and Henry began to lead the way. He went close up to the old tower, and stopped before a large mass of ivy, which, half covering the tower, was extremely thick, and projected a long way over the grass at the roots. Pushing it aside at one place, he crept in followed by Valentine. They crawled along on hands and knees, among the matted branches, till they came to a place where the shoots of the ivy formed a little arch over a hole in the ground, but the leaves overhead were so thick that the moonlight did not get through. It was perfectly dark, and Henry only found the place by groping with his hands. He let himself down into the opening till his feet rested on a block of stone below.

"Let yourself down after me steadily, and you will find footing."

Valentine obeyed.

"Keep quite still while I strike a light, or you will fall into the dungeon."

It took a little while to strike a spark with flint and steel, and then Henry lighted a little horn lanthorn he carried in his pocket.

The light showed down into a deep and dismal pit, the old dungeon of the tower. They were on the highest of a flight of stone steps that led down into it. Leaping from one to the other, they got to the bottom. The feeble rays of the lanthorn did not penetrate the whole of its gloomy dimensions.

"What a horrible place!" said Valentine shuddering. "It freezes me to the bone. This is not our place of refuge, is it?"

"No, no; we are going up to a snug room. But, Valentine! men—and those our ancestors—have thrown other men into this dismal hole to pine and die, and that's a dreadful thought!"

"Well, do not think of it now. 'Tis quite enough to be here ourselves. What is that sound?"

"The dropping of water."

Henry now led the way across the dungeon, to a small opening in the wall, and crept through it, followed by Valentine. Then they found themselves in a large square place, which they crossed again, and began to ascend a very steep, winding staircase hewn out in the wall. At the top they found a landing place, and a strong door which opened by a spring that Henry understood. Within, he was able to secure it by a bolt, so that it could not be opened by any one outside. They had reached their place of refuge at last.

"Now I have thee safe. We have escaped in truth!" cried Henry exultingly.

He set the lanthorn down on a table that stood in the middle of the room. Its light fell upon many things that brought back to his memory, in a moment, the events of former days: his own sufferings, his mother's love, Mr. Russell with all his goodness and strength, and affection. He had to rouse himself to action, or he could have sat down and dreamed over it all.

There were many comforts in the room that had been brought down by Mr. Russell for Lady Carewe's use, besides what the doctor had before. It looked sumptuous to the tired wanderers; the air also was neither damp nor close, though there was no window. The immense thickness of the walls kept out cold and wet entirely, and besides many openings for ventilation, there was a wide chimney communicating with the outer air, skilfully constructed in the wall, and permitting the smoke to escape among the ivy boughs in such a manner that it had never yet excited observation. Nevertheless, in the day time, it was necessary to be cautious in lighting a fire.

At present, however, there was no occasion to fear it, and Henry, remembering where all the treasures were, went to a great heap of dry wood in a corner, piled it up, and lighted it on the hearth. The cheerful glow sent such a brightness over everything, that Valentine's spirits rose high; he drew a chair close to the blazing fire, began to laugh over their adventures, and to pile up more logs.

"Now, then, for our supper!" said Henry. "Come, Master farmer! turn out your pockets! 'Tis mighty convenient to play the farmer and wear a frieze jacket for the sake of these capital pockets."

They had soon spread on the table a supply of bread, half a ham, and some cheese.

"But what are we to drink?" asked Valentine, looking up in consternation as Henry, who had been purveyor, took out his last parcel.

"You cannot think the contriver of this good room forgot the need of water to drink?"

"Water! Is that all we are to have?"

"We could scarcely carry a barrel of ale, or even a beaker of sherry-sack, I would suggest to your lordship."

"Well! I knew it would be sorry cheer! But where's the water?"

"For that I must go down into your favourite place, the dungeon, again. Now for the pitcher we left."

He groped in a corner and found a water pitcher, and with it prepared to descend the stair again.

"Thou wilt not come to look at the spring?"

"No, not to-night. I am so tired and the fire is so pleasant. Make haste back. Thou needst not be long."

Henry was half way down in a few minutes carrying his pitcher and lanthorn. When at the bottom he crossed the dungeon to that corner whence the sound of dropping water came that had startled Valentine. Here flowed a little

spring out of the dark rock on which the tower was built,
glancing bright as a diamond in the light of the lanthorn.
He placed his pitcher beneath it, and waited while it filled,
and while waiting he held up the light and looked into the
depths where the water fell. It had worked a deep chasm
for itself. He threw in a piece of stone, and it sounded loud
and hollow from the bottom. As he looked, the idea occurred
to him that dreadful deeds might have been done there, and
that if he could fathom that gloomy pit, he might find human
bones in it. The sound the stone had sent up even seemed,
to his imagination, as it echoed through the vault, to have
changed into hollow groans. A cold shudder ran through
him, and a feeling of superstitious dread and horror got hold
of him, so that he stood trembling there in the darkness, and
forgot his water pitcher, which was running over.

The lanthorn fell from his hand. This accident roused
him. Its loss would have been a serious misfortune. He
stooped and picked it up, and as he raised it, the light fell
again on the sparkling water flowing from the rock. It
seemed to say to him, "God is good. He ever gives good
gifts to His children flowing from His heaven, like this pure
water. It is they who abuse His gifts, and turn them into
the means of crime and misery."

Plainly, as though the words had been spoken, did Henry
feel the heavenly message in his soul, and with it came words
that his mother had read to him the very last day he was
with her : " I will give thee that living water." He knelt
beside the spring, and out of the depths of that dungeon
rose his prayer, " Let me not abuse Thy gifts, oh Father !
Open my heart to the living waters of His love, whom Thou

didst send to us. Forgive me, whom Thou hast blessed with this great deliverance of my brother, for my faithless fears."

Then Henry rose strong and joyous, and scarcely felt the ground beneath his feet, nor knew he was carrying a heavy weight up difficult steps, till he heard Valentine's voice call—

" I thought thou wouldst never come back !"

They ate and drank merrily ; deciding that though no flourish of trumpets had ushered in the ham and bread and cheese, they enjoyed their supper as much as if they had both been archbishops. Then they piled on logs enough to keep in the fire, put out their lanthorn, lay down side by side on the bed, and slept soundly for nearly twelve hours.

CHAPTER XVIII.

The brothers spent their Christmas-day in their strange silent room, but not in any melancholy mood. They were glad to rest, and the feeling of security was delightful and sufficient for the day. They could at least burn their yule log, as Henry said; and as to their dinner, they must remember the good old saying, " Enough is as good as a feast," and they had enough, though none to spare.

So now when night was come, Henry must go forth and try to find Woodruffe. He could be trusted like a brother, and it was to him they must look for a supply of food and all else they wanted. Above all, in Henry's estimation, was Woodruffe's help necessary to communicate with their family, to tell them Valentine was safe, and to receive their father's commands what to do next.

Henry waited till eight o'clock to set out.· He wished that every one in the village should be in bed and asleep by the time he got there, and in that quiet place this hour was considered quite late enough to go to rest. He knew that they would all have had their Christmas beef and ale sent down from the Hall, and he hoped they would sleep soundly after it. He intended to go softly to Woodruffe's window and tap at it and awake him. No one but Woodruffe himself and his old mother, who was deaf, lived in his cottage, and Henry hoped he could manage well. Though he knew that every one in the village would be true and faithful, he wished if possible to conceal the fact of Valentine's concealment from every one but Woodruffe. Valentine always called him King Solomon, when he said so, but he did not care for that. He knew it was safer, because, however faithful they were, some of them might be indiscreet.

It was a stormy night. The frost was breaking up, and the clouds scudding across the sky, and, ever and anon obscuring the moon, made alternations of darkness with her silvery light, as Henry, cautiously moving aside the ivy leaves, looked out over the snowy park. No living creature was to be seen, so he crept out and stood upright.

The nearest way would have been to cross the park to the avenue, but a dark figure moving across the white ground would have been seen at a great distance there, whenever the moon shone out, if any eye was open and happened to look that way; so he made a circuit, keeping carefully under the trees.

The way he took led him by the church, which, as has been said, was close to the park wall, forming, in fact, a part of its boundary; and the burial vault of the Carewe family abutted into the park, and had a separate entrance by a narrow grated door from it. All around it there was a thick plantation of yews and cypresses.

Henry thought that he was perfectly secure against meeting any one in this path. No one would go near the vault, nor even approach the grove of dark trees near it, after nightfall.

It was an age in which a belief in ghosts, witches, and sorcery was nearly universal; but Henry, with his earnest purpose in his mind, and the strength that came the night before, and which had set up a steadfast power within him, walked firmly on, fearing nothing.

The wind whistled and moaned among the yew trees. It moaned so like a human moan, that he could scarcely believe it was only the wind. Then a large owl flew close past his face, in its strange noiseless flight, and its wild unearthly cry came back on the wind like a sobbing wail. It was echoed by a groan from the vault. Yes, it was a groan; there could be no mistake about it; and, strange to say, the iron door was open, and a faint light glimmered within.

Henry's knees shook under him. A cold sickly dread crept over him. But it was only for a moment. The strength that was in him supported him, and he shook off his fear; walked on slowly but steadily, and looked into the vault.

There was a dark figure within, and a torch set against the wall; and from the figure came words, mixed with sobs and moans. " Have mercy! have pity! Let not the young life be taken! If one must die, let it not be Master Henry!"

"Woodruffe!"

The figure started round. It was Woodruffe, but he seemed paralysed with terror. He spoke again.

" Oh, what wouldst have? I will serve thee, living or dead, my dear young master!"

Henry rushed forward; but Woodruffe drew back, and had reached the utmost end of the vault before Henry caught him by both hands. He was trembling from head to foot.

But now his feared changed to extravagant joy. He laughed, he cried, he shook Henry's hand, he clapped him on the back, and at last found voice to declare that he cared for nothing now, since it was Master Henry himself that was come.

"I did think it was your spirit; and no wonder, after what we had heard."

"What have you heard?"

"But, Master Henry, why have you come to this fearsome place?"

"Come out of this place—come under the trees with me, and I will tell you everything. I was in search of you to tell you. But first, what had you heard? Put out the torch, and come under the trees and tell me."

Woodruffe obeyed, and at last ceasing to shake and tremble, said—

"Ditchly came yesternight, and told us the news from Lunnon. Says he, 'Master Valentine's Star-Chambered!' That was bad enough; but I stood that, and hoped some way he'd get off. 'For trying to kill Colonel Lunsford,' again he says. He will never let alone, thinks I in to myself, 'till he's done it, but I said nothing. 'Master Henry has got him out o' prison,' he goes on. 'He's gone off wi' him to Portsmouth, and they are both taken, and both sentenced; and they will be beheaded.' That I couldn't stand no way. I was like a madman. I knew it was just like you to go and break prison to get him out, and just the most likely thing that you would be taken. Not a man, woman, nor

child has tasted their Christmas beef and ale this day.
There has been a fast instead of a feast, and I came here
this night to pray for mercy, and mercy I have received."

Woodruffe, strong man as he was, was completely overcome, and unable to speak ; and Henry again seized both
his hands, and stood long holding them, while his own tears
flowed fast.

"We are all right now, everything is right, Master
Henry, now you are here your own self again," Woodruffe
went on.   " Who invents all the lies ?"

"They are not all lies, though."

"What! Don't say those things to me !"

"Listen to me, Woodruffe," said Henry ; and then
warning him first that he must be secret, Henry told him
what had really happened, and the perilous situation in
which Valentine stood, and then what service was required from him.   Henry could not tell him the place where
they were concealed, having come under a solemn engagement with his father never to reveal it without special permission.   This he explained to Woodruffe, feeling that, but
for this engagement, boundless trust might have been placed
in his faithful servant.

"We want food regularly brought to some safe place,"
said he. "Nowhere is so safe as this vault.   Let it be here
in this hollow old yew."

"The owls will have it."

"You must pack it safe in a box or basket."

"Well, if needs must, it shall be here."

"Above all, I want you to go off to London in the
morning."

" How to do that, and take care o' you at once, I cannot see."

" But I must send by you a message to my father, and I dare not write. No one but you can take it."

" I need not be long gone, riding post-haste. But to go by morning ! Where's the food to come from ? I have it. Mother's Christmas beef and ale you shall have, and I will satisfy her somehow."

Henry would not hear of this. On the contrary, he must tell her, and all at the village, that the news was wrong, and Master Valentine had escaped, and Master Henry was all right, and she must eat the beef herself.

" I have it, again. Can you cook meat, if meat you have ?"

" Surely. We have plenty of wood for firing."

" Then wait about ; get up i' the old yew where I was to put the meat, till I come again, and you shall have a quarter of a good fat buck as Ditchly is to take in the morning. It seemed little good to send it ; but Ditchly he said, ' What then ? Sir Arthur must eat, come what may !' "

" That will do. Here I am, up in the tree. Some bread thy old mother will spare to two poor hungry lads."

" That will she, and the beef too, if you will have it."

" That I will not."

" Could you manage a flask of ale ?"

Henry thought of Valentine. " I will try ; but a flask of oil is more important. Bring one if you can."

" Knives ?"

" We have them, our two good pocket knives ; and as for the new fashion of forks, why, we do without them."

" Forks ! What be they ?"

Henry explained.

" There's many a thing made for the penny," said Woodruffe. "What will they think of next ? Well, Master Henry, I shall not be long. Old mother's asleep by this time, and will not hear me go to cut up the buck."

In a wonderfully short time, Woodruffe was back ; and Henry had, meanwhile, time to think what message to send to his father. It was a brief but distinct one. " We are safe! Where—you know. Send us your commands, and all you can tell us of yourselves, and your blessing !"

Woodruffe had to repeat these words several times, to be sure of them. Then he loaded Henry ; the venison slung on his back ; the bread in his pockets ; a flask in either hand.

" 'Tis well you have a strong back, Master Henry."

" Good night, and God speed you, Woodruffe ; and meet me here, three nights from this time, with my father's commands."

So saying Henry set forth, under cover of the trees again, and reached the ivy safely. It required some contrivance to get into the hole in the dark, loaded as he was ; but on the top step was his lanthorn. Having lighted it, he was at no loss. It required only two or three journeys up and down, and he knocked at the door for admittance, with all his booty.

The sight of ale and venison, the means of light, and the excitement of Henry's news and adventures, raised Valentine's spirits in a moment. He sat Henry down, and dubbed himself cook, having learned to rough it for himself a little in the campaign against the Scots ; and they were soon enjoying a feast and very merry over it, and very soundly they slept after it.

The three days that had to be passed before Woodruffe would return were trying, however. Valentine grew restless and impatient. Already he had begun to urge Henry to go to nurse, and gain a secret admittance for them both into the Hall itself. "Nurse could be trusted, of course! It was mean and suspicious to doubt her."

Henry, who knew that a far easier plan was open to him, and that he could have taken Valentine up into the chamber above, was much troubled by all this. He did not dare to tell Valentine of that secret opening without permission. Crairy had only brought permission for him to disclose the secret of the one they were in ; and he felt, besides, how unsafe it would be to take Valentine to the other. A heedless laugh, a loud tone, and he might have betrayed himself, should nurse have been wandering about in the passages. And dearly as he loved, and well as he trusted her, he feared her tongue. So he had to bear complaints, jeers, and entreaties as well as he could. He was King Solomon, a puritan, and a marplot. Well! He must keep his temper as best he could.

At last came the appointed time to go to Woodruffe. Henry lighted his lanthorn, and descended to the dungeon, crossed it, and had his foot on the first step when a voice from above distinctly said, "Henry!"

He stopped. It must have been fancy! No! it came again, in the soft musical tone of a woman's voice.

"Henry!"

"Edith!" He could say no more, but hurried up to her. It was Edith indeed, who threw her arms round him and leaned on his shoulder. "I could not let him go without seeing him once more. Take me to Valentine. Woodruffe is close behind me. Thou mayst trust him in everything, and bring him in."

Still bewildered with the amazement he had been thrown into, Henry assisted Edith, and afterwards Woodruffe, whose hand he grasped with an affectionate pressure, down to the first step. Then he helped her, trembling as he could feel she was, to descend to the bottom. The strength of her affection alone supported her, brought up so delicately and guarded so carefully as she always had been, to brave such an adventure as this. Woodruffe followed her close, so as to shield her from any peril he could.

"It is a fearful place, Henry. Let us go up to the room they tell of. Is he well?"

"Yes! well. What will he feel when he sees thee?"

He led her up, then knocked. "Open again, Valentine! I have come back!"

Valentine's astonishment when he had opened the door was so great, that for a moment he held back, but he was soon clasped in Edith's arms.

"Oh, I could not let thee go without seeing thee once more, my brother!"

"Edith! I am not worthy of such love!"

Well would it have been for Valentine had those words of his, uttered in a moment of real feeling, from a conscience touched, for once, deeply, remained in his memory and borne fruit. Some minutes passed before he spoke again.

" Before I go ? Am I, then, to go ?" he said.

" I will tell thee all soon, but now—I cannot yet."

She was half-fainting ; and her brothers were both ministering to her in a moment. She was released from the warm and heavy cloak that covered her ; stretched on a couch, once her mother's, and now brought close to the cheerful warmth of the fire ; her cheeks and forehead tenderly chafed by Henry's hands ; and she soon smiled on them. Her golden curls and lovely face seemed to light up the room.

She was soon able to speak to Woodruffe, who, after laying a large bundle on the floor, was watching his young mistress with the deepest anxiety, and to tell him that now he might safely leave her, and go to do his part of the work ; he therefore went, only saying he would be ready.

" How hast thou fared in this cold and dreary season, and so long a journey ? Oh, Edith, it was a loving heart and a noble courage that brought thee !" said Henry.

" Was it womanly to attempt it with this rustic for sole company ?" said Valentine.

She looked at him long in silence. Then rose from the couch. " It is womanly to be ready to do whatever a woman can do, and is called to do. I came not merely for my own heart's ease to see thee again. It was needful to assist thy flight, and for either my father or my mother it would have been dangerous to leave London, and would have led to suspicion that they came to thee. Of my absence no one takes heed."

Valentine stood silent before her, and she went on.

" We have not a moment to lose. In half an hour your

P

came with me besides Woodruffe, will prepare the servants in the morning to receive me in the Hall.   He, also, is in our confidence."

"There is nurse to tend thee, but—"

"Our father will come in a few days."

"Ah ! my sister, thou wilt then be safe. Thou camest last night—where then hast thou been all day ?" asked Henry.

"I have lain hidden in the vault."

"What a place for thee, my Edith !"

"What matters it, compared with the sorrow we have suffered, and that which is to come ? Thou knowest well, Henry, that it is nothing."

He pressed her hand.   They quite understood each other.

The brothers sat down to eat, and persuaded her to join them, but the attempt was vain.   She said she had already had enough.   Her heart was full now, for the minutes were fast fleeting.   They extinguished their lamp, lighted their lanthorn, and closed the door behind them.   Valentine supported Edith through the dungeon.   "I shall not have her long !" he said ; " give her quite up to me, Henry."   He was much affected.   Perhaps in all the world it was Edith he loved best—after himself.

They walked very quickly, and found Woodruffe waiting with three horses ready.   The old mother was there to receive Mistress Edith.

"Henry, my own brother Henry, come back to us safely ! What should we be without thee ? I dare not even touch his hand again, lest I be seen and cause suspicion. Give him his Edith's love and farewell !"

These whispered words from her aching heart were all she could say. Woodruffe, who was strongly armed himself, gave sword and pistols to Henry, and then to his fellow-servant, and both assisted their young master to mount. He moved off, slowly at first and looking back; then seeing Edith at the cottage-door with the old dame, and Valentine mounted and by Woodruffe's side, set spurs to his horse, and dashed away, followed by his two attendants. The moon was up, and the weather fine though very cold.

CHAPTER XIX.

A JOURNEY.

WHEN, on the afternoon of the second day, they reached
Oxford, they found the inn occupied by the party they
expected, and Henry was a welcome guest with all.
To Mr. Henry Vane, who was among them, he was well
known; but Valentine, as it chanced, had not been in his
company since he was a boy. Everything had gone on
smoothly and successfully thus far. Henry thought much
of Valentine, and gave Woodruffe many charges to attend
to his comforts. "A little knocking about will do my gentleman no harm," thought Woodruffe to himself; but he obeyed
Henry nevertheless.

But they were not destined to leave Oxford without an
alarm. Henry was awakened in the night by shouts and
yells, and Woodruffe came to his door, with a face of terror,
to say there was "hue and cry after some one; pray heaven,
it was not—"

"Hush!" said Henry, starting out of bed, and going to
the window.

"The house is on fire, anyhow," said Woodruffe.

There was, indeed, a red glare flashing in at the windows,
but it came from the torches of a crowd in the court of the

MUMMING IN EARNEST.

old inn, which was built round a quadrangle, and much ornamented with balconies and carved wood, having been, in its past days, the residence of some dignitary of the church.

"For my part," said Woodruffe again, "I think 'tis a goodly company of witches and sorcerers. Nothing else ever made such yells as these ; and no woman, but a witch, ever was so tall as that one with the light."

"I know what it is. They are mumming. Do you not see hobby horse, the bishop, and all the rest ?"

"Ay, but it's mumming in earnest. They have got two prisoners, bound with cords, in the midst."

Henry saw, with horror, that it was so ; and from the cries, it became evident the prisoners were catholic priests, who had got into the hands of this furious mob. Scarcely, however, was there time to think, when a strong party of constables, headed by a number of students of the university, came to the rescue. There was a desperate scuffle, and some shots were fired. It was, however, soon ended, and the priests were saved, and carried off in triumph by the students, the rabble rout dispersing in all directions. Woodruffe disappeared early in the fray, and Henry supposed he had joined in it; but it turned out that he had been keeping guard on Valentine, lest he should be rash enough to do so.

Henry knew much more of the distracted state of the country than he had known, when, long ago, the difficulty that Justice Croke had to contend with, when he resolved to give a true judgment, had surprised him. In his office of secretary to his father, he had learned that there was no toleration in England except among one party, and that the smallest.

This party, the independents, acknowledged no head or master to the church but Christ alone, and suffered no interference of men in the worship of their Creator. In all others there was persecution. The episcopal church persecuted the puritans and the catholics. All that majority of the puritans who were called presbyterians, were ready to persecute the church if they had the power, and did persecute the catholics, who, but for the secret favour of the queen's party at court, would have been treated on all hands with even greater rigour than they were. This mob had only shown an example of it. Henry went to bed again, and fell asleep wondering how all these wrongs were ever to be righted.

The whole party set forth early next morning on their journey to the north. Riding fast, and changing horses at each posting-house, they reached Hull in three days. Their party was too strong to permit of any risks or dangers, except from "winter and rough weather," and they were all hardy and stout, and cared not much for that. Many a time did Henry look back at the servants riding behind, and exchange a glance with Valentine; and each night Woodruffe had to drive him away from the kitchen of the hostelries at which they put up, for fear he should raise suspicions by seeing after his groom's supper, but no misfortune happened on the way.

The whole party was received into the governor's house with all the old English hospitality; and when Sir Henry heard that a young son of Sir Arthur Carewe's was among his guests, he came forward to shake Henry by the hand, and give him the most affectionate welcome. Henry had

despatches from his father to deliver, and in doing so, requested a private audience, which was immediately granted.
The result was that the very next morning it was told in the
household that one of Master Carewe's grooms had taken
ship for Calais, in a vessel that dropped down the Humber
by early tide.

The parting had been so sudden, and there had been so
much to do to get all the comforts that could be got for
Valentine, that there was no time to think till he was
actually gone. Then Henry took a solitary walk to some
high ground to watch the ships moving down seawards with
the tide, and wondered which was bearing his brother away
from him. It was a relief, a great relief, that he had succeeded in getting away. But he was gone from his home
and his country. When to return? How to fare while
away? "He makes friends no less than enemies," thought
Henry, "wherever he goes; and he seemed not very
heavy at heart; but it is very wretched to think that he is
gone from us."

The party at Sir Henry Hotham's was gay and numer-
ous; and though Henry was not in spirits to enjoy it at first, yet
after a time, when he had heard by an express that arrived
that all was well at home, and had written to tell them his
mission was safely accomplished, he spent some pleasant
weeks at Hull. The sea was new to him; and the north
country of England, so different in every way to that he had
been used to, was something to see and explore. The party
he had come with delayed their return till the middle or end
of March, and tried to persuade him to wait for them. But
he had other plans in his head. That journey was an ex-

pensive affair. "Why," thought he, "if my father is strait-
ened for money, should he be put to such charges for me?
Why not get into one of the ships that are often trading
between Hull and London, and go by sea for a trifling
sum?"

Sir Henry opposed his plan; reminded him of the
shipwreck of Sir Patrick Spens, who went to sea "at the
wrong time o' the year;" and told him the discomforts of
these vessels were such as he had no idea of. Henry per-
sisted. He thought •if Valentine could brave and endure
dangers and discomforts, surely he could.

He and Woodruffe, therefore, employed themselves in
choosing a ship, and found that by far the best was one that
went to Yarmouth, a short voyage, and one that would give
them a trial of the sea, and they could take ship again for
London if they pleased at Yarmouth. Woodruffe liked the
adventure mightily. They sold their horses for a good price,
laid in a store of provisions, bought good thick sea jackets
and blankets, to keep them warm in their hammocks—
Woodruffe much admiring the woollens of this north country
—and sailed the beginning of March.

Henry enjoyed the deck and the sea. He had not been
so happy and free for a long time, as he felt when seated at
the stern, watching the coast and the sea birds. Woodruffe
soon made friends with the sailors, and got in good store of
fearful tales of shipwrecks, of Sallee rovers, of whole villages
on the coast being pillaged by the pirates, all the women
and children carried off for slaves, and all the men killed.
In return, he told them tales of robbers and poachers; of
disbanded soldiers committing murders: of witches tried by

fire and water; of the evil deeds these witches had committed, in causing diseases among cattle, and the pining
away and death of poor people's children : so the voyage
passed, though the wind was contrary, and kept them tack-
ing about for three days and nights. Then, as they neared
Yarmouth, came a storm; such a storm as would have made
Henry think of home with a fear that he should never see it
again, if he had not been too ill to think of anything, as he
swung in his hammock, down in his dark berth below. At
last they got safe into Yarmouth Roads, and landed.

"Right glad am I to set foot on dry land again," said
Woodruffe, as he trudged after Henry with the baggage,
from the pier up to the town. "If you'd have told me how
Master Russell thought the sea spun round the earth, and
we all ran round th' other way, I'd have said Ay, to it;
but don't tell me this good ground we tread on be running
away from under us. Happy be lucky it is not ! But now,
Master Henry, what are we to do next, for we are a long
way from Lunnon yet, not to speak of our home."

The first thing was to find an inn where they could dine,
for appetites such as they had they had never felt before.
Hunger being appeased, Woodruffe set off to explore and
inquire, and returned with the advice that they should
ensconce themselves in the long waggon for Norwich. After
getting there, they could do as they liked. 'Twould be
tedious, but a mighty good rest after all their turmoil.

Henry thought the idea good, as the waggon started the
next morning, and did not repent it. The waggon, drawn
by eight good horses, with bells on their heads, went on
slowly, it is true, but steadily, defying ruts and holes. The

March winds had dried the roads, such as they were, and he
liked walking by the waggoners up the hills and having a
talk with them; and peeping under hedges for the early
primroses; and exploring up green lanes, and taking long
runs over breezy commons. At night the waggon was a
capital place to sleep in, among bales of goods and great
packages of various kinds. There were several passengers
besides themselves, some of whom were good company too;
but among them the great talk was of troubles in the country, and the hope that everything would be put right by a
parliament. Sometimes, in spite of March winds, they came
to a stand still in some bog or morass, and then every man
there had to put his "shoulder to the wheel," and help the
horses by poles pushing behind, or by what ways they could
contrive, to get the heavy waggon on. Norwich was reached
safely at last, however.

Between Norwich and Bedford the chief traffic was
carried on by pack-horses, the road being too bad for the
waggon; and Henry resolved to join the next train that
started, and for this purpose hired two horses; and, accompanied by Woodruffe, repaired at the appointed time to
the hostelry where the carriers put up, Woodruffe carrying
the saddle-bags. They found a party of about fifty horses
in all, the greater number loaded with their packs, but about
some ten bearing travellers, who, like themselves, took this
opportunity for company's sake, rather than enjoy greater
speed with the drawback of fear of highway robbery.

All being ready, they started in single file, the leader
being an old and experienced horse with a bell. The way
for many miles was over a paved causeway, having on either

side a thick sludge of mud; so that if any horse became restive, or if by any accident he stopped, there followed a floundering in the mud and a terrible confusion. If, on the other hand, any unlucky single traveller met the long train, he had to turn off and stand by till they had passed, his horse perhaps up to his knees. Whatever happened in the rear, however, on went the steady leader, undisturbed by anything.

When this causeway had been passed, they came to one of those heathy commons that were so much to Henry's taste, where the track guided the train of horses, and where he could try the mettle of his hired steed by a gallop over the turf.

In this way the country through which they passed varied, and the journey was interesting, though it was slow. Sometimes they would pass over dreary stretches of moorland, and towards evening the mists would rise, and as darkness came on no track would be visible. Then the carriers trusted entirely to the leader, and he deserved their trust. For safety's sake, the whole train was ordered into line, the leader in front. On he went, his bell serving as guide to all the rest, not missing an inch of the way, never leading into a bog, till turning into some miry lane they saw the lights of the village or town where they were to put up. The old and feeble horses lagged far behind, but came up at last. Never did they fail, bending under the packs, to do their duty and their appointed tasks, and stories were told of some that had dropped down dead as they entered the inn yard.

Thus travelling, they reached Oxford early one day, to put up till the following morning; and while Henry was taking a walk about the city, and admiring the splendour of the colleges, he found himself suddenly clapped on the shoulder, and heard a friendly voice. Turning quickly round, he found it was Mr. Henry Vane.

"And so we have overtaken you, Master Carewe," said he. "Where do you put up, and how are you travelling?"

On being informed, he seemed much amused at Henry's primitive modes of conveying himself about, and told him he had none of the courtier or the fine gentleman about him, but would do well for the New World with its wild freedom, whither he should himself return if matters improved not at home. "But," said he, "there is good hope they will improve. Writs are issued for a parliament, and thy father will sit in it. But thou must join our company now to London. We stay here only a week."

No! Henry would not desert his pack-horses, and meant to be home before four days were over.

"Come, then, with me to the house of Col. Thornhaugh, where I am kindly received. There is gay company there, and good cheer; and while they drink their toasts after dinner, you and I can wander out again among these old colleges, and talk over your home affairs, for I know a little of them, and over the amended hopes of the friends of liberty."

Henry gladly accepted the invitation, and found as pleasant a party as he had been promised, but was glad to obey Vane's signal and walk out to hear what tidings he had.

He heard that confidence had revived in the country in prospect of a parliament, and that Sir Arthur Carewe had been able to sell his Cornwall property to good advantage, and thus to recover the shock that his great loss of money had occasioned to his fortune. That he would assuredly sit

in parliament, and that he was totally engrossed by public affairs, and much longing for Henry, whom he missed terribly.

Henry was the more resolved to make no delay. He would gladly have put spurs to his horse and rode post to London, but his friend would not hear of it. The frequency of robbery and violence on the road, especially near the metropolis, would render such a proceeding unsafe. " I know thou wouldst brave many more dangerous passes, Henry," said he, "if need were; but here is no need. A day or two makes little difference; but a murdered son will do little for his father."

So Henry returned to his hostelry, just as Woodruffe was getting very anxious about him.

"I am glad to see thou hast thy honest, steady servant with thee," said Vane, who had walked with him. " I liked not thy young groom as well. He was a handsome fellow, but upstart and insolent. I am glad he hath taken his departure."

"I also am glad," said Henry; "and yet I was sorry to part with him."

The train of horses, considerably increased in number, was on its way by six in the morning; and with no more serious accident than an occasional loss of a shoe or roll in the mud, at last reached Hagbush Lane, the bridle road from the north into London, leading by Holloway, into what is now called the City Road. It was a deep hollow lane, with high hedgerows on either side, and meadows much higher than the road, and was more muddy than all the rest of the way. Here, at the top of Gray's Inn Lane, the carriers put up; and having given up their horses, and paid the very moderate hire, Henry and Woodruffe walked at a rapid pace towards the Strand, and Henry rang at the door just as the watchman's cry to light up was heard. That night there was joy in the house, such as made up for many a past sorrow. Woodruffe was telling his adventures till he was too sleepy to talk any more, and Henry had brought as much happiness with him as he felt himself.

CHAPTER XX.

THE TOWER.

BUT the brighter prospects which seemed to open for the country, and the hopes of all who loved the ancient constitution of England, her monarchy, and her parliament, were doomed to disappointment, for the parliament which met in April, 1640, and the king who summoned it, had two different aims in view.

The king called together the houses of Lords and Commons that he might obtain from the Commons a grant of money without farther departure from the constitution of the realm in levying taxes by his royal will. Twelve years he had done so ; but now, when a second Scottish war was nearly certain, and his necessities greater than ever, the temper of the country was such that he dared no longer continue it.

The parliament, on the other hand, assembled with the purpose to redress the grievances of the country ; to annihilate ship-money, and all illegal modes of raising revenue, to put the constitution on a firm basis, and render it impossible for any king henceforth to attempt to govern without his parliament.

Neither party would give way ; and the result was a dissolution of parliament by the king in twenty-one days.

"There could not," to quote Clarendon, "a greater damp have seized upon the spirits of the whole nation than this dissolution caused, and men had much of the misery in view which shortly after fell out."

Distress and discontent now spread throughout the country. Levies of soldiers had to be made for the Scottish war; it was difficult to raise them; money must be had to pay

them; the people murmured at their forced loans and taxes. They carried in to the justices their poultry, their produce of any kind, in hopes to satisfy the sheriffs; they sent their sons to the army unwillingly, for never was war so unpopular. It was a religious war, undertaken to set up episcopacy in Scotland, and the whole of the large puritan party in England disapproved of the attempt; while the people at large, and those who belonged to the church, disliked it, for they believed that though episcopacy was talked of, popery would follow. The soldiers, when collected together, would not serve under officers who could not clear themselves of the charge of popery, and even rose upon and killed some who could not.

There were some tumults. In London, a mob of apprentices, to the number of five hundred, attacked the palace of Archbishop Laud at Lambeth, at midnight, with intent to sack it. He effected his escape, and the rebels were dispersed, but not without bloodshed; and one wretched victim was put to the rack to try to discover if any more important persons had instigated the riot. Nothing, however, was discovered. This atrocity was committed in the Tower, and the warrant for inflicting it still exists in the State Paper Office. It should be remembered as the last instance in which the torture was ever legally applied in England.

Several members of the house of Commons were committed to prison by the king, immediately after the dissolution, and the papers of Lord Brooke were seized, and his study and desks broken open.

At this crisis, one man stood eminent in supporting and aiding the king. That man was Lord Strafford, once known as Sir Thomas Wentworth, the friend and supporter of liberty; afterwards as Lord Wentworth; now as Lord Strafford, lord-lieutenant of Ireland and president of the council of the north, in the latter capacity despotic over all the northern counties of England. He urged the king without wavering to employ the policy known between them by the word "thorough;" meaning, by that word, the application of force to obtain his will in every department of the state. He promised to bring over a large body of the wild Irish to assist him. The queen also urged to despotism, never forgetting the usages of her native court.

It is September of this disastrous year, and Lady Carewe, pen in hand, sits writing to her husband's dictation. But they are not in the fine old library at Crewhurst, nor in the pleasant room overlooking the river in the Strand. Sir Arthur Carewe is a prisoner in the Tower of London. Here he has spent the whole summer. His room is gloomy, and he has suffered in health from want of air and exercise, but has been cheered by the permission granted him to see his wife and son daily. They live in a small lodging near the Tower. Edith is at Crewhurst, where, assisted by nurse, she takes charge of her little brother and sister, and educates them, and takes her mother's place in guiding the household and superintending the servants, and caring for the people and the poor.

There is no longer luxury or grandeur at Crewhurst, yet the place looks like its former self. The gardens are full of plants and flowers; every room in the Hall is in order; the park and the chase are in their former beauty; the old servants are still in their places; the village is as cheerful as ever. But there are no horses in the stables; nor hounds in the kennels; nor falcons on the perches; nor plate in the cupboards. Valentine could no longer have shown off the

glories of the property to which he was heir; but if he had
known how much greater a thing it is to be poor for conscience' sake, and for the truth, and to preserve a noble in-
dependence in comparative poverty, than to be rich and
live sumptuously by giving up honour and principle, he
would have been prouder of his father, a prisoner and im-
poverished by losses and fines, than if he could have seen
him in all his former state; and prouder of his beautiful
sister Edith fulfilling her round of duties, a sweet influence
to all, the comforter of the poor and the afflicted, the idol
of her dependents, and the guide and darling of her brother
and sister, to whom she is as a mother, than if his wish had
been gratified, and he had seen her shining and admired at
court. She is melancholy, because so loving a heart cannot
be glad in separation from all she loves best, but she does
not show it, she allows no sadness to gloom over the young
lives she has to cherish, and constant occupation helps her
to endure her solitude.

The quiet of the small prison room where no sound had
been heard for the last hour, but the low voice dictating and
the ready pen transcribing, was interrupted by the unfasten-
ing of locks and bars, and Henry was ushered in by the jailer.
His presence always cheered his father, who extended a hand
to him, and held his while finishing the sentence he was
dictating.

" And now, Henry, what news hast thou collected in thy
wanderings ?"

" Much news, my father. Some public news, very heavy,
yet mixed with hope too ; and some which concern us nearly,
being of Valentine."

this weary prison; so Mr. Hampden saith. 'All our state prisoners,' these were his words, ' will be released.'"

"I do rejoice with thee in that, Henry, for myself and my brothers in captivity. I pine for liberty, and often have I thought of that eloquent and heartfelt outburst of indignation with which Sir Robert Philips moved for the committee to petition his majesty against these arbitrary imprisonments, in the parliament held now thirteen years since. 'I can live,' he said, 'although another who hath no right be put to live with me, although I pay excises and impositions more than I do; but to have my liberty, which is the soul of my life, taken from me by power, and to have my body pent up in a jail, without remedy by law, and to be so adjudged —oh improvident ancestors! oh unwise forefathers! to be so curious in providing for the quiet possession of our laws and the liberties of parliament, and to neglect our persons and bodies, and to let them lie in prison, and that during pleasure, remediless! If this be law, why do we talk of liberties? Why do we trouble ourselves with a dispute about law, franchises, property of goods, and the like? What may any man call his own if not the liberty of his person?'"

Henry was deeply affected by these words, and by the depth of his father's emotion as he uttered them, and no one spoke again until the summons of the jailer obliged him and his mother to leave their dear prisoner in his solitude for the night. Already had Henry's interview with Mr. Richard Eliot that morning tried his fortitude, for their discourse had been of the gloomy days when Sir John Eliot, the father of this young gentleman, had given up his life in that very room where now Sir Arthur Carewe was pent up; and this although petition was made to the king that for the sake of his health and to save his life, he should be liberated under promise to return when he had recovered. His son remembered the day he carried up that petition and was refused; and another sadder day when he carried up the petition to remove his father's body, for burial in his own vault, and was again refused. Henry's heart was full of these things, but he did not remind his father of them.

And Henry had not to endure such bitter grief himself. But a few days after that conversation, joyful news was brought to the prisoner in the Tower by two men, the most influential men of those days, Mr. Pym and Mr. Hampden. The petitions for a parliament throughout the country could no longer be resisted; twelve peers had drawn up one to his majesty, and despatched two of their number to York to present it to him; the petition from the city of London alone was signed by ten thousand names, and carried to York by members of the common council; the gentry of Yorkshire, when called upon to support the train-bands for two months, had replied by humbly petitioning for a parliament; upon all this the king and Lord Strafford had yielded, though so unwillingly, that the two lords who carried the petition had like to have been shot for it,—only that Lord Strafford was told there was danger the soldiery would not obey the order; and the writs were issued.

Only a few days more and Sir Arthur Carewe was released from prison. He was received immediately, together with Lady Carewe and Henry, into the house of Mr. Hampden in Gray's Inn Lane, and thence they went on to Crewhurst.

It was a day of rejoicing indeed when they arrived. The

commonest gifts of God to man—the free air, the green fields, the open sky—become miracles of goodness to one long pent up in a prison; but besides these, there was the joy of the re-union of the whole family, only excepting him they had lost, but never ceased to regret; and the awakening hope for the country. Sir Arthur was returned to parliament. His wife would have had him decline the duty, but it was in vain she tried to persuade him on the score of his ruined health and the danger of the fatigue and excitement to his life itself. "The country needs the best service of all her sons," he said. "While life lasts, I must do my duty."

"It is hard to bear," she replied; "and I have an ill-boding heart; yet would I not my husband should desert his post."

Parliament was summoned for the 3d of November; and Lady Carewe and Henry would accompany Sir Arthur to London, leaving Edith again to her duties at Crewhurst. They took a lodging near Mr. Hampden in Gray's Inn Lane; but before going up they joined a large meeting of the parliamentary leaders, at the mansion of Lord Say in Oxfordshire. At that gathering, whither Edith accompanied them, they once more met their friends the Willoughbys; and Lady Willoughby returned to Crewhurst with Edith for a while, when her lord went to London.

THE MEETING AT LORD SAY'S.

CHAPTER XXI.

THE WAR BEGINS.

On the morning of the 4th of January, 1642, Henry, when he went to the house of Commons with his father, according to his usual custom, did not take leave of him after they had passed up Westminster Hall and go to his own studies in the Temple as usual, but entered the house with him, and took his station in the strangers' gallery. He stayed, anxious to hear the debate on this important day, for on the day before, the king had sent by message of a serjeant-at-arms to require of Mr. Speaker five gentlemen, and they being delivered to him, to arrest them for high treason. Their names were Denzil Hollis, Arthur Hazelrigge, John Pym, John Hampden, and William Strode; and at the same time, in the house of Lords, the king had by message of his attorney Herbert, accused the Lord Kimbolton of high treason. The Lords had appointed a committee to consider precedents, the Commons had returned a message by Lord Falkland to the effect that the members would be ready to answer any legal charge. The Commons also having heard that the studies and papers of their five members had been sealed up by order of the king, had sent their serjeant-at-arms to break open those seals.

The house of Commons in which Henry sat that day, existed till it was destroyed by fire, and gave place to the present one; in the year 1834.   It was a narrow, dingy, ill-lighted room, running at right angles with Westminster Hall, and having a passage into it at the south-east angle. The Hall shared in all the excitements of the House, and nothing of interest went on in the one, without an eager sympathy in the other.

At the western end, the entrance was between rows of benches, passing the bar, and underneath the gallery.   At the east end, a little in advance of a large window looking on the river, stood the speaker's chair.   In front of that stood the clerks' table, at which sat Henry Elsyng and John Rushworth, with their faces to the mace and backs to the speaker.   On benches stretching to right and left of the speaker, were assembled the honourable members.   There they sat, puritan and courtier, the first and foremost of the gentlemen of England, with bearded faces, close cut and stern ; or more courtier like, with flowing hair and peaked ruff, and all wearing steeple-crowned hats, Spanish cloaks and swords; their faces for the most part worn with anxious thoughts and fears, heavy with toil, responsibility, and care, often pale with long imprisonment.   The speaker, Mr. Lenthall, was in costume like the rest.   Mr. Pym was in his usual place near the bar, just beyond the gallery on the right hand side of the house at entering.   Hyde (Lord Claren-don) and Falkland sat together on the left hand ; Sir Henry Vane on the right.   John Hampden behind Pym; then Edmund Waller, then Henry Martin ; Oliver Cromwell, member for Cambridge, on one of the back benches ; Denzil

Hollis near him ; Selden, member for Oxford University, under the gallery.

Lord Falkland reports, in answer to their message, that the serjeant-at-arms, in requiring the five members of Mr. Speaker, did no more than his bidding. Then Mr. Hampden made an eloquent speech, and was followed by Sir Arthur Hazel-rigge ; and the house committed to custody those officers who had sealed up the studies and papers of their five members.

At the dinner hour, between twelve and one, there was as usual a rush of members into the hall, and Henry, then joining his father, did not afterwards return to the gallery, but remained in the hall. Many of the members too re-mained for some time walking up and down, or gathered in knots talking earnestly, until the serjeant was sent with his mace to collect them. Henry had an anxious foreboding of coming dangers, caused by rumours that had got afloat, no one knew whence ; rumours that the king had feasted at Whitehall, the previous evening, a large assemblage of reck-less, violent spirits, such as were called in those days reforma-does ; that a hundred stand of arms, and a large quantity of gunpowder, had been sent to Whitehall from the Tower that morning. It was known, too, that to the petition of the house to be allowed to appoint a guard, the king had replied by saying he would himself appoint them a guard. There-fore, an awful sense of some coming evil, more terrible sometimes than the evil itself, took possession of Henry, and he felt it so keenly, because he knew his father's shattered health could stand no painful excitement. It was an un-healthy season ; the plague was in London ; and the anxious course of public affairs had worn and wasted away the

little strength that had remained to him after his imprisonment.

The course of public affairs had been sufficient to try a
strong man's strength, and had brought the king and his
parliament to an attitude of open defiance. The king's
usual demand for supplies at the opening of parliament had
been answered by the appointment of committees of grievances to consider petitions; and from north, south, east, and
west, flowed in the petitions, complaining of the sufferings
of the country. The mutilated victims of the Star Chamber
had been released from their dungeons, and brought into
London, escorted by many thousands, with banners flying
and much rejoicing, and grief too, to see their scars and the
sad state of one who had lost sight and hearing, and nearly
the use of his limbs in his captivity. By a solemn judgment
their sentences were reversed; and then the courts of Star
Chamber and of High Commission were for ever abolished.
When, at the Christmas of that year, the wassail bowl was
carried round, the wassailers congratulated each other on
these great events, and there was rejoicing throughout the
country.

Retribution, stern and solemn, had been visited by
the parliament on the doers of these deeds. The all-
powerful minister, Lord Strafford, who had urged the king
to the " thorough " policy, and promised to support it by
his army of wild Irish, was in his grave ; beheaded
after trial by impeachment, and warrant signed by the king.
Charles had struggled hard to save him, but yielded at last,
and Strafford's exclamation thereupon has never been forgotten—" Put not your faith in princes !"

Archbishop Laud, and many of the bishops and clergy of his party, were in prison, but there were no disgraceful scenes of torture and mutilation; these had vanished for the present from England. The unjust judges of Hampden had been deposed; two members of the government had fled.

The king, on his part, had gone to visit his Scottish subjects in the summer of 1641, and had been well received; had held his court and a parliament in Edinburgh, but had been recalled by a terrible catastrophe that struck horror throughout the country. The Irish catholics had risen with the intention to massacre every protestant in the country. That wild Irish army that Charles had delayed very long to disband, in spite of the parliament, had speedily reunited, and become the ready instrument of atrocities too horrible to repeat. Men, women, and children were ruthlessly murdered by them, till the Shannon was choked with dead bodies; and though the forces hastily sent over, and the stand made in Dublin, checked the slaughter, it broke out again and again for two years. No one believes now that the king was privy to this horrible business, but the name assumed by the Irish assassins of the " Queen's army," and the supposed leaning of the court to popery, naturally made the people suspect him.

In November the parliament presented to the king, and printed and published to the country, their celebrated " Remonstrance of the State of the Kingdom," containing, in a long preamble and two hundred and six clauses, the calamities and the wrongs of the country throughout his reign, and the remedies they had applied by the measures of the present session. The first answer of the king seemed to give earnest that though Strafford was dead his policy was living, and that henceforth "force" was to be the arbiter between crown and parliament. He deposed the trusty Sir William Balfour from his post of governor of the Tower, and put in his place that Colonel Lunsford of whom we have heard, and who was ready for any desperate deed; but the appointment lasted only a few days. The lord mayor reported that the apprentices were about to rise to carry the Tower by storm, and there were dangerous tumults, with some bloodshed, in Westminster. The keys of the Tower were therefore taken from Colonel Lunsford again.

This was the state of matters when the Commons' petition for a guard was answered by the king "that he would appoint them a guard," and he sent to arrest the five members for high treason ; and this was the state of things, well known to Henry in his capacity of secretary to his father, which made him wait in Westminster Hall, that 4th of January, with an awful sense of some approaching crisis.

The assembling of the members after dinner was shortly succeeded by a hurried message from without, brought by Captain Langres, and then a stir within the house, and a hasty departure of some of the members, which of them was not exactly known. Immediately after this, the king's coach entered New Palace Yard, escorted by his guard of gentlemen pensioners, and followed by a train of about five hundred young men, courtiers, officers, and soldiers of fortune, armed with swords and pistols. These armed men entered the hall, and after them the king, striking such a terror into all those that kept shop there as they instantly shut up. Booksellers, law-stationers, sempstresses, and the like, ceased to utter their usual "What d'ye lack?" and gathered up their goods in silence. The armed band now made a lane up the middle of the hall, and the king walking fast along it, and up the stairs to the door of the house of Commons, knocked hastily and was admitted, taking in with him his nephew, the Prince Palatine Charles, and was heard, as he entered, to order the armed men "for their lives!" not to follow him. But they remained crowding round the door.

In the sudden rush of such a multitude into the hall, Henry was borne backwards, and it was some minutes before he could move. Then he succeeded in clambering up some of the stone-work so as to see over the heads of the crowd. For what purpose had the king, contrary to the privilege of parliament, made this entrance into the house? Why had he brought with him that desperate band? The answer rushed through his brain in a moment. The king has come to seize the five members he has accused. The house will not give them up. There will be a dreadful scene of violence and bloodshed.

The thought drove all the blood to his heart, and made him turn deadly pale. Then he called up all his resolution to think what he could do. If these armed men pressed forward into the house, among them he would go, and by some means would get to his father's side. He held himself ready for a spring, and at the first move he would be among them; in the very midst of them.

In this attitude he remained watching with steady eye. He could see impatience, a reckless demeanour, a swaggering manner, among the men; but they were not summoned;

there was no move to pass up the stairs, and enter the door.

Suddenly there was a recoil to right and left. The men who had crowded up after the king were hurrying down. The lane was made again, and the king came forth, followed by his nephew; and walked fast, and with an air of sullen passion, back to his coach, the word "Privilege! Privilege!" sounding through the open door. Murmurs of disappointment and oaths were muttered among his train, but they followed him, and the hall became nearly empty. Then, in a short time it was full of honourable members. The house had adjourned.

Henry hurried to his father's side the moment that he appeared, and saw him with flushed cheek and excited eye, leaning on the arm of Henry Vane.

"We have had a great deliverance, my son!" he said, as he took Henry's hand. "Thank God, for our great deliverance! Was there large force of armed men?"

"They must have amounted to many hundreds," said Henry.

"I have a coach here that shall set you down," said Vane. "Thy father must have no more fatigue this day."

Henry gladly accepted the kind offer, and they were speedily at home with Lady Carewe, who was watching for them anxiously. She led her husband in, stretched him on his couch, brought him refreshment, and made all tranquil around him. Her cares are not for long. He will never enter the house of Commons again. The sand is running low, and his "long day's work" is nearly done, and his wife knows it, and he knows it well.

But now, with animated voice and manner, he tells her and Henry the events of the day. "We had scarcely assembled after dinner," said he, "when it was communicated to us that during our hour's adjournment Mr. Pym had received secret intelligence that the king was coming to seize the five impeached members by force; and farther, that Lord Essex had sent to advise those five members to absent themselves this day. There was a debate on this. It was interrupted by a more pressing message still, brought in by Nathaniel Fiennes. Captain Langres had clambered over the roofs from Whitehall to call him out of the house, and tell him to warn it that the king was approaching at the head of a large body of armed men."

"Even among the resolute men of our house of Commons, it must have been an awful moment. I tremble as thou tellest."

"On this it was moved that the five members have leave to absent themselves, and they went instantly—Strode only resisting, and having to be forced away by a friend—and took boat at the stairs. Scarcely had they gone, and Mr. Speaker had instructions to sit still with the mace lying before him, when a loud knocking was heard, then a rush of armed men, and above all the voice of the king commanding 'upon their lives not to come in.'"

"That I also heard," said Henry, "and saw the demeanour of his hundreds of armed followers. I watched all from without."

"Thou also hast had thy awful moments, then," said Lady Carewe; "but let us listen to the rest."

"The king entered immediately with the Elector Palatine, while the door was kept open, leaving visible a party, of whom some had left their cloaks in the hall, while most of them were armed with pistols and swords."

" All, nearly all, my father."

" As the king entered, we all rose and uncovered, the king also removing his hat. His glance and his step were in the direction of Mr. Pym's seat close by the bar. Not seeing Mr. Pym, his majesty proceeded up the house to the chair. The speaker rose and dropped on one knee, then rose again, and stood, as did we all, and the mace was removed. His majesty then cast searching glances among us, but could nowhere see those he sought."

" Oh, what mercy it was that they had been warned ! What a dreadful scene might have ensued, where men resolved in principle, became opposed to brute force ! To whom do we owe the discovery ?" asked Lady Carewe.

" 'Tis well believed that 'twas the Lady Carlisle, to whom some indiscretion of the queen may have revealed the king's intention, but this is uncertain, and known only to Pym. His majesty then made a short speech in much discomposure, in which he said not much that I remember, except that he had sent for five persons and expected obedience and not a message, and that there is no 'privilege' in cases of treason. Then he again looked round the house, and said to the speaker, ' Are any of those persons in the house ? Do you see any of them ? Where are they ?' Then the speaker fell on his knees and said, ' May it please your majesty, I have neither eyes to see, nor tongue to speak, in this place, but as the house is pleased to direct me, whose servant I am.' His majesty then again cast his eyes round the house, and his next words I remember well. They were, 'Well, since I see all the birds are flown, I do expect from you that you do send them to me as soon as they return hither,' and then he said more, not much to the purpose, as that he never meant any force ; but at the last he said again, ' I do expect you to send them to me as soon as they come to the house,' adding, ' otherwise I must take my own course to find them.' Then he moved to retire, and passed down the house between two rows of stern faces, with eyes all fixed upon him, and as he passed there was from many the loud cry of ' Privilege !' "

" That I heard," said Henry, " and observed in the king much angry passion, as well as smothered disappointment in his train."

" By this act," said Sir Arthur, " the king hath drawn the sword and thrown away the scabbard. He hath made his attack and failed, but he will rally and renew it. From this moment, that becomes certain which hath long impended. We shall have civil war in England."

Sir Arthur was so deeply moved as he said these words, that his strength failed him in an alarming degree, and Lady Carewe motioned to Henry to keep perfect silence, while she sat watching her husband's wasted face, and holding his hand in hers. As Henry looked on the two faces he loved best in the world, the one scarcely less worn and wan than the other, a feeling of dread entered his heart ; for the apprehension rushed on his mind for the first time, that he was about to lose his father. Utterly unable to control himself, he stole softly from the room, shut himself into his own, and gave way to a flood of grief and tears. The constant companionship of two years had reared up a great love

R

between father and son ; and Sir Arthur's misfortunes had wrought a great change on his character. Still as stern and unbending in principle as ever, he was gentle and affectionate in his family, and reposed such perfect trust in Henry, and loved him so well, that to look forward to his father's loss and the cessation of their happy intercourse, was a trial he had not dreamed of, and now that it suddenly came upon him, it seemed too much to bear.

He remained alone for some time, then roused himself, and tried to think more calmly, and to hope. This time had been too full of stern anxious business for his father's strength, and besides he had never recovered Valentine's departure. His father must have rest at Crewhurst, and Valentine must come home. For this he would try hard. He could come now. The Star Chamber and its judgments were swept away. His father should soon be better !"

So said Henry to himself, and when he went down again, and his mother smiled as he entered the room, he cast off his fears entirely.

CHAPTER XXII.

THE TRIUMPH OF MIND.

"I AM going to make thee my envoy to the city to-day," said Sir Arthur, as Henry entered his room on the following morning. "Already I have heard by special message from Mr. Hampden that he and our four other friends are safe in the house in Coleman Street in which they had resolved to take refuge. The king, he informs me, hath not given up the contest. He hath sent orders to stop all the sea-ports, in the imagination (which indeed shows how he is deluded) that they will attempt to flee. He hath also sent warrants to the lord mayor to arrest them, and announced his intention to visit the Guildhall this day. Thither I would have thee go. I would not willingly send thee into danger, but there will be none. The city is too firm to permit the possibility of any contest. The king, doubtless, deceives himself, and imagines it will support his course because it feasted him and gave him a loyal welcome on his late return from Scotland. But he will find it is not so. There are nowhere more loyal subjects than the citizens of London to a constitutional king, but a king using force against his parliament, and himself attempting to execute his own warrants contrary to all legal usage, they will not support. If the king persist in this fatal course, he will find that he hath lost the capital of his kingdom."

"And if we do come to this dreadful civil war you so much dread, my father, will London side with the parliament?"

"I am well assured it will. But go and observe well for me all that falls out this day. It is a great day, and one that will have great influence on those days that are to follow."

According to his father's direction Henry repaired straight to Temple Bar, and there waited within the gate. He found a considerable crowd collecting, and on looking up Fleet Street saw that all the shops were shut. He was informed also that there had been great excitement through the night, and that a body of citizens had remained under arms; rumours having reached them of an intention to search their houses, seize their arms, and even to fire the city. Presently there was a movement among the crowd, and it was announced that the king was coming, and his coach came quickly up without any guard. It was evident that the king had expected a good reception; but they who watched his face saw how rapidly it was overclouded, for no sooner had his coach passed Temple Bar than the crowd pressed around it with confused cries of, "Privilege of Parliament!" So it passed on the whole way to the Guildhall; and Henry, entering with the people, got a good place to observe the proceedings. There had been only one tumult on the way, when a man was taken into custody who had thrown a paper into the coach. As appeared afterwards on his trial at the sessions, the words were written on it, "To your tents, O Israel!" the

war-cry of the ten tribes when they revolted from Reho-
boam.

The lord mayor and the common council were assembled,
and received his majesty with every mark of loyalty and
homage, whereupon he made a speech, in which, declaring
and protesting many things as to his respect for the privileges
of parliament, he repeated many times that he must "question those traitors."

During the speech Henry carefully noted the behaviour
and looks of the assembly. There was perfect, indeed ominous, silence. As it ended the silence ceased, and the cry,
"Parliament! Privileges of Parliament!" resounded through
the hall, even the common council joining in it. Presently
another cry was heard, " God bless the king," and these
two cries continued both at once a good while, till the knocking for silence was at last obeyed.

The king then commanded that whoever had anything
to say, should speak.

" It is the vote of this court that your majesty hear the
advice of your parliament," said a voice.

" It is not the vote of this court, it is your own vote,"
said another.

" Who is it that says I do not take the advice of my
parliament?" replied the king. "I do take their advice,
and will ; but I must distinguish between the parliament and
some traitors in it, and these I will bring to trial—*trial*."

There was again a silence in the hall, which lasted for
some time. This silence was broken in a manner that was
almost ludicrous, and but for the grave nature of the circumstances, would have raised a laugh. A bold fellow of the

lowest rank got upon a form, and in a loud voice cried, "The privileges of parliament!" "Observe the man—apprehend him!" cried another voice, but no one obeyed.

"I have and will observe all privileges of parliament," the king mildly replied to his ragged subject, "but no privileges can protect a traitor from a trial—*trial.*"

This closed the proceedings. The king rose and was escorted to the door, passing through a ruder crowd in the outer hall, who instantly set up a greater cry of "The privileges of parliament!" He went not straight to Whitehall, but drove to Sheriff Garrett's, where he dined, and it was said was magnificently entertained. Henry waited among the crowd without till he saw the coach moving on again, and then followed with the stream, "Privilege! Privilege!" sounding from the lips of thousands the whole way.

"The king hath made his last throw and lost the stake," said Sir Arthur, when Henry, returning to him, told the events of the day. Henry Vane, calling in the evening, informed them, however, that a proclamation was issued by the king enjoining the seizure of the accused, and prohibiting others to harbour them. He had, therefore, not yet thrown up his game; but in two days the formal answer of the corporation of the city was delivered to him, which closed it. They advised him to "consult with his parliament, to desist from military preparations, and to proceed against the accused only in form of law."

On the following morning the "Perfect Diurnal of the Passages in Parliament," one of the weekly newspapers which at the opening of the Long Parliament first appeared in England, informed its readers of what had occurred in the house while these events took place in the city. The house had met as usual, and had voted a declaration after some patriotic speeches, adjourning the sitting of the house to the 11th ; but empowering it to meet in committee meantime, in Guildhall.

To Guildhall, therefore, Henry now went, in his capacity of envoy, to observe proceedings for his father, and was there before the members, who punctually arrived at eleven o'clock, and sate in the room within the court to which juries withdrew ; while a feast was laid out for them in the hall, at which they made great cheer at the hour of twelve, without having to slip out to dinner, as usual. By application to his friend, Henry Vane, Henry was admitted to hear the proceedings, at which were some important speeches to the effect that they wished not to protect any members in any crime, but to object to their being proceeded against except in a legal way.

On his way, Henry had observed that the shops were still shut. On the breaking up of the committee, the streets were found to be filled with armed men, who opened a way for the members to pass, and thus he moved on more easily than he would otherwise have done. There had been a rumour of an attack upon the house in Coleman Street, and forty thousand men were instantly under arms, besides at least a hundred thousand armed with clubs, halberds, swords, and the like. The Tower was now under command of Sir John Byron, and the better to secure it, the sheriffs of London and Middlesex were ordered to send a sufficient force to watch it by land and water, and Major Skippon, a trusty and experienced officer, was put in command of the city militia.

It was to see a peaceful demonstration that Henry
stood in the London streets on the following Saturday. On
that day petitioners began to crowd into town from the
neighbouring counties. Several thousands came with a
petition for the protection of Mr. Pym, and Buckinghamshire alone sent four thousand squires and freeholders, who
rode in procession to petition also, but also to live and die
with Mr. Hampden. On Sunday the 9th of January there
were strange groups in London streets, strange visitors in the
London churches. Men not known to each other but by the
purpose that lighted up each face, men who were complete
strangers, grasped hands firmly and passed on without uttering
a word. Many a firm and silent pressure of his hand did
Henry receive and return as he mixed among these men
with a face as earnest and enthusiastic as theirs. How had
these men, when their fellow-townsmen or villagers selected
them to go and represent them in the metropolis, received a
parting cup and pledge, and so been speeded on their way in
that wintry season before the moon had faded !

The following day was a great one in Guildhall. On
that day Henry did not fail to be present, for the five
members had been invited to attend, and to-morrow the
house would meet again in Westminster. After resolutions
had been voted against evil counsellors, against royal pro-
clamations and warrants under the king's own hand, came
in a deputation of seamen, with a petition signed by a thousand hands offering to escort the committee to Westminster
on the morrow, which was accepted. Then came the city
apprentices in great numbers, offering their services as a
guard ; but it had been resolved to go by water, and this was

THE BUCKINGHAMSHIRE MEN.

declined. A military escort was, however, engaged to move along by land as the procession moved by water. Scarcely was the business all settled, when the shouts without announced the approach of the five members. It was a moment never to be forgotten in Henry's life, when he saw them enter and take their places among their fellow-legislators; and Sir Arthur's face lighted up with the fire of his early days, and Lady Carewe's grew bright again, as they listened to the description he gave them in the evening.

"To-morrow," said Sir Arthur, "will be a great sight. Thou shalt see it, Henry, from the garden of my Lord Essex, who hath given me that favour, and afterwards thou wilt be admitted to the gallery of the house. Thou dost live in wondrous times, among great deeds, and dost look upon the faces, and hear the words, of a band of men, the greatest geniuses for government that ever existed—clear, resolute, temperate, who have not yet made a single mistake as to end or means. It is a privilege for thee that thy youth witnesses their deeds; may thy manhood bear the fruit, my son, and well I believe it will."

Lady Carewe's glistening eyes were fixed with something of pride in them on Henry, and her heart echoed the words "well I believe it will."

On the morrow, the morning of January 11th, 1642, a day to be ever remembered in the annals of England, Henry went out to see the five members return to the house in triumph, guarded by their fellow-citizens; and in the evening he returned, with a face still beaming with the excitement of the day, to his father, and found him looking almost as he used to do, strong and earnest in expression of face;

while Lady Carewe, forgetting in the public rejoicing her private grief, sat beside him, to listen with intense interest to all Henry had to tell. The echoes of the triumph, and the thronging multitude in the streets, had already told them much.

"There were," said Henry, "innumerable thousands in the streets from early morning, so that I had no small difficulty to reach my Lord Essex's; but the sight I had there was worth any crush to get at it. Surely never did the Thames, from London Bridge to Westminster, present so great a spectacle. The members of the committee, the 'five' among them, as also my Lord Kimbolton, were conveyed in one of the city barges, through a fleet of vessels and boats, armed with ordnance, and dressed up with waistclothes and streamers, as ready for fight. But fight there was none; nought was heard around but shouts of rejoicing, between the volleys they fired all the way, as the barge passed along between. Then on shore, keeping pace with the barge, there marched a strong body of the militia, every man bearing on his pike, that was attached to his musket, a printed copy of the solemn protestation. I have brought thee a copy of it, my father; it binds all who take it to the rendering up life itself on behalf of the liberties of parliament and the maintenance of the protestant religion."

"It is a solemn protest," said Sir Arthur, "and religiously it will be kept. Woe to them who have driven Englishmen to make it."

"These printed papers flapped like little white banners about the pikes and around the ensigns and colours; and so they moved all the way to Westminster among the people,

who thronged around by thousands, shouting, and, as it might
be said, echoing the volleys from the river, and so on to Westminster. And when the barge stopped at the old port at
Westminster, then landed the members, among dense, shouting crowds; and well I know how thick was the press, for I
was in the midst of it, and shouting too till I was hoarse ;
and so they passed up the hall, and up the lobby stairs, and
into the house."

" A great moment! And thou, I warrant me, wert not
far behind !"

" I was in the gallery among the first, and saw how the
speaker and the members, after first all standing up, took
their accustomed places, and how then arose the ' five,'
silent and uncovered. It was a moving thing. Many men,
as they sat and looked, had the tears on their cheeks."

" I well believe the tears ran down thine, to judge by
thy eyes now," said Lady Carewe. " But was there no
speaking ?"

" It was Mr. Pym who spoke; the others continued to
stand silently till he had finished. What he said was in
earnest language. I cannot even try to repeat it ; but he
returned hearty thanks to the citizens of London, and said
eloquent words to the effect that the house would protect
and defend them from all evil consequences, and great impression was produced by his speech. Then the house sent
for the sheriffs of London, the masters and officers of ships,
Sergeant-Major-General Skippon, and some of the gentlemen
of Buckinghamshire, and they all and each received the
thanks of the house ; and the Buckinghamshire men pressed
in, and so great was the press of them, that it was long

while before they could get out, and when their spokesman returned thanks, he said they were six thousand strong."

"Nay, four thousand, I have heard; but that matters little."

"And he added that they could tell the Commons of England that they were ready 'to die at their feet.'"

"And did the proceedings close thus?"

"Oh, no; another and most strange thing I have to tell you, my father. It was announced in the house, before it rose, that yesterday evening the king and queen and all the court suddenly left Whitehall, and have removed to Hampton Court."

"Is it possible? He hath left his capital, then! When or how to return? Never—but as a victor trampling on our liberties, or a captive in the power of his subjects! Oh, madness, to have driven us to such an issue! Long and vainly have we struggled to avert it!"

The pale and worn expression of face had returned as Sir Arthur said these words, and Henry almost started when he looked up and saw it, but the face lighted up again.

"This has been a great triumph," he said. "The triumph of mind and spirit over force. I would I might have been allowed to see it. Yet no! unworthy that I am to say so! I ought rather to rejoice that I am permitted to hear it through thee, my son, and to know that thou wilt be ready when thy time comes to carry on the great work thus begun. But before thy time comes, a dreadful conflict has to be fought. This day has ended our great war of mind. That war was sure to end in the triumph of liberty and truth.

THE TRIUMPH OF MIND. 273

Now we begin the fearful struggle of bone and sinew, of steel and bullet; now will man grapple with his fellow-man and murder his brother. In this awful strife 'the race is not always to the swift, nor the battle to the strong,' and yet I well believe we shall triumph even in this. Was Cromwell in the house to-day?"

"He was, my father. I saw him in his usual place."

"I often remember now that speech of Hampden's concerning him, and he knows him well, being, indeed, nearly related. When Lord Digby one day, in the last parliament, before that change which now unites him with the court, said to my friend, 'Pray, Mr. Hampden, who is that man? for I see he is on our side by his speaking so warmly to-day;' then Hampden answered : 'That sloven, whom you see before you, hath no ornaments in his speech ; but that sloven, I say, if we should ever come to a breach with the king (which God forbid !), in such a case, I say, that sloven will be the greatest man in England !' "

"My husband," said Lady Carewe, "think not more on these matters to-day, nor speak farther on them. Thou art exhausted. Let me persuade thee to go to thy repose."

He held out his hand to Henry to wish him good night ; and as he moved, his weakness seemed so great that he leaned for support on the arm of his son. Then again returned that dread, now become almost a certainty, that had before appalled Henry. He was, indeed, about to lose his father. He was still sitting alone, buried in his uncontrolled grief, when, after the lapse of an hour, a knock at his door roused him. It was his mother who had come.

"Thy father hath fallen into a sweet sleep," she said,

"and I am come to thee. Oh Henry, my son,—my own dear son—it is coming; this bitter trial ; thou seest it at last."

She could say no more. Henry had thrown his arms round her, and, for long, they remained in silence, letting their sorrow have its way, till he, mastering himself for her sake, was able to speak, was able to try to entreat of her to look at him again, and tell him she would let him try to be a comfort to her.

She did look at him through her tears, but it was with an expression of such great sorrow, it had almost overcome him again. She only pointed upward, as if she meant to say, "There was all her hope," and left him, for she could not speak. Henry, therefore, composed himself, and went softly to sit by his father till she should be able to come, but how great was his surprise to find her there at her post, calm, watchful, without any outward sign of suffering, except the traces of the tears she had shed ! Then he understood that she might long have known of the sorrow that was coming, though her fortitude prevented any one from discovering it; but he did not know yet, how great a comfort his sympathy had been, nor how much relief to her had been those tears she shed when they sat side by side.

CHAPTER XXIII.

FORCE AGAINST FORCE.

THE hoar frost lay on the ground, and the bare branches swung to and fro in the wind, as Edith and Henry walked together slowly and mournfully across the park at Crewhurst, from the chapel where their father lay buried, and where they had been looking at the tablet that was raised to his memory. Their talk, which had long been of him they had lost, was now of Valentine.

"If Valentine do come to us on receiving thy letter, Henry," said Edith, "I cannot hope that he will be happy with us. Thou dost fancy he will, because thou so much wishest his company; but we live so simply, so very quietly, and in such perfect retirement, that after the life of gaiety and vanity he hath led, he will not be able to endure it."

"But will he not like the change? Would he not, if he were once with us for this little while, and had time to think of our father's noble principles, and read the journals I have written of his life, and the records of his speeches, would he not begin to sympathise more in his course, and feel more as we do?"

Edith shook her head, and said she was very hopeless about it, but would like to hear the letter Henry had written. They therefore went in together to the library, where Henry now sat for many hours daily, finishing certain tasks his father had left him to do, arranging his father's papers and books, and going on with his own studies. Here, having thrown some logs on the fire, and seated Edith in an armchair, he took out his letter and read it. It was directed to Sir Valentine Carewe, at the court of the Prince of Orange :—

"DEAR BROTHER,

"The first letter I sent to thee after our great loss, left me so heavy with grief, that I could not say much to thee besides the grievous news it took to thee, but now I will send thee our father's will and wishes for thy consideration, for he would not say 'commands.' 'Only make known to him my wishes,' that was what he said.

"'Tell him,' so said my father to me the last day of his life, 'tell my dear son Valentine, that I leave him my blessing and forgiveness for all the sorrow he hath caused me ;" I like not to grieve thee with that word 'sorrow,' but I must give his message truly—' and that when he attains the age of twenty-one, he will find himself possessed of my estates and property, such as they are, after many heavy losses and fines, which have greatly lessened the amount ; and after deducting the provision made for the rest of my family. But tell him it is my wish that during the year that intervenes he will live at Crewhurst with his mother, who is his sole guardian, and that he will in no way meddle in public affairs. This year of cool thought he needs in these distracted times, before embarking on either side in the strife which agitates our country, and if in the course of this year he would apply himself to study the causes of the present discontents, where thou canst point out to him the way, I die in the hope that he might abstain from throwing his life and fortune into a cause, which, as it is the cause of despotism against liberty, cannot prosper in England for long, though in the chances of war it may for a time.'

"These words, my brother, I took down and noted carefully as his lips uttered them, and if thou wouldst come to us, I tell thee the truth when I say it would be a day of rejoicing to us all, and go far to cheer our mother's spirits, which, though she hath a wonderful strength and fortitude, yet fail her often. She occupies herself much in teaching our little Alice and Martin, and they prosper bravely in her hands; thou wilt scarcely know them again, so grown and improved are they. Edith is——"

"I think not best to read what I have said of thee! I might make thee proud."

"I wish to hear it, Master Henry. Thou hast no right to send a character of me, and I not know of it."

"I shall not read it, though. It means that we at Crewhurst have an angel to guard and cheer us."

"Ah, Henry!" said Edith, "thou dost make me humble, not proud, if thou hast said such things as that," and the tears stood in her eyes. Henry went on with his letter.

"Do come, Valentine. I want to see thy face again; nay, I long for it. I do wish thou wouldst come. There are now no horses in stall, nor hawks on perch. What then? We can still enjoy much. We have strong legs

8

of our own. Dost not remember how we ran, once upon a
time, when we feared to look who might be behind us ? We
can play bowls too; and Woodruffe is a good fellow, and will
contrive sport for thee. I have some hard work to do, but
some hours a day given to it earnestly for a few months will
finish it; and I am going on besides with Greek and the
mathematics, under our new vicar, who is a learned man,
and to whom I go daily; but still I shall have good time for
thee. Ever I think on Mr. Russell, and long for him, when
I look upon my books. Shall I ever see him again ?

"I want thee, in short. And so do all here. Our
mother sends her blessing, and bids me say she trusts thy
father's wish will be a law to thee, and that she will see
thee soon among us. Thy loving brother,

"HENRY CAREWE."

This letter did not receive a very immediate answer, and the
answer, when it came, was not such as cheered Lady Carewe,
and sadly disappointed Henry. Valentine promised to obey
his father entirely as to abstaining from entering into public
affairs until he was of age, but he would remain abroad till
that period. He tried to give some reason for this that
should not look unkind or unaffectionate, but he did not
succeed. His refusal cast a gloom over the whole family
for some time, but in their round of duties and the occasional intercourse with some dear friends, such as the Willoughbys and Hampdens, they partly recovered their spirits.

But these friends had now little time to give to aught
except the troubled affairs of the country. Preparations for
the impending war, mixed with negociations in the vain

hope of averting it, occupied them and all men of note on both sides. The king had retired to York, where he held his court, and where many joined him, both of his courtiers and of those who had belonged to the parliament, till the prospect of taking arms against their sovereign made them desert it. Amongst these, the most eminent were Lord Falkland, and Hyde, best known as Lord Clarendon, who now gave themselves entirely to the royalist side. The words addressed by Sir Edmund Verney, the king's standard bearer, to the latter and recorded by him, doubtless express the conflict in the mind of many an honourable man in those days, though Sir Edmund thought they applied only to himself. They were uttered in explanation of his melancholy, about the time of the erection of the royal standard at Nottingham, which event took place in August of 1642.

" My condition is much worse than yours, and different, I believe, from any other man's, and will very well justify the melancholy that possesses me. You are satisfied in your conscience that you are in the right; that the king ought not to grant what is required of him, and so you do your duty and your business together. But for my part, I do not like the quarrel, and do heartily wish that the king would yield and consent to what they desire, so that my conscience is only concerned in honour and in gratitude to follow my master. I have eaten his bread, and served him near thirty years, and will not do so base a thing as to forsake him ; and choose rather to lose my life, which I am sure I shall do, to preserve and defend these things which are against my conscience to preserve and defend."

The king now put forth the "Declaration of his Cause," and issued his commission of array. The queen was in Holland, where she had carried the crown jewels, and pawned them to procure ammunition and arms. The two princes, Rupert and Maurice, the nephews of the king, had joined him. A great portion of the gentry and aristocracy declared for him, sent in large contributions to his treasury, and brought in their tenants and retainers to swell his army. The spirit of his army was chivalrous, loyal, brave, haughty and self-confident, dissolute—partly from the habits of the times in men of their party, partly from opposition to the puritan strictness—and reckless of the people's lives and properties. Prince Rupert, whom the people learned to call "Prince Robber," possessed of dauntless courage, carried pillage, ravage, and murder to the same height to which he had been used in the ferocious German wars; and his sword was dripping with English blood in every skirmish and every battle, and pitiless in pursuit and after defeat.

The parliament, on the other hand, published the ordinance to marshal the militia of the country, and voted the necessary supplies. The metropolis continued firm in the people's cause; and the navy declared for it from the first. Scotland, also, was in alliance with the parliament; though at a later period the Marquis of Montrose's extraordinary feats in favour of the king became an important part of his warfare. In many of the counties—as, for instance, Buckinghamshire—the parishes and hundreds, often with their preachers at their head, marched forth to training. Subscriptions in aid also flowed in, not only from the rich, but the poor, and even from women; so that the cavaliers called it, in derision, "the thimble and bodkin army." But they soon learned that this army was not to be despised. Many distinguished men—among them Hampden, Lord Brooke, and Lord Willoughby, raised bodies of men, who became distinguished for their courage and discipline; and Oliver Cromwell, who had purchased the commission of a colonel of horse, raised a regiment in the eastern counties, that was celebrated, from the beginning of the war, for its superior training. The spirit of the parliament's army was stern, enthusiastic in religion and in the cause of liberty, and was strictly observant of discipline.

The people were harassed, as a matter of course, by the contradictory and conflicting orders, and when the two parties met, as sometimes happened, with the king's commission of array on one side, and the parliament's ordinance on the other, drawn up, according to form, for the "Defence of the king and parliament," they knew not whom to obey; and conflicts, often leading to bloodshed, were the consequence.

The foreboding of his death was fulfilled very soon in the case of Sir Edmund Verney. In the first battle of this war, the battle of Edgehill, fought in October of that same year, he was killed; one among four thousand Englishmen slain by each other's hands, who were left on the bloody field. It was observed, by those who have left records of that day, that there was a long pause before either army opened their fire. They stood drawn up in their opposite ranks, as if some awful sense of the horror of brother being opposed to brother had oppressed them. Skirmishes there had been before, affairs of outposts and sudden attacks, and the king had already appeared in arms before Hull, and made an unsuccessful attempt to enter it ; but this was the first pitched battle. It was the guns of the army of the parliament which at last began it ; and, sanguinary as it was, it effected little or nothing for either party. Both claimed the victory; while, after it, the king took no advantage of his opportunity to advance upon London, nor did the Earl of Essex (the general for the parliament) make haste to throw himself between the royalist army and the capital.

It was on one of those calm, bright autumn days, that sometimes make October the most delightful month of the year, that Lady Carewe and Edith sat reading, under the green shade of an oak tree in the park, the account of this battle, in one of the parliament's " Diurnals." The two children, not far from them, were playing happily ; the pale autumn roses on the wall spread a sweet scent through the air ; everything around spoke of beauty and peace. Henry, a little way from them, leaning on the stone that supported a sun-dial, seemed to be full of conflicting thoughts and feelings. He had brought the paper to them, and had already read it himself.

"Edith," said Lady Carewe, looking up after a long silence, "I hope that had God called me to the trial now heavily pressing on many a mother and wife in England, He would have found me ready. I hope, too, I am not cowardly, nor shrinking in heart from this work, if I feel deeply grateful that my husband was called away before this dreadful war began, and that my son is too young to take part in it. Look at him now ! Whatever work he is called to do, he will do it strongly, not sparing himself, fearing nothing. Oh, may God preserve him !"

" In His hands he is safe, my mother."

They rose as they spoke, and Henry joining them, they walked to the house. He knew more than they did of the probable results of the approach of the two armies towards London, and of the peril of the country about them, should Prince Rupert begin his system of recruiting and pillage. His thoughts were often employed on how to protect the tenants on the estate, and his mother, sisters, and little brother, should danger come near them. Sometimes he thought they ought to go to London, but Lady Carewe could not bear to think of it. " I trust Crewhurst to thee, to preserve it in its beauty for Valentine;" so her husband had said to her; and it became a sacred duty with her to obey him, and to remain there till she gave it up to his successor.

Only a month after this time Henry received letters from Lord Willoughby giving hopes of peace. Lord Essex's army was now in and about London ; the king's, near Brentford ; and he had received the overtures of the parliament graciously, and a truce had been declared. The joy which this news spread through the family is scarcely to be described.

" The skies do not sympathise with us," said Edith. " How dense is the fog, and, but that it is wintry weather and cold, I should say I hear thunder."

Henry had been listening attentively for some minutes at an open window, and he now spoke.

" The sound we hear," said he, " is the distant roar of artillery. Strange sound during a truce ! I cannot understand it."

The ominous sound continued at intervals till night, and

then ceased; and was followed soon after by the news of
that treacherous attack on Brentford, with intent to proceed
to London during the truce, from the disgrace of which the
king was never able to clear himself, and which was only
thwarted by the resolute bravery of the parliament's pickets
who maintained the place, fighting from street to street, till
Hampden and Lord Brooke came up, and afterwards Lord
Essex, at the head of the London train-bands, and repulsed
the royal troops.   The king then retired to Oxford, and all
thoughts of a peace were at an end.

There were no thoughts of Christmas festivities that year.
The winter passed heavily, and with much distress among
the people.   Their green corn had been trodden down, or
cut for forage; their cattle, sheep, and swine, seized and
killed by the cavaliers; their sons were enrolled in the ranks
of one party or another; sometimes a family had the double
distress of seeing one son opposed to another from having
taken opposite sides. So opened the year 1643, and in spring
began hostilities again.   But bright and beautiful came the
summer on, and the leafy month of June was close at hand,
and the sun shed his light and warmth on the evil and the
good.

On the tenth of June Valentine would attain the age of
twenty-one.

It was with much anxiety that Lady Carewe had looked
forward to this time.   Had all gone on well with the family,
it would have been a season of rejoicing when the heir of
the house attained his majority; but she shared with many
others in those disastrous times the sorrow of divided opinions
and principles among those nearest and dearest to her.   She

had reason to believe, from his latest letters, that Valentine
would come home immediately, and that he would take arms
in the king's service. She had written to him that he would
find her at Crewhurst, anxious to receive him, and would
find her and all his family full of love for him, and longing
to see him; but she had privately made up her mind that if
he did indeed embark in the war on the royalist side, she
would retire to London, with all her family, at first, and
afterwards, when the troublous times were over, would take
up her abode in Devonshire, at a property there which Sir
Arthur had left to her, and which would belong to Henry at
her death. This she had resolved to do, as soon as she had
fulfilled her husband's desire to make over Crewhurst, in all
its beauty, to his son, and as soon as Henry had performed
his promise to deliver certain urgent messages from his
father, intended to enforce on Valentine the paramount duty
of examining well into the causes and aims of the war before
he embarked in it. The cause for which her husband lived
and died was sacred to her, and she could not preside over a
household opposed to it.

Edith and Henry were acquainted with all her inten-
tions. The old servants of the family looked forward to the
change of masters with the greatest apprehension; and many
a consultation went on among them without their being able
to come to any conclusion, except that wherever my lady
went, or wherever she stayed, there they would go or there
they would stay. Woodruffe stoutly maintained that he
would never be separated from Master Henry; and poor old
nurse likened herself to the beautiful young Ruth when she
said to Naomi, " Where thou goest will I go; where thou

diest will I die, and there will I be buried. God do so to
me, and more also, if aught but death part thee and me."
"And so," said nurse, "shall I say to my pretty ladybird,
my sweet Mistress Edith."

Everything in the village bore the same look of comfort
and peace that it had done in the best days of the family.
Lady Carewe had sent in her contribution to the parliament
handsomely, but had, by her influence, prevented writs being
issued for any of her servants to enter the militia, on the
plea that she held the property only in trust for her son.
What would happen when he took possession, remained
uncertain.

Things were in this state, when alarming rumours of
fresh ravages by the cavaliers issuing from Oxford, began to
fly through the country. It was therefore with a face of
alarm that Freeman opened the door of the parlour, on the
evening of the 9th of June, and announced that a party of
royalist cavalry were galloping up the avenue.

Henry instantly went to the door, where Woodruffe,
always on the watch, was already posted; and saw, indeed,
a party of eight horsemen coming. His mother was soon at
his side, with beating heart, for the idea that immediately
entered her mind was that Valentine was among them.
But it was not so. The sergeant in charge of the men
ordered a halt as soon as they reached the door, and in
answer to Henry's question as to the purpose of their visit,
replied, civilly enough, that they came to demand quarters
for the night, by command of his highness Prince Rupert, at
the hospitable mansion of his friend Sir Valentine Carewe,
who would himself arrive on the morrow.

There was no question as to the necessity of compliance. Woodruffe was directed to show the men to the stables, and provide forage for the horses, and Freeman to supply supper and beds for the men. In less than half-an-hour they were

seated in the great hall carousing, and making it resound with shouts, and oaths, and noisy songs.

The presence of these men alarmed the whole household. Woodruffe, Boult, and Leeson, left their cottages and came up to the Hall, where they remained the whole night ; and the women left their spinning-wheels, which usually hummed the whole evening through, to the sound of their songs and light-hearted gossip, and crowded into the room next to their lady's, having obtained permission. Edith and the children were all in their mother's own room, and Henry, quite unable to sleep, sat in her dressing room.

It was not till very late at night, when all were asleep but her and himself, that he had come to a resolution how to act under the circumstances which he believed were threatening. He then begged her to come to him.

"I think you know, my mother," he said, "that I am not easily frightened, nor would I alarm you needlessly; but I feel certain that great calamities are hanging over us, unless I can take some speedy steps to drive them away."

"I cannot think so. Valentine, if he comes to-morrow, will ensure our safe departure; and I cannot doubt that he will forward our views with regard to our people. It is grief enough to know he is called 'friend' by Prince Rupert, without additional alarms being allowed to harass us farther."

"But these alarms, I fear, are well grounded. Hateful as the company of these men was to me, I went to them, and remained with them for some time, to try to make out what they are here for, and I fear I have found out."

"You alarm me, indeed, Henry, now!"

"They talked openly enough, after they had drunk ale for an hour; and then I discovered that Rupert himself is coming with Valentine, and that he is going to recruit among our people. What he calls recruiting, is seizing on the men he wants, and hanging at their doors those who will not enlist. You know full well, my mother, that none of our men will enlist under him. The cause that their master died for is their cause, and against it they will never fight. Rupert will ravage and burn the village, and murder the people."

Lady Carewe turned pale and trembled. Still she said she could not believe that Valentine would permit such atrocities.

"He would not. No, I know he would not. That is what I must do. I must find him, and rouse him before it is too late. When Rupert is down upon us like a flood, it will be too late. I must go to their head-quarters, only ten miles off, they say, and see him. I must rouse him with our father's message to him. I must insist on his giving us time to leave this place, and take away our people in safety."

"Thou must not go. Thou wouldst run into perils innumerable."

"I should not run into any, I fully believe. My name would protect me."

"Take then Woodruffe and Leeson well armed."

"I will not take a single man from this place. You will want them all. These troopers will leave early in the morning, and take up a post on the Oxford road, to wait for their commander. The moment they are gone, let every woman and child, and the old and feeble, leave the village and come up to the Hall. You will feed them and lodge them safely, my mother, I know. The men must stay to defend their homes if attacked. But I may, if it please God to permit me, prevent it."

"My Henry, can I bear to see thee go?"

"And can I bear to leave you, my mother? Yet I think —I trust and believe—you cannot be in any danger when Valentine is near you. But keep all doors and windows fastened. Woodruffe and Freeman must stay in the house; and, in case of the worst, you remember the secret chamber. I must now try to rest for an hour. I have told Woodruffe to come to me at sunrise. I know the paths in the forest so well that I can go by short cuts, and shall reach their quarters in little more than an hour. You will try to sleep, my mother?"

She promised to try, but no sleep visited her eyes, nor did she close them after she had seen him mount and ride away in the early morning light. The dew lay on the grass; the lark mounted into the sky; it was Valentine's birthday; but what a heavy sigh did she give as that thought entered her mind !

What bitter grief it was to feel that the wide domain on which her eyes rested had passed away from under her influence, and now belonged to the son who had deserted his father, and who would turn its resources to the purpose of opposing the liberty his father had upheld through life ! How gladly would she have given all up to Valentine had it been otherwise !

"But I must learn to submit," she said to herself. "I must learn to respect my son's opinions, though I cannot share them. May he do his duty in the cause he has chosen ! Then I shall go far hence, and see beautiful Crewhurst no more ; but my heart will be resigned, though it cannot be joyful."

CHAPTER XXIV.

THE BIRTHRIGHT.

RIDING at a rapid pace, by forest paths and over heathy wastes, leaping every obstacle in his way, and keeping a steady watch in all directions, Henry reached the road as he had expected in little more than an hour, and found himself very near the encampment of Prince Rupert. Without slackening his pace, he went straight on, and was speedily challenged by a sentinel. To the challenge, he gave his name, and said he came to visit his brother, Sir Valentine Carewe, and desired that his name and wishes should be carried to the prince.

He was ordered to wait, and was kept waiting for nearly an hour : at the end of which time he was conducted to the tent of Prince Rupert, and found himself at once in the presence of that man, only too well known in England.

The prince rose as he entered, and received him with a politeness of manner and a courtesy almost overstrained and excessive, and quite out of keeping with his large person and awkward carriage ; smiling and assuring him in broken English that he was honoured by this interview. Henry answered to this politeness with a cold gravity. There was something harsh and repulsive in the countenance of the prince, seldom to be equalled in so young a man, for he was only three and

twenty, and besides, all that Henry knew of him was calcu-
lated to inspire aversion.

It was not long therefore before the two parties in this
interview felt a desire to bring it to a conclusion, from a
mutual dislike ; and Henry very quickly stated that his object
was to see his brother, and that if agreeable to his highness
to allow them the opportunity of a private interview, he
should be greatly obliged.   To this the prince replied that
he was extremely grieved to say that Sir Valentine Carewe
was on duty at a considerable distance.

Henry was much surprised at this announcement, and
looked so incredulously in the face of the speaker, that a
sudden flash of passion darted from Prince Rupert's eyes,
and uttering a coarse oath, he seemed about to say something
violent, but checked himself.

"My men will put you on the way homeward, Mr.
Carewe," he then added.   "You will see your brother there
more conveniently and surely."

"If I cannot do my errand to my brother," said Henry,
"may I be permitted to do it to your highness?"

"Certainly."

"I have been informed that your highness intends to
visit my brother's village to-day and to recruit there.   I
earnestly beg for the delay of only one day.   The men now
there will not enlist in your service ; my brother may gladly
put in others that will.   Suffer me to withdraw these men.
Crowhurst has become my brother's this day ; if your highness
will grant me, besides the request I have made, the favour of
a private interview with him at the first possible moment, it
is all I ask."

The prince bowed courteously; summoned an orderly to his presence; gave him some command in German, and motioned to Henry to follow the man, who waited.

"Your highness has not replied to my requests," said Henry.

The only answer was a volley of oaths and the command to " go " in a thundering voice.

Henry had no choice but to obey. He went out and asked the orderly for his horse.

" There under the trees," said the man.

Henry walked in the direction of the trees, the orderly keeping close by his side, and soon found himself in the midst of a crowd of soldiers, and perceived in a moment that he was their prisoner.

Aware that he was entirely in their power, and that remonstrance was useless, he uttered not a word, but seating himself on a fallen tree, remained in silence a prey to the most wretched forebodings, and so he remained for about two hours, which appeared to him like twelve.

The insolence with which Henry had been treated by Prince Rupert in this short interview, exasperating as it was, sank into insignificance in comparison with the anxiety which it awakened. What was this man going to do, that he so carefully guarded against a meeting between two brothers, who had been separated so long, and must naturally desire to see each other? Would he go on to Crewhurst, and was it possible that Lady Carewe would be subjected to some insolence too?

" Why did I leave her!" groaned Henry inwardly. " Why did I come on this insane errand! Oh that I were but with her, to stand forward and save her from the slightest communication with this ruffian. I cannot bear that he should even look at her or speak to her!"

He rose and cast his eyes warily round for the chance of escape; but instantly two pistols were pointed at his head.

He flashed back the look of defiance that he met from the men round him, and folding his arms, leaned against a tree, and there remained perfectly quiet, but attentively observing everything that passed.

"I shall keep my senses 'awake," thought he. "This watchfulness of my guard tells me plainly enough that Valentine is hereabouts. I may get a glimpse of him, or hear his voice. If I do, I will shout to him, and make him aware I am here, though they lay me dead the next moment. The sight of my body would at least arouse him to the villany they are plotting, whatever it be."

The time, however, went on without sight or sound of Valentine.

Horses were brought out at last, and the whole party mounted, ordering him to do the same. Still keeping him in the midst of them, they put themselves in motion, and took the road to Crewhurst.

At first the road was winding and skirted by trees, but as soon as they reached a more open part of the country where he could see half a mile in advance, he observed a strong body of cavalry moving forward in the same direction with the party which guarded him, and he believed that one of the horsemen who rode in front was Prince Rupert himself, while the cavalier at his side had the air and manner of Valentine.

Forgetting for the moment that he was likely to meet with nothing but insolence, he asked the soldier nearest to him, " Is not that Sir Valentine Carewe ? "

He received no answer. They continued at the same steady pace.

Suddenly there was a distant sound of musketry in front, and Henry thought he observed that the soldiers about him were startled at it ; still they went on.

They were soon within half a mile of the village, and from the top of the hill they were mounting, it would be visible. They reached the top ; and below them, instead of the neat cottages and their gardens, was a mass of flaming and smoking ruins.

Scarcely had Henry lifted his hands to heaven in his mute despair, when he perceived that the body of cavalry in front had come to a halt, and were in a state of extraordinary confusion. At the same time his guards quickening their pace, the distance between the two parties was rapidly lessened, until he could distinguish the gleam of swords flashing in the sun, and hear the report of pistols.

Presently another cause of disorder unexpectedly arose. A strong and compact body of infantry in green uniforms, advancing from the burning village, marched in double quick time upon the cavalry ; but before they had time to fire a single volley, Prince Rupert and his whole force disappeared across the country with the speed of the wind, and Henry's guard instantly following, he found himself free.

Putting his horse to its full speed, he galloped madly towards the scene of ruin in front of him, but before he reached it, his bridle was caught by Woodruffe.

T

"Now may God in heaven be for ever praised," exclaimed his faithful servant, "for bringing you back to us!"

In a moment Henry was surrounded by the detachment of soldiers who had put Rupert to flight; they belonged to Hampden's regiment; friendly faces were round him, friendly hands helped him to alight, kind voices uttered words of sympathy.

"They came to our rescue, Master Henry. They followed on the heels of these robbers, who have pillaged Buckinghamshire from end to end; they have saved us from greater woes. Our homes are destroyed, but not many of us have lost our lives; and our wives and children, our old mothers and fathers, thanks to you and your thoughts for us, are safe at the Hall. There our kind lady gives them food and shelter."

"Safe! Oh, my God, then Thou'hast heard my prayers! At the Hall it is safe."

Henry was too much overcome for some time to move or speak again, till suddenly raising his head, he told Woodruffe to follow him.

"I must go," said he, "to that rising ground to the left. Something dreadful happened there. I cannot rest till I know what."

They went together, passing over dead and mangled bodies—poor Leeson lay there, shot through the heart—among trampled gardens, smoking rafters, broken implements of industry, smashed pieces of furniture, dead animals, and wasted bread, and the little stores of rye and barley scattered on the miry and bloody earth. The sight might have sickened a lover of war of the dreadful work.

THE VICTIMS OF WAR.

They drew near the spot to which they were bound. Two dead bodies lay in the way as they ascended the eminence, and a wounded man lay moaning and imploring for water as they went on. Henry knew of a little spring in a hollow near at hand, and hurried there, carrying with him the soldier's steel cap to fill it.

As he began to descend into the hollow, he heard a groan. He looked about, but could see no one near. He went lower, moving aside the bushes and searching about. Again came the groan, but more feebly now. It came from a deeper hollow yet. Thither he clambered down, and saw—oh what a sight he saw!

"Valentine, my brother, my brother!"

His cry was so agonised, so wild, that Woodruffe heard it, and rushed to him.

The brothers lay together on the ground. Henry had clasped Valentine tightly in his arms, and was calling for help to bind up the wounds—to save his brother!

Alas! no human aid could save him! His face, once so full of manly beauty, was distorted with agony; his long curls were glued to the ground in his blood; his hands were full of earth and grass that he had dug up in his frenzy; his eyes were growing mad; he did not know Henry.

They brought him water and got some drops within his lips. Then Henry wiped his clammy forehead, sprinkled cool water on his face, opened his hands, poured water over them, called him by his name, in accents of tenderness and love; tried to fix his eye.

He succeeded at last. Valentine's eyes grew softer, and

looked into his, and they exchanged one look—one look never to be forgotten. The next instant, Valentine was gone.

"Oh, Valentine, is it thus thou enterest on thy birthright?"

A voice said those words; and the same voice said other words: words of love, of consolation, of pity, of sorrow. For a long while Henry lay immovable on the ground beside the dead, his whole frame quivering with anguish; long sobs and groans issuing from his aching heart, and whenever he did hear the words that were addressed to him, they only gave him an impression that he was mad, because the voice seemed Mr. Russell's.

At last a strong arm raised him from the ground, and eyes full of affection and sympathy were fixed on his. Still he only felt that he was mad, for the eyes were Mr. Russell's.

"Henry! my own dear Henry, strive to rouse yourself. Try to bear your cross. It is very hard, very heavy; but think of his mother, and what she has to bear; think of his sister, and the bitter sorrow of her loving heart. For their sakes, rouse yourself!"

"Mr. Russell, it *is* you! I am not mad! God has sent you to help me. My second brother—much more than brother! But Valentine! Oh, I cannot bear it!"

Again Henry sank on the ground and gave way to passionate grief, but at last he was able to listen again to Mr. Russell.

"Let it be a consolation to you to know," he said, "that it was poor Valentine's indignation at the ruin of the village,

and the murder of his people, that caused his death. One
of the wounded men, who is but slightly hurt, has told us so.
When the cavalry reached this height, and the burning
ruins came in view, Prince Rupert coolly avowed that his
purpose had been fulfilled in clearing out a set of Roundheads
and making room for a loyal body of retainers. Valentine
could not bear it. He drew upon the prince, who had to
defend himself from the infuriated attack, and by some
hand—whose we know not—the death-blow was given."

It was a consolation in after days, when Henry looked
back upon this dreadful time ; but now, he found no comfort
in anything.

" Go to them, Mr. Russell. Tell my mother, tell my
Edith. I will follow with *him*. I cannot leave him. Woodruffe will stay with me, and do you send us help."

Mr. Russell complied ; and it was long afterwards, when
the evening twilight had almost given place to night, and the
stars were coming out, that a mournful procession approached
the Hall. The rough bier was carried by Woodruffe, Freeman, and two other men ; the hand of the pale corpse that
lay on it was tightly clasped in Henry's. He walked close
to its side.

The men of Hampden's regiment, who kept guard by the
door, mutely saluted as the bier passed them. The bearers
set it down in the hall, and silently departed. No one was
by when the mother and sister embraced the beloved dead,
and kissed him, and wept over him. No one, save Henry
alone.

He had sunk at his mother's feet, and knew that she
blessed him ; and Edith's tears and kisses were fast raining

down on the two clasped hands now held in hers, the one cold and still, the other trembling with deep feeling.

Valentine had, indeed, entered on his birthright; but Sir Henry Carewe was lord of Crewhurst. Of his future history, it can only be recorded here that he realised the wish of his best friend, and that in manhood he was true to the dream of his youth.

THE END.

LONDON:
HENRY VIZETELLY, PRINTER AND ENGRAVER,
GOUGH SQUARE, FLEET STREET.

www.ingramcontent.com/pod-product-compliance
Lightning Source LLC
Chambersburg PA
CBHW031340070726
47496CB00017B/1386